Diesel Death

J. Douglas Lynn

PublishAmerica
Baltimore

© 2005 by J. Douglas Lynn.
All rights reserved. No part of this book may be reproduced, stored in a retrieval system or transmitted in any form or by any means without the prior written permission of the publishers, except by a reviewer who may quote brief passages in a review to be printed in a newspaper, magazine or journal.

First printing

This book is a work of fiction. Names, characters, places, and incidents are the product of the author's imagination or are used fictitiously. Any resemblance to actual events; locales; or persons, living or dead, is coincidental. The author uses the name of a real California regulatory agency in the story, but character names and places are strictly fictional. While the story line of *Diesel Death* is fiction, the problem of pollution from diesel exhaust is real.

ISBN: 1-4137-4659-4
PUBLISHED BY PUBLISHAMERICA, LLLP
www.publishamerica.com
Baltimore

Printed in the United States of America

To Pat:
My life didn't work without you.

Acknowledgments

I wish to thank my late wife Pat and my daughters Martha, Susan, and Sarah for reviewing and editing the *Diesel Death* manuscript and for their unflinching support. I want to give special thanks to Bob Dodge for creating and managing my web page: www.douglynn.net, and to my daughter-in-law, Margaret Lynn, for preparing the downtown site plan for my fictitious city, Riverside, Connecticut.

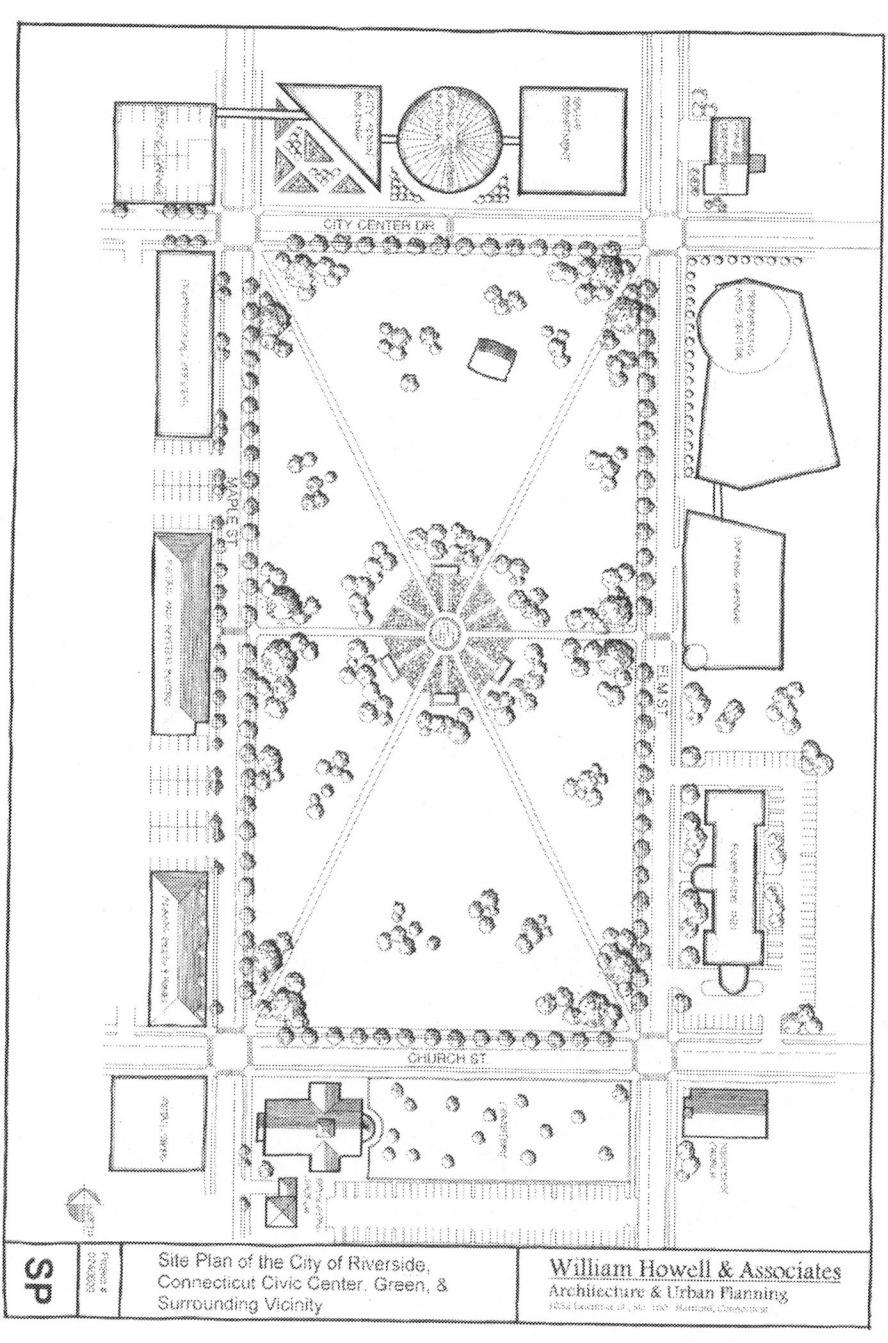

Prologue

Rose Nardello stepped through the revolving door at the main entrance to the Riverside Inn, stopped, and waited while Dr. Julius Simpkins conferred with the front desk clerk. When Dr. Simpkins joined her, Rose asked, "Everything okay?"

"Yes. The suite that Frank requested just became available. They'll move my things after lunch."

"Good." Rose looked up into the late September sky, and then at the trees surrounding the "Green" across the street. "What a magnificent day, Doctor. Look at those trees. The fall colors are beginning to take over."

The "Green," as it was affectionately called by the citizens of Riverside, Connecticut, was a 100 year old, 20-acre park at the very center of the city. A large fountain, surrounded by four war memorials honoring veterans of WW I, WW II, and the Korean and Vietnam wars, served as the focal point of the rectangular park. A concrete sidewalk encircled the park and four additional walkways crisscrossed the Green and connected at the fountain. Elm trees formed a canopy above the diagonal walkways, while maple trees shaded the sidewalk that encircled the Green.

Wearing black slacks, black flats, a white blouse, and a lightweight black sweater, Rose took a deep breath, reached out, and grasped Dr. Simpkins' arm. They descended three steps and walked down a winding sidewalk to Elm Street, passing a series of colorful flowerbeds on the way, and stopped at the curb. Dressed in gray slacks, a blue blazer, and University of California tie, Dr. Simpkins lifted his head toward the sky.

He shielded his eyes from the glare, and remarked, "My father used to call a day like this 'football weather.'" He turned toward Rose and added, "It's so pleasant, it'll be tough working indoors today. I'd love to walk around the Green before our meeting, but we don't have enough time."

Rose looked at her watch. "Unfortunately, you're right. The meeting starts in 15 minutes. Why don't we visit the monitoring sites later? I haven't seen the Laser Trail equipment yet."

"Good idea. We'll visit both sites after lunch."

As a sign of respect and friendship, Rose smiled and squeezed the 66-year-old African-American's arm. Simpkins returned the smile, and thought, *It's been awhile since an attractive young lady held onto my arm.* They turned right and began the short walk along Elm Street toward the Riverside City Center.

Approaching the entrance to the Elm Street Parking Garage, Rose turned her head and asked, "Are you satisfied with the initial test results from the Laser Trail system?"

"It looks like it will be even more reliable than Charlie Olson forecast. Come to think of it, I should give him a call today. I'm sure he'll be pleased."

"Will the system provide enough data to satisfy the attorneys?"

"So far, I'd have to answer with a qualified yes. The data collected during the first four days appear to support the city's complaint. From what I've seen so far, I predict that our findings will show that D.E.C. engines are the dirtiest diesels on the road. I can't see how D.E.C. can come close to achieving the 2007 requirements set by the E.P.A. without achieving a significant technological breakthrough. In spite of the impressive data collected so far, it won't be enough to satisfy a jury. The university statistics professor you retained said that we'll have to test at both monitoring sites for at least 30 days if we are to achieve the level of statistical reliability we need to support the pathology report. But, I'm confident we'll have enough data to convince a jury after 30 days. I have one word of caution, however. First results during a test like this can be deceiving, Rose."

Passing the entrance to the Performing Arts Center, Rose saw Dr. Simpkins smile. "I feel pretty good, Rose. Working with the city of Riverside is a far cry from what I've been doing the last six months. I feel like I've been reborn, like I'm accomplishing something, something important. Sitting around the house, twiddling my thumbs gets old pretty fast. My wife told me a few weeks ago to stop moping, and go out and volunteer my time for some worthy cause. I told her I didn't want to just give away my knowledge and experience. 'Well, write a book,' she said." Simpkins laughed. "I guess retirement isn't my cup of tea." Rose saw a look of satisfaction on his face. His chest was thrust forward, and even his step seemed to communicate confidence. Rose smiled when she realized she had to increase the length of her stride just to keep up.

Suddenly, her peripheral vision saw Dr. Simpkins' head snap forward. He stumbled and began to fall. Rose's momentum carried her one step further before she was able to disengage her arm from his, and right herself. Simpkins collapsed face down on the sidewalk. When Rose saw a pool of blood begin to form around his head, she placed her hands on her cheeks, and screamed.

Two men, who'd been jogging together around the periphery of the Green, rushed across the street in response to Rose's cry. One man had a cell phone attached to his belt and dialed 911. The other man knelt down next to Dr. Simpkins. He saw a hole in the top right side of his head and shouted, "He's been shot!" He lowered his head further to get a better look. He gasped. There wasn't much left of the lower left side of Simpkins' face: most of it was splattered on the sidewalk and in the gutter.

Instinctively, the man with the cell phone whirled around and looked up toward the roof of the parking garage, and then turned to look toward the roof the Performing Arts Center. He grabbed Rose around the waist and pulled her toward the protection provided by the entrance to the P.A.C.

1

Rose Nardello's father, Mario, was just six years old when he and his family emigrated from Sicily to Pawtucket, Rhode Island, in 1946. Like many children of immigrant parents, young Mario was immediately thrust into a difficult situation: since his family spoke Italian at home, Mario struggled with English. His parents were unable to help. Because of the language liability and his out-of-the ordinary wardrobe, Mario became the butt of jokes and ridicule during the first and second grades. Mario lost interest in schoolwork, retreated within himself, and became combative. Not a week went by that he didn't arrive home with raw knuckles or a bloody nose. Mario's academic performance continued to slide as he progressed through elementary school. Even when he applied himself, he was not an especially good student. Mario's interest in athletics, however, soared. By the time he entered his junior year at North Pawtucket High School, Mario had matured into a strong, 200 pound, 6' man that happened to reside in a teenager's body. The general consensus around Pawtucket was that Mario Nardello had the potential to become one of Rhode Island's all-time, premier high school football players. Those predictions proved accurate: Mario was named to the Rhode Island All-State team during both his junior and senior years.

The military draft caught up with Mario within weeks of his graduation from high school: he spent the next two years in the United States Army. He didn't end up in Viet Nam like many of his fellow draftees, however. He broke his leg in two places during a climbing exercise while undergoing basic training at Fort Dix, New Jersey. A steel bar was inserted in his right femur to hold it together. He was given an administrative assignment and remained at Fort Dix until his tour of duty ended. Any aspirations that Mario might have had about playing college football after his tour ended were also shattered because of the leg injury.

Unlike Rose's father, her mother, Teresa, was born in the United States. Teresa's parents, Leonardo and Angela Aquavia, immigrated from the southern part of Italy to the United States before the onset of WW II. Within days of settling in Pawtucket, the ambitious couple acquired custodial jobs at the local telephone company and commenced saving for the day they could afford to open a restaurant.

The Aquavia's were determined not to allow the language barrier to interfere with their economic aspirations. They convinced a high school English teacher to tutor them for an hour every afternoon before they went off to work. When the couple's English proficiency enabled them to converse comfortably, they began implementing their business plan. They purchased a vacant two-story building on a busy street between the cities of Pawtucket and Providence, gutted the interior, and constructed an upscale restaurant they named "The Palermo." When the restaurant was completed, the Aquavia's renovated the second floor and created suitable living quarters.

The Palermo featured upscale Sicilian cuisine and quickly gained a reputation for serving quality food at reasonable prices. Unfortunately, the restaurant also became a favorite of the Providence area underworld. The Aquavias had mixed emotions about the Palermo becoming a gangster hangout. On the one hand, the mob was good for business: they were free spenders and loyal patrons. On the other hand, their presence was bad for business: conservative elements of the general public would leave and not return when they saw the cigar-smoking, rough-looking patrons, and overheard the occasional cursing.

The Aquavia children, Teresa and her younger brother Mark, would spend most of their free time after school helping their parents in the restaurant. The underworld customers delighted in observing Teresa and Mark at work: waiting tables, busing dishes, or just cleaning up their messes. It didn't take long for Teresa and Mark to be on a first name basis with each of them. The mobsters even developed games that were tied to the children's performance at school. They'd forecast the children's grades before a test and bet on the outcome, or they'd gamble about the children's chances of achieving certain academic goals.

A typical exchange between their leader, Vito Summa and little Teresa might have sounded like this: "Teresa, come tell your Uncle Vito what youse did in school today."

"I was teased by Jackie O'Brien, Uncle Vito. And he pulled my hair."

"Them damn Micks, they don't know no better. Do what my boy Tony does. He punches the little creeps in the mouth. How'd you do with that arithmetic test, Teresa?"

"I got an A, Uncle Vito."

"Good for you, young lady. Hear that, youse jerks? Teresa got an A. That makes me the winner. Who's got the pot?"

Fortunately, the attention the gangsters lavished on Teresa and Mark had a positive effect: it created a competitive environment that actually motivated the children. Throughout elementary school and high school, both Aquavia children earned high grades and were consistently listed on the school's academic honor roll. With the aid of the many scholarships and financial awards the children earned from local service and non-profit organizations while in high school, the parents were able to send both children to college: Teresa to St. Mary's School of Nursing; and Mark to the University of Rhode Island, and then on to the Southeast School of Law. Mark graduated from the law school, passed the bar, and to the dismay of his parents, became a successful counsel to the underworld customers he'd befriended as a child. Attorney Mark Aquavia was short, like his mother: he never grew taller than 5' 8". One could tell at a glance that he was from Italian stock. He was slightly overweight, had a dark complexion, jet-black hair, chunky face and nose, and a serious disposition.

Teresa was an inch taller than her brother. She also was dark with black hair. But, unlike her brother, Teresa was very attractive, possessed a marvelous sense of humor, and had an infectious smile and laugh. Six months into nurses training, Teresa married her high school sweetheart, Mario Nardello. She was able to continue her studies after the marriage because Mario held a secure job as a warehouseman with Mayflower Van Lines.

After graduating with honors, Teresa made arrangements to take the state exam for certification as a registered nurse. She scored a significantly higher grade on the state exam than she'd anticipated and earned her certification. Seven months later, Teresa delivered her only child, Rose Frances, on schedule and naturally.

2

By the time Rose Frances reached her early teens, she possessed her mother's smile; her dark, shoulder length hair; her mother's gray/blue eyes; and her father's Mediterranean coloring. The general consensus within the Nardello neighborhood was that Rose would mature into a beautiful woman. Beauty was just one of Rose's assets, however: she was an inquisitive and gifted student as well. Each school year her academic scores would place her in the top ten percent of her class.

Rose understood at an early age that extra-curricular activities could be just as important to her future as good grades. When she entered high school, she tried out for the cross-country team and discovered that she possessed the endurance required of a long distance runner. She embarked on a disciplined training regimen that included after school workouts with the team and running two miles on her own most mornings before school. Rose would run on the streets in her neighborhood on even days. On odd days she'd run through the industrial district of Pawtucket near her father's business.

It didn't take long before Rose became aware of the numerous homeless people that were hanging about the streets near her father's business, especially on the street that ran between her father's truck yard and the loading docks of the Diesel Engine Corporation. She saw men curled up in the fetal position in doorways, women pushing grocery carts overflowing with clothing and junk, men rooting through garbage cans, and especially elderly men and women shuffling along going nowhere and seemingly in a trance.

Rose focused on the activities of one elderly man in particular. *I see him every time I run through this section of town*, she thought. *He must make his home somewhere around here.* The old gent was not very tall; wore a knit cap; tattered pants; and an ankle length, stained raincoat that touched the tops of his mismatched shoes. He muttered as he walked, sometimes in a loud voice, as though he were arguing with himself.

One cold morning in late October, as Rose approached an intersection next to the main parking lot of the Diesel Engine Corporation, she was forced to stop and wait for a traffic light to turn. While she waited, she saw the same old timer walk up to a beat up car parked on the street only a few yards from the intersection. The man leaned over and knocked on the window. Rose watched him for a moment and then observed a woman sitting on the driver's side motioning for the man to move on. Rose walked toward the car and noticed that the woman was in the process of dressing two small children. Rose thought, *I wonder if that man is going to cause trouble.* A sudden sensation of concern for the children caused her to move even closer. She stopped abruptly, realizing that the developing situation was none of her business, turned around and went back to the intersection.

The scene she'd just witnessed, however, kept replaying in her mind as she completed her run: *How can the woman care for the children while living in an automobile?* Rose had been agonizing for days about a subject for a writing assignment at school and decided to investigate the plight of the homeless as an appropriate subject. She'd return the next morning and try to talk with the woman living in the car.

The car wasn't where Rose expected it to be the following morning. She jogged around the block and down a side street toward the rear of her father's property to see if maybe the woman had moved the vehicle. She found the car parked on a street behind her father's business. The woman was squatting on the sidewalk talking to the children. Rose could see that she was wearing threadbare slacks, a beat-up green sweater, and a baseball cap. Her hair looked unwashed and greasy. Both of the children appeared to be dressed in old clothes as well: long pants, worn sneakers, and jackets. In contrast, Rose was wearing new running shoes and sweats, with North Pawtucket High School printed across the front.

Rose stopped in the street on the opposite side of the vehicle, and looked inside. She saw an unorganized collection of clothing on the passenger seat and two small pillows on the back seat. Rose thought, *I wonder where the woman sleeps? I guess sitting up in the driver's seat.* Containers of food were piled on the floor in front of the passenger seat and on the floor of the back seat. Rose walked around to the other side of the car and said, "Excuse me." The woman looked up, but didn't reply. Rose continued, "I'm sorry to intrude. May I ask you a few questions?"

The woman stood, placed her hands on her hips, and scowled. Sensing danger, the children, a girl and a boy, clutched the woman's legs and placed their heads against her thighs. The woman stared at Rose. Her scowl slowly softened and was replaced by a questioning look. She asked, "Why?"

"I passed your car yesterday and noticed a man looking in your window. Does he bother you?"

Recognizing that the teenager wasn't threatening, the woman smiled and answered, "Uncle Jimmy? No. He's a harmless old fellow." She reached down and caressed the heads of the children. "He loves my children. He'd never hurt them or me."

Observing that the woman's hostility was beginning to melt away, Rose smiled and reached out with her right hand. "My name is Rose Nardello. Is there anything I can do to help?"

Taking Rose's hand, the woman said, "My name is Rita Fernandez." Rita shifted her feet, and put her arms around the shoulders of her children. "If you really want to help, help me find a job so I can take care of my children." Rita studied Rose for a few more moments, and asked, "Are you a student?"

"Yes, ma'am. I'm a senior at North Pawtucket High." Rose squatted in front of the children and looked at the little girl. "My name's Rose. What's your name?"

The girl lifted her head and searched the eyes of her mother. Rita nodded. The girl said, "Elizabeth."

"What a beautiful name. How old are you Elizabeth?"

"Four."

Turning her head to face the boy, Rose said, "Now it's your turn young man. What's your name and how old are you?"

The boy straightened, pushed out his chest, and replied, "My name is Jon, and I'm five and a half."

"Well, I guess you're the man of the family." Rose stood up and said, "I've got to go home and get ready for school. I'll do my best to help you, Rita. It'd help if you could write down on a piece of paper what you're qualified to do. I'll talk with my father first."

Rita searched the eyes of the teenager to detect the level of sincerity. Believing the request was legitimate, she said, "I'll write up something and give it to you in the morning."

"Will you be here tomorrow morning?"

"Probably, unless the police run us off."

Rose shook Rita's hand, waved at the children and resumed her run.

3

"Dad, here is the information that Rita Fernandez gave me this morning. It looks like she earned an AA degree from the local junior college, then married when she was 21, and had both children before she turned 24. Her husband took off after the birth of the little girl and left her with nothing. It doesn't look like she's had much work experience."

Mario Nardello studied the two-page, handwritten note. "She says that her degree is in computer science. That could fit with what I have in mind. What's your opinion of this Rita Fernandez?"

"I haven't talked with her enough to comment one way or the other, but my gut says that she may be very smart. If you can find a place for her in the company, I have a gut feeling that you wouldn't be disappointed."

Mario sat quietly for a few moments. "I sure could use more support with dispatch. Keeping track of my drivers is becoming a problem. I need more visibility. It's hard to firm up a schedule for the next day when you're not sure where the drivers are today. We've got to develop a better system to control their whereabouts." Mario sighed. "I'll talk with her, Rose."

"That's great, Dad. How about tomorrow afternoon after school? I can bring her over to your office."

"Okay, if you'll watch the children. I want to meet with her alone."

Rita liked the middle-aged man immediately. Mario was relaxed, which in turn, helped Rita relax. Although Mario asked some penetrating questions about the courses Rita completed while attending the junior college and about her knowledge of computers, he seemed to be more interested in how she cared for her children. Rita liked that. Mario, in turn, was impressed with Rita's knowledge of computers and her verbal communication skills. However, he was having mixed emotions about offering her a job. On the one hand, he was proud of Rose for attempting to help a homeless mother and her children, and he wanted desperately to support that effort. On the other hand, he realized that he'd be taking a flyer if he hired her: Rita had no meaningful work experience.

Mario ran out of questions and sat quietly looking at the top of his desk. He began to fidget: he knew he couldn't delay a decision any longer. If he offered Rita Fernandez a job, he knew that he'd have to do more than put her on the payroll. She couldn't work for him and continue to live in an automobile. Mario looked up into the eyes of the obviously stressed young mother and asked, "How'd you like to work for Nardello Trucking?"

A broad smile creased Rita's cheeks. She sat up straight. "I'd jump at the chance to work for your company, Mr. Nardello."

"We could set up a special training program for you so you could learn the business and the duties of a dispatcher. Could you start the first of the month?"

"Yes, sir!"

Mario stood up and reached across the desk to take Rita's hand. "Welcome to Nardello Trucking. The first thing we've got to do is find you a place to live and some one to take care of the children while you're at work. I'll talk with my wife and my daughter this evening. We'll get back to you in the morning. Call me around nine, or stop by the office."

Equipped with a written job offer and a written commitment from her father to pay first and last months rent and a damage deposit, Rose and Rita were able to find an inexpensive, vacant apartment on the second day of their search.

Furnishing Rita's apartment became a labor of love for the Nardellos. Teresa convinced Mario to donate a few chairs, a table, and an old chest of drawers stored in their basement. Then she purchased three inexpensive beds from a local furniture store. Before the end of the week, Rita and the children were able to move into their new home. The Nardellos were so pleased with the turn of events they celebrated by buying new clothes for the entire family, and hosted Rita and the children to dinner at the Palermo, now regarded as one of Pawtucket's finest restaurants.

Mario assigned the responsibility for Rita's training to the company's traffic manager and requested weekly reports on her job performance. Initial reports were very positive and complimentary: Rita was learning the nuances of the trucking business quickly. The traffic manager suggested that she'd be able to assume the duties of a dispatcher within a matter of weeks.

Rose was so proud of her parents for helping turn around the life of a homeless mother, she wrote a story about what they had done and submitted it to the local newspaper in the form of a letter to the editor. The letter caused quite a stir. A reporter from the local public radio station called Mario and requested an interview. Instead of accepting praise for their act of charity, Mario shifted the credit to his daughter and to Rita Fernandez. "My wife, daughter, and I are pleased we could help a young mother find a job and provide for her children. We helped Miss Fernandez furnish her new apartment and Mrs. Nardello cared for the children for a few weeks while Rita got on her feet. Miss Fernandez worked very hard. I'm proud to report that she now holds a responsible position with Nardello Trucking. The person that deserves most of the credit is the mother, Rita Fernandez. She's a remarkable lady!"

The news report resulted in an invitation for Rose and Rita to meet with the Mayor. In front of TV cameras, the Mayor honored Rose with a good citizen award. That award, coupled with being named valedictorian of her senior class and her many extracurricular activities, resulted in Rose being awarded five separate scholarships from local service clubs and fraternal organizations during the North Pawtucket High School graduation ceremonies. Rose could have attended any one of the prestigious private universities in New England, but she selected the University of Rhode Island. U.R.I. offered the kind of public administration major she was searching for.

4

A heavy, persistent rain had fallen during the night. Rose looked through the window of her Graduate Center dormitory room and frowned. *The ceremony will have to be moved indoors. I guess it doesn't matter, as long as I get my degree.* Rose had two hours to kill before her parents were scheduled to arrive. She opened her desk drawer and retrieved the orientation material she'd just received from the city of Riverside, Connecticut. A smile of satisfaction lit up her face as she reread the letter from the city manager offering her a job as the city's first ever administrative trainee.

> Dear Miss Nardello:
> The Riverside City Council has approved my request to create a new administrative trainee position. Because of your academic achievements and community involvement, the Council has directed me to offer the position to you.
> This letter will serve as my formal invitation to you to join our administrative staff starting Monday, July 5, 1998. An employee contract is enclosed. Call me if you have any questions about the terms of the contract. Please sign both copies of the contract and return it to me at your earliest convenience.
> Sincerely,
> Frank Mancuso, city manager

The significance of their daughter's graduation from the University of Rhode Island Business School monopolized Mario and Teresa's conversation as they drove from their home in Pawtucket to the campus in Kingston. They were pinching themselves because their only daughter was about to receive a master's degree in public administration. As they drove south on Interstate 95, Mario and Teresa would sneak glances at each other and smile like two children. The idea that a member of the Nardello family would ever earn a master's degree in anything could only have been described as a dream 20 years ago.

Their euphoria slowly shifted to nervousness as they approached Kingston: the rainstorm had slowed traffic to a crawl. When they drove onto the U.R.I. campus, they were already ten minutes late for the graduation ceremony. They needn't have been concerned, however. Everything was running late. The rain had disrupted all the graduation activities. Dozens of chairs that had been set up on the grassy area in front of the Administration Building to accommodate family and friends had to be moved into the new indoor tennis facility.

Mario hugged Rose at the conclusion of the ceremony. "Your mother and I are so proud of you." Turning to face his wife, Mario added, "Can you believe it, Teresa, our daughter just received a master's degree?" Turning back to face Rose, Mario said, "I think we got some good pictures of you while you were receiving your diploma. Now, I want a picture of the three of us together. Let's ask one of your friends to take our picture."

Picture taking completed, Rose turned in her cap and gown and rejoined her parents at the entrance to the Tennis Center. Mario asked, "Is our favorite daughter hungry?"

"I'm famished, Dad."

"Let's drive over to Newport and splurge on lunch at the Beach House Restaurant." As they left the parking lot, Mario said, "You may remember me talking about the home of my neighbor, Winston Osborne, the C.E.O. of Diesel Engine Corporation. While we're in Newport, we'll drive by his waterfront home." Mario chuckled, "Winston has more money in his checking account than I'll earn in a lifetime." He sighed. "Unfortunately, Winston told me the other day that his latest physical didn't go well. His doctor told him that he may have prostate cancer, and until he knows for sure, he instructed Winston to cut back on his work load and to begin turning over the day-to-day management of the business to his son."

Teresa said, "I'm so sorry. He's such a nice man."

"What kind of a person is his son, Dad?"

"He's not like his father. In my opinion, he's a spoiled brat and a pompous ass. I'm worried that he may try to scrap the services contract that his father and I signed last year." Mario looked in the rear view mirror, and said,

"Enough about the Osborne's. Rose, give us an update about that job offer from Riverside."

"I'm really proud of the offer, Dad. I'll be the first management trainee the city of Riverside has ever hired. The salary isn't much, but it'll give me an opportunity to train under the wing of one of Connecticut's best city managers, Frank Mancuso. Frank's designed a special program for me. He wants me to spend at least two weeks in each city department, including the police and fire departments before he'll allow me to become his administrative assistant." She laughed and added, "He'll be a tough boss, but a good one."

Teresa said, "It sounds like this Mr. Mancuso wants you to stay around for awhile."

"He does, Mom. Frank and I talked about that. He's aware that I could demand a higher salary in private industry. That's why he committed to the training program. It partially substitutes for a higher wage. I think it's a brilliant idea."

"When do you start?"

"I report for work the week after next, Mom. Could you drive over to Riverside with me next week and help me find a place to live?"

"Certainly, honey. I'll be available whenever you decide to go."

5

After an eight-year courtship that began in high school, William "Bill" Rado and Ethyl Mary Anderson decided to marry in the spring of 1985. Bill was a handsome young man: high cheekbones, firm jaw, and a Mediterranean nose. His dark eyes were accentuated by black curly hair, olive complexion, and a perpetual smile. At 6' 1", but weighing only 180 pounds, Bill's parents believed he was too thin to play football, so he concentrated on basketball and baseball at Riverside High School. He was outstanding in both sports and earned all-state honorable mention as a second baseman during his senior year.

Ethyl Anderson was from Swedish stock: short at 5' 2" with blond hair, creamy white skin, and blue eyes. She was voted the prettiest girl in her senior year by the entire student body. Ethyl went on to earn a degree in nursing after high school. She passed the state's licensing exam and joined the staff at Riverside Hospital. Because of her unflinching dedication to pediatrics, she was promoted to day shift supervisor after only three years on the job.

Meanwhile, Bill was earning an accounting degree from the University of Connecticut. He, too, passed the state licensing exam and was awarded certification as a public accountant. His one-man practice catered to Riverside's small business community. Bill was proud of his practice: he could count on one hand the number of times a client of his had to suffer through an IRS audit.

Two years after their marriage, Ethyl gave birth to their first child. They named him Robert (Bobby) after Ethyl's uncle, a municipal court judge in Massachusetts. They purchased their first home, a vintage 1950s house, before little Bobby celebrated his second birthday. The house was located in a middle-class neighborhood at the end of a cul-de-sac, nestled in the hills to the west of State Route 10 and just south of Riverside Hospital. A vibrant row of rose bushes provided a sea of color across the entire front of the house. Hedges framed the triangular shaped yard, one running along side the driveway and the other straddling the property line from the mailbox to the beginning of the back yard fence.

What was to become a close friendship between Rose Nardello and Ethyl Rado began at a Soroptomist International luncheon meeting in Riverside. They joined the service club for professional women after having been guest speakers. Rose, substituting for her boss, City Manager Mancuso, talked about the city's economic development initiatives. Ethyl, substituting for the hospital administrator, discussed the Riverside Hospital's growth plans.

The new friends looked forward to the weekly luncheon meetings and would make an effort to sit at the same table. During those luncheons, they'd talk about many things: developments at City Hall; Soroptomist activities; and especially, the current subject of Ethyl's concern, the deteriorating health of her son Bobby. The boy had begun experiencing respiratory difficulties soon after his fifth birthday. Like most parents of very young children, the Rados weren't overly concerned at first over the boy's occasional cough and breathing difficulties. After all, it wasn't unusual for a kindergartner to bring home colds and other maladies from school.

Rose asked, "How's Bobby?"

"I'm concerned, Rose. Bill and I are beginning to think he might be asthmatic. We hope not, but I had a grandfather who suffered with asthma until he reached adulthood. Dr. Panotti diagnosed it as a seasonal allergy, not that unusual during the spring."

When the frequency of Bobby's coughing spells increased, however, Ethyl's uneasiness grew. She told Rose that it pained her to watch her son breathe: his chest would rise and fall like he had just run a mile. Ethyl stopped attending Soroptomist luncheons and discontinued accepting shifts at the hospital. She began to check on her son while he slept, or she'd sit next to his bed and hold the little guy's hand.

The Rados revisited Dr. Panotti. He prescribed a stronger medication, but it became apparent quickly that the new drug was equally ineffective. Not knowing what else to do, Dr. Panotti recommended the Rados take Bobby to Dr. Sydney Bernstein, a pulmonary specialist at New Haven Hospital to undergo extensive tests.

"Are you ready to call it a day, Claire?"

"I've been ready since 4:00, Rose. I can practically taste the merlot."
"Let's walk over to the Bistro for a change. I'll meet you in the lobby."
"See you in five."

Claire Pasternak and Rose Nardello became friends within weeks of Rose's arrival at City Hall. The training program Frank Mancuso set up had her moving from one department to another every two weeks. Although she was meeting a lot of people, she wasn't staying around a department long enough to get to know anyone really well.

Rose was sitting alone at a table in the small City Hall cafeteria eating her lunch, a sandwich she'd purchased from a deli on the way to work, and reading an issue of Cosmopolitan when she heard a small voice ask, "Mind if join you?" Rose looked up. Standing across the table was a short, slim, almost skeletal woman Rose judged to be in her mid-twenties. She had a narrow pointed chin, high cheekbones, brown eyes and closely cropped black hair that seemed to accentuate her thin neck.

Rose smiled and answered, "Certainly."

The young woman placed her tray on the table, sat down and extended her hand. "I'm Claire Pasternak. I work over in the Building Department. Did I see you over there last week working with Chris Butler?"

"Yes, I was in your department last week." Returning Claire's handshake, Rose introduced herself. "I'm Rose Nardello, Frank Mancuso's administrative assistant. He has me visiting with each city department for a period of at least two weeks." Smiling, Rose added, "I guess he wants me to become the city's expert in everything." Rose closed the magazine. "I just finished the article I was reading and was about to get a cup of coffee. Can I get you one?"

"Yes, please. I'll take it black."

They sat at that table and chatted long after they'd finished their respective lunches. They talked about their jobs, joked about fellow employees, and discussed their personal lives. The chemistry between the two was evident immediately. A friendship was born.

Claire and Rose received a warm greeting when they approached the Bistro hostess. "I haven't seen you two for awhile. Good to have you back."

Claire said jokingly, "We have a civic responsibility to spread our business around town. Is Charlie Mancuso in? We'd like to say hello."

"Charlie won't be back for about an hour. I'll tell him you're here when he gets back."

When the friends were settled on stools at a small round table in the bar, Claire asked, "Have you talked with Ethyl Rado lately? I've heard that her son Bobby is still having breathing problems."

"Ethyl is really scared. They can't seem to put their finger on Bobby's problem. Their family doctor recommended that she take the boy to a pulmonary specialist in New Haven. Frank is very upset about what's happening to Bobby."

"Why is Mr. Mancuso upset? Is he a relative?"

"No. That's not it. It's the smog situation. Ethyl told him a few days ago that three more children were treated in the emergency room last week with symptoms similar to Bobby's. Frank is beginning to suspect that the children are getting sick because of the pollution that hangs over the city. Even I'm beginning to have trouble breathing. Frank's totally frustrated, Claire. He's fearful that Riverside is becoming another Los Angeles, and he admits that he doesn't know what he can to do about it. He was so upset yesterday he called the E.P.A. in Washington and talked with one of their officers. The lady told him that the Riverside's smog is probably no different than the smog in Los Angeles: a buildup of vehicle emissions, especially truck emissions. She said emissions contain a lot of unhealthy crap that can cause asthma, lung disease, and even cancer. Unless he was willing to limit vehicle traffic within the city, she said there wasn't much he can do about the problem."

Rose Nardello's new apartment was 22 miles west of Riverside. She'd found the vacancy the day Frank Mancuso announced that he wanted her to assume the city's economic development responsibilities. "Dick Wallace will retire at the end of the July. I want you to begin working with him immediately and be ready to take over when he leaves. You know what the city needs, Rose. I'm confident you'll do one hell of a job."

"I'm flattered, Frank, and very excited. I enthusiastically accept the challenge."

"It won't be easy, Rose. Delta Brass is scheduled to complete its relocation to South Carolina in September. The loss of jobs will hurt this community and make a big dent in city tax revenues. Filling the job void has got to be our highest priority."

Rose was jubilant when she left City Hall that day: the promotion was exactly what she'd been seeking for the past few months. She decided to drive west into the countryside, locate a country inn, and treat herself to dinner. The gentle rolling hills, not unlike the swells one would see on a calm ocean, were replete with green grass and trees as far as the eye could see. She noticed everything, especially the horses grazing in the fields in front of large fenced horse farms and the well-maintained country estates. Many of the older homes, closer to the road, featured colorful flower gardens and signs indicating when they'd been built. She found the type of restaurant she was looking for in the village of Westwood, a small community on the eastern side of the Housatonic River. A sign on the front lawn read "Westwood Inn, 1834." The white, two-story building featured black shutters, and four dormers on the second level. A windowed porch extended across the entire front of the building and served as a second dinning room. While Rose waited in the lobby for a table in the main dinning room overlooking the River, she noticed a bulletin board filled with all sorts of notices: cars and trucks for sale, homes for sale, and apartments for rent. One item in particular caught her eye: an apartment vacancy in an old, rebuilt country house. She called the number listed in the ad from a pay phone in the lobby. The owner, James Bishop, invited her to stop by after dinner to check it out.

When Rose drove up the circular drive in front of Bishop House, she was surprised by the size of the structure. It was a very large, three-story colonial mansion that had been converted into five apartments: two on each of the first two floors and a single one-bedroom unit on the third floor in what used to be the attic. Jim Bishop met her at the front entrance and guided her up the stairs to the vacant unit on the third floor. In spite of the inconvenience of climbing stairs, Rose fell in love with the one-bedroom apartment. The view from the large front room window was exhilarating: undulating hills as far as the eye could see, interrupted only by a barn, a farmhouse, or an occasional open space between the trees.

They descended the stairs back to the ground level and walked around the building to the back yard. Green grass and flowerbeds dominated the space. A hammock swung from two large branches of a maple tree. A small dog looked up from where it rested next to the hammock. When the dog saw Rose, it wagged its tail and rushed across the lawn to greet her. Rose squatted down. The dog continued to wag its tail while it licked Rose's hand. Rose turned and looked up at Mr. Bishop. "What kind of a dog is that, Mr. Bishop?"

"It's a mutt, Miss Nardello. Name's Alice. She's a harmless little creature. She's been with us for quite a few years now."

Rose decided that this was the home she wanted, despite knowing the drive to and from work would take at least a half hour each way. Without further hesitation, she agreed to rent the apartment.

6

Ethyl and Bill Rado sat in the waiting room while Dr. Bernstein reviewed their son's medical history and conducted a thorough physical examination. They tried to read magazines but found that it was difficult to concentrate. An hour passed, and the anxiety grew. When Dr. Bernstein finally reentered the waiting room, he was holding Bobby's hand. He informed the Rados that he'd sent a blood sample to the hospital laboratory for analysis. In spite of the priority he'd placed on the sample, he expected that it would take over an hour to run the tests he'd requested. He suggested that they visit the hospital cafeteria, buy Bobby some ice cream, and come back in an hour and a half.

When they reconvened in the waiting room, Dr. Bernstein asked an assistant to take Bobby for a walk around the hospital while he met with the parents. "Mr. and Mrs. Rado, I believe in being forthright when the situation is serious. It's not fair to you or me, for that matter, to beat around the bush. Based on the information provided by your family doctor, a review of your son's medical record, and the results of the blood test, your boy's breathing difficulties have become a very serious matter." Bernstein pushed back his chair, stood, walked around the desk, and sat on the edge with one leg dangling. "When I listened to his breathing, I was alarmed by the sounds I heard. I'd hoped that it was an indication of a severe allergic reaction. Now, I'm convinced it's more serious than that, and the blood test confirmed what I suspected: Bobby is suffering from chronic obstructive pulmonary disease. In other words, he is suffering from a severe case of emphysema. I recommend that we keep Bobby here for observation and further tests."

The Rados looked at each other and both nodded. Bill spoke first. "I think that's probably a good idea, Dr. Bernstein. His breathing has been so labored the last few days, none of us sleep very well."

Ethyl added, "Can you give him something to help him breathe, Doctor? He's struggling so...I don't know what to do." She lowered her face into her hands and began to weep.

Bill reached over and wrapped his arm around her shoulders and said, "We did the right thing bringing Bobby here." Then, turning to look into Bernstein's eyes, he added, "Dr. Bernstein will do whatever he can to help."

"Mrs. Rado, Bobby will have access to the best medicine available in the United States. Be assured, whatever should be done, will be done."

Before the Rados were out of the hospital parking lot, Dr. Bernstein had dispatched Bobby's medical history to New Haven Hospital's environmental epidemiological medical team.

7

Mario Nardello clipped an article from the Providence Journal and sent it to his daughter. The article described the expansion dilemma faced by Pulmoco, a Providence area medical instrument manufacturer. The article quoted the President of Pulmoco, Dr. Austin Knowles. "Pulmoco has outgrown our only building in Providence: an old, converted textile factory that we've occupied for six years. We're faced with two alternatives: split the operation and relocate a portion of the business to another old, vacant building near the existing facility; or, build a new facility outside Providence and move the entire operation." Dr. Knowles stated further that he would be traveling to New Haven, Connecticut, at the end of the month to attend a medical equipment conference, and while he was there, he'd talk with city officials about moving his entire operation to New Haven.

Mario Nardello, keenly aware of his daughter's new economic development responsibilities, suggested that Rose might construct a package of incentives to motivate Pulmoco to relocate to Riverside. Mario attached a note to the article. "Corralling a quality organization like Pulmoco might serve as a foundation for a biotechnology center in Riverside. You should make plans to attend the medical equipment conference and introduce yourself to Dr. Knowles."

Rose liked her father's idea. But, she was also a realist: Riverside lacked the basic conditions conducive to establishing an important biotechnology center, namely, a university with a respected biology department. Rose was confidant Riverside could provide engineering expertise, but the paucity of knowledgeable biologists and bioscience professionals represented a major stumbling block. She recognized another obstacle: while respected for its quality care, Riverside Hospital was not a research hospital.

Rose was not deterred, in spite of these shortcomings. She responded immediately to her father's suggestion and sent off a request for a registration packet. She signed up to attend two panel discussions on the first day of the conference. The first panel, scheduled for 8:00 a.m., featured four noted medical experts who had been asked to discuss the causes of lung cancer. Rose didn't expect much in the way of economic development information from that panel, but because of what Frank had said about the smog buildup in Riverside, she was intrigued by the subject matter.

Rose arrived at the New Haven Convention Center before 7:30; ordered a cup of coffee and a bagel from one of the concessionaires. As she reread the information about the first panel, she tried to recall why the name of the panel's moderator, Dr. Sydney Bernstein, a professor from the New Haven Medical School, was familiar to her. She was not able to make the connection, however, and returned the conference brochure to her briefcase, and left the concession area.

She located the room reserved for the first panel and selected a front row seat directly in front of four name cards on a raised table that identified each panelist. Dr. Bernstein was already seated studying his notes. Rose tried again to recall why his name was familiar. *Have I seen him before?* she thought. He was a swarthy man, probably in his mid-fifties. His hair was still mostly black but was beginning to show signs of gray in the sideburns. Rose focused on the man's eyes: they appeared to be brooding under thick, unruly brows. His nose was fairly large. Although he was seated, Rose thought Bernstein to be of medium height and looked as though he possessed a muscular body. He wore dark gray slacks, blue blazer, and a conservative tie. *Probably a product of Yale*, she thought.

After the remaining panelists took their seats, Dr. Bernstein announced, "Ladies and gentlemen, before I introduce the panelists, I want to issue a warning. We may shock you this morning with some startling and controversial information. We will discuss the negative health effects of a technology that you live with every day: diesel power." Rose sat up straight. Dr. Bernstein looked to his left at the other three panelists, smiled and added, "Ladies and gentlemen, we have irrefutable evidence that the exhaust from diesel engines is more than just black smoke. It's poison!" Bernstein waited for the murmuring to die down. Bernstein raised his voice, and added, "Diesel exhaust is not only dirty, it's toxic and carcinogenic. It's a major cause of lung cancer and many respiratory diseases, especially in children. Seniors are also very vulnerable to this poison, but we're most concerned about children. Just think of the number of school playgrounds that are close to a major truck route in this country, and you'll begin to understand why we're concerned.

"Suspecting industry collusion to cover up this problem, the California Air Resources Board recently brought an enforcement action against diesel engine manufacturers. The agency fined the manufacturers millions and directed the industry to introduce cleaner engines on an expedited schedule." Bernstein picked up a report he'd placed next to his microphone. "C.A.R.B. said, and I quote, 'Diesel engine manufacturers have conspired to circumvent existing regulations in California by using faulty electronic timing devices. The industry ignored existing regulations, and may be held accountable for respiratory illnesses caused by pollutants emitted from their diesel engines.' The statement went on to question the accuracy and integrity of emissions data published by the manufacturers. Last year, the California Air Resources Board identified diesel emissions as the direct cause of close to 2,000 deaths in California." Bernstein dropped the document on the table, looked up at the attendees, and added, "That's a powerful charge, folks." Dr. Bernstein scanned the audience of over 20 people, including a member of the New Haven press. For over one hour and thirty minutes, Dr. Bernstein and his fellow panelists presented incriminating and convincing data from a variety of sources to support their contention that diesel emissions represent a serious health risk to children and seniors.

At the conclusion of the time allotted for the panel, Rose stood up and approached Dr. Bernstein. "Doctor, my name is Rose Nardello. I'm the new economic development director at the city of Riverside. May I speak with you for a few moments?"

"I have about ten minutes, Miss Nardello, and then I have to get back to the hospital."

"I think that will be enough time, Doctor. Our city manager is becoming increasingly concerned about diesel truck traffic passing through Riverside. If you look at a map, you'll see that Interstate 64 and State Route 10 intersect in the center of the city. About six months ago, the city asked a statistics professor at the University of Connecticut to put together a sampling regime so we could count the number of long-haul trucks that pass through that intersection. Based on the professor's statistical model, we sampled at various times of the day for an entire month. We discovered there is a lot more truck traffic than we originally thought. I can't remember the exact number, but something in the neighborhood of 8,000 trucks per day pass through that intersection."

"Now that's very interesting! That kind of truck traffic is probably the crux of your smog problem, Miss Nardello. As you just heard from our panelists, diesel engines emit very harmful pollutants." Rose looked confused. She didn't know how to respond to that statement. Dr. Bernstein smiled, revealing a mouth full of well-proportioned white teeth. "I'm sorry, Miss Nardello. When I talk about diesel emissions, I tend to get a little worked up at times." Dr. Bernstein patted Rose on the shoulder. She didn't flinch. Looking into his eyes, she recognized that his intent was not sexual, but rather, fatherly. Dr. Bernstein continued, "Your count at the intersection of I-64 and Route 10 is close to one tabulated by the California Department of Transportation last year at the intersection of Interstates 5 and 405, just south of Los Angeles. The department counted over 10,000 trucks per day and found that over 90 percent of the trucks were powered by diesel engines.

"The scientific community is becoming increasingly concerned about the harmful effects of diesel emissions, but the public remains unaware of the severity of the problem. We have an environmental epidemiological team right here at New Haven Hospital. We're beginning to share data with the California Air Resources Board, Harvard University, and numerous other research groups. Unfortunately, our governmental agencies, especially at the federal level, aren't doing much to inform the public about the diesel problem."

Rose blurted out, "I just made the connection. Are you the specialist who's caring for five year old Bobby Rado?"

"Yes, I am."

"I'm a friend of Ethyl Rado. She told me the other day that her boy is not doing well. She said that he has emphysema. How serious is that, Doctor?"

"I'm sorry, Miss Nardello. I'm only able to discuss the Rado boy's condition with family members."

"I understand. But, my friend is very discouraged. Is she overreacting, Doctor?"

"No, she isn't overreacting. I see little that would allow me to be optimistic. My colleagues and I have consulted with specialists at the Mayo Clinic, but we still can't seem to arrest the onslaught of the disease. I know I shouldn't be telling you this, but since you are a close friend, you'll find out soon enough. We believe that the poison emitted from diesel engines near the

Rado home is the root cause of his emphysema, and we don't have a remedy for that, Miss Nardello."

"If the Rados were to move away from Riverside wouldn't that solve the problem?"

"Unfortunately, moving him now would have little effect on the boy's health. All we can do now is ease his pain and help him breath. If things don't improve within the next two days, we plan to send him home."

Rose was momentarily stunned. Not having children of her own, Rose couldn't even imagine what it would be like to lose a child. Her thoughts then segued to thoughts of her father's trucking business in Rhode Island: most of his trucks were powered by diesel engines. She wondered how the health risks associated with diesel emissions might affect the future of his trucking business. Rose asked, "What do you think will happen to the trucking industry, Doctor? My father owns a moving company in Pawtucket. Will the government ban diesel trucks? How will these new findings affect his business?"

"I wouldn't be concerned about that, young lady. We're a long way from legislation that would ban, let alone restrict, the use of diesel-fueled engines here in New England. I'm sure that only a few politicians are even aware that there's a health problem, and when they become aware, the trucking industry will do everything in its power to disrupt attempts to restrict the use of diesel fuel. Organizations like C.A.R.B. can influence change in California through mandates, incentives, and court challenges, but it will take years for similar initiatives to appear here in New England."

"I'm sure my city manager would like to hear what you just told me about diesel emissions, but I'm not qualified to repeat it accurately. Could you send me documentation?"

"I'd be happy to, Miss Nardello. I'll pull together copies of articles and reports and send them off early next week. My schedule is pretty loaded up right now, but I imagine I could drive up to Riverside and meet with your city manager after he's had time to review the material."

"That'd be great, Doctor. Here's my business card."

Looking at his watch, Bernstein said, "I've got to get back to the hospital. I've enjoyed talking with you, Miss Nardello. I wish I'd had better news about the Rado boy."

During the drive back to Riverside from the New Haven medical equipment conference, Rose kept reviewing the conversation she'd had with Dr. Bernstein. His declaration that there was a direct connection between lung disease and diesel engine exhaust troubled her greatly, especially when she thought that her father's trucks might be adversely affecting the health of innocent children. *I should have realized that the black crap spewing out of my father's trucks had to be harmful.* Rose slammed the flat of her hand against the steering wheel. "Damn it!" she shouted. "How could I have been so stupid? It's unconscionable!" *What can I do? I can't talk to Dad about it yet: I don't know enough. He'd just wave me off and say that the lung disease/ truck exhaust connection is just another liberal challenge directed at small business.*

It was difficult, however, for Rose to think negatively about trucks: trucks played such a positive role during her childhood. Her father, a strong, tough Italian immigrant, would tenderly lift her up to sit in the truck cab next to him and patiently explain why he had to shift gears. He even taught her how to read road maps, and at times, depended on her to navigate. The experience of riding along in the truck cab with her father inspired Rose to take an interest in all forms of transportation. While attending elementary school, she and her mother would visit the Pawtucket library and borrow books about trucks, trains, and airplanes to read at bedtime. Before she was ten years old, Rose's bedroom walls were a gallery of posters displaying trucks, aircraft of all kinds, and trains. She could recite which airlines serviced the Providence Airport, as well as the schedules of passenger trains that passed through Providence on their way to and from Boston.

Rose unlocked the front door to the apartment, moved through the living area into the kitchen, placed her brief case on the counter, and entered the bedroom. She changed into more comfortable clothes and slid her feet into slippers. Returning to the kitchen, she uncorked a bottle of merlot and poured a glass. The kitchen, large for a one bedroom apartment, had been designed to optimize counter space: one side of a two way counter ran perpendicular to the sink and provided space for food preparation and other kitchen chores, while the opposite side was used as a casual eating surface.

Rose sat at the counter and began to sort through the material she'd collected during the conference. She reviewed the annual report of Pulmoco Incorporated, and then read the material from N.E.I. Rose had been impressed with N.E.I.'s marketing executive that she'd talked with while visiting the company's booth. She was intrigued that N.E.I. had the same problem that Pulmoco had: their facility in New Bedford was bursting at the seams. They were considering a move to more spacious quarters somewhere in Rhode Island or Massachusetts.

She attempted to read the N.E.I. material a second time, but her ability to concentrate stalled. Dr. Bernstein's remarks about the harmful effects of diesel emissions elbowed all other thoughts from her mind. She placed the N.E.I. material on the counter, stood up, and walked into the living room to look at her favorite view. Normally, she'd be captivated, but not today.

She began to mentally explore the consequences of unchecked diesel emissions. *I wonder if vehicle emissions are any worse than second hand smoke? Both spew life-threatening stuff into the air that people ingest involuntarily. Dad can't be aware of the problem or he'd do something about it. Is it my responsibility to talk with him, and if it is, how can I do it without alienating him? I'm still his innocent little girl. I've always deferred to his judgment about things. Maybe if I could just show him the facts that support Dr. Bernstein's conclusions, he'd listen.* Rose realized she couldn't resolve the dilemma until she learned much more about the subject and enlisted the help of someone with credibility to accompany her when she talked with her father.

The Rados were becoming physically and emotionally drained. Working a full day and driving to and from Riverside to the New Haven Hospital every night to visit their son was beginning to take its toll. Bill would close his accounting office at 5:00, pick up Ethyl at Riverside Hospital, and drive to New Haven without stopping for dinner. On the fifth day of Bobby's hospitalization, the couple decided that Ethyl should take a leave of absence from her job and rent a room in a motel near the hospital. Ethyl telephoned Rose at City Hall and asked her to please stop at her house after work to check for telephone messages and mail. "Bill won't get home until after 10:00, and he'll have to leave for work before 8:00. If there is anything urgent, call me on my cell phone."

"Not a problem." Rose hesitated before asking. "What are the doctors saying, Ethyl?" Ethyl didn't respond right away. Rose suspected that Ethyl had placed a hand over the mouthpiece to hide her sobs. Rose's heart sank. She closed her eyes and waited patiently for an answer.

"It's not good, Rose. They're telling us that Bobby has emphysema." Ethyl didn't bother to cover the phone with her hand this time. She cried openly. Rose placed her hand on her forehead and closed her eyes.

When Rose thought Ethyl had stopped crying, she said, "Bill has enough on his mind, Ethyl. I'll arrange for someone to take care of the yard if you want."

Ethyl blew her nose before responding. "That's a good idea, Rose. I'm sure Bill would appreciate that."

The Intensive Care Unit at New Haven Hospital was an intimidating sight: one large open space filled with all sorts of equipment to monitor heart, blood pressure, oxygen levels, and respiration. Dozens of intravenous poles stood next to beds like security guards watching over their patients. Curtains hanging from stainless steel bars affixed to the ceiling separated patients from one another, and if a curtain weren't available, the nurses would use a portable screen.

Dr. Bernstein gave Ethyl permission to sit next to Bobby's bed most of the day. She'd stroke his arm and head and speak to him softly. Ethyl found the I.C.U. personnel to be competent, compassionate and helpful: they seemed to be fully aware of the stress and pain she was experiencing. The nurses tried to mitigate her stress by talking about her nursing duties at Riverside Hospital. Ethyl understood that their questions were intended to reduce the agony and frustration she was experiencing as she watched the health of her only child deteriorate before her eyes. When a nurse came to check the monitors attached to Bobby, or tend to his bodily needs, they'd ask Ethyl to sit in the waiting room until told it was all right to return. The noise from the numerous monitoring devises would occasionally give Ethyl a headache, and she'd be forced to leave and walk the corridors or take the elevator to the cafeteria.

Bill would arrive at the hospital between 5:30 and 6:00 p.m. and join Ethyl at Bobby's bedside. Ethyl would report on Bobby's day, but unfortunately, she was never able to report any improvement. Beyond that, the conversation was limited as both parents sat quietly wrestling with their own inner grief and praying for a positive change in his condition. They'd both sit by Bobby's bed until approximately 9:00 p.m. Bill would drop Ethyl off at the motel and drive back to Riverside.

On the tenth day of Bobby's hospitalization, Ethyl decided that she couldn't stand being alone in the motel one more night: she wasn't sleeping well and she needed Bill's shoulder to lean on. She didn't say anything until Bill was ready to leave the hospital and return to Riverside. Bill understood immediately. They stopped at the motel, picked up Ethyl's things, but didn't bother to check out: it was too late in the day for that anyway. They'd have to pay for one more night's lodging regardless. Bill said he'd call the motel in the morning and settle the bill over the phone. Bill activated the electric door opener, pulled the car into the garage, and followed his wife into the kitchen.

Ethyl asked, "Are you hungry?"

"No, thanks. That cafeteria sandwich was enough. It's after 10:00 p.m. If I eat any more, I'll have indigestion all night."

"I'm exhausted, sweetheart. Why don't we get into bed and catch up on the news?"

"That sounds good to me. I'll check to see if we have any email messages first."

Bill switched off the light around 11:00. Instead of lying down to sleep, the couple remained seated in their bed chairs, holding hands. There was enough moonlight streaming through the bedroom window for them to distinguish an array of framed photographs of family members that covered the wall in front of their bed. Their eyes were focused on one photograph in particular, the one at the center of the group. It was a large professional portrait of their son Bobby taken just six months earlier. The boy's face wasn't clear in the moonlight, but it didn't matter: his features were etched into their memories. They continued to hold hands until Ethyl's head tilted back, and she fell asleep.

Bill awoke with a start and looked at the bedside clock: 4:00 a.m. He swung his legs off the bed and onto the floor. He ran his fingers through his hair and thought, *Damn it! I'm exhausted, but I can't sleep.* He turned and looked over his shoulder at Ethyl. Her eyes were wide open. He smiled.

She returned the smile and mumbled, "I guess you couldn't sleep, either." Neither said anything for a few moments. Ethyl whispered, "Do you realize Bobby may never come back to us. He may be gone forever." She tucked her head under the covers and began to sob uncontrollably. Bill leaned over, reached out with both arms and hugged her. When she finally stopped sobbing, she asked, "How will we cope, Bill?"

"I don't know." Not knowing what to else to do, he let go and resumed his position on the edge of the bed. He leaned over and picked up a slipper, but he didn't put it on his foot. He just sat there and held it in one hand.

Bill was not unfamiliar with the emotional strain and sadness associated with death: his mother had died of breast cancer six months earlier. This was a decidedly different feeling, however. Losing a mother who had lived a long and productive life was completely different than losing a five-year-old child: his sorrow was so deep he hurt physically. He could only imagine how Ethyl felt. A father's loss was one thing. A mother's loss had to be more than devastating.

He turned toward Ethyl and said, "I guess we might as well get up. I'll check to see if the newspaper is here, and then I'll make a pot of coffee." Bill shuffled to the kitchen wearing a pajama bottom and a T-shirt. He flicked the light switch and unconsciously shielded his eyes from the sudden glare. He stood by the sink preparing a pot of coffee when the telephone rang. A cold chill ran through his body. He nervously lifted the instrument off the wall fixture and practically whispered, "Hello."

"Mr. Rado, Nurse O'Brien here. We think you'd better return to the hospital as quickly as you can."

"We'll be there within the hour, Janice."

Fifty minutes later, the Rados sat nervously thumbing through magazines in the I.C.U., waiting room. Bill looked at his watch for the umpteenth time. He stood and moved to a water cooler tucked in the corner of the room. He filled a paper cup, drank a sip, emptied the rest down the drain, and sat back down in a chair next to his wife. Ethyl watched Bill's movements, but his movements weren't registering. When he sat back down, she resumed flipping through the magazine pages. Ethyl's mind was so absorbed with concern for her son's health she hadn't noticed that the hospital had begun to redecorate the waiting room to make it less somber. Tube light fixtures had been interspersed between ceiling tiles. Old, beat up chairs had been replaced with new effulgently upholstered furniture and a few colorful reproductions of contemporary art had been hung on each wall.

The Rado's skittishness caused them to jerk to attention when the door from the I.C.U. opened, and Dr. Bernstein walked in. They attempted to stand, but he waved his hand, and said, "Please remain seated." He sat down in the chair nearest the door. "Mr. and Mrs. Rado, your son is not doing well." Dr. Bernstein stopped, looked at his hands for a moment, leaned forward, and continued, "I've been with him since 4:00, and I'm concerned. His expiratory flow is labored. It's much more difficult for him to breathe than it was just a few hours ago."

Bill Rado asked, "How concerned, Doctor?"

"We've been able to suppress the coughing and phlegm production somewhat, but the labored breathing has gotten worse." The doctor looked from one to the other, and sighed. "Your son's chances are now less than 50 percent."

Ethyl's eyes glazed over, and she fainted. As her body began to slump in the chair, Bill grabbed her arm so she wouldn't fall onto the floor. Dr. Bernstein jumped up, gently lowered Ethyl's head forward, and held it until she regained consciousness. Ethyl raised her head slowly and looked at her husband. She placed her hands over her eyes, moaned, and began to rock back and forth.

Rose Nardello's phone rang just as she was about to shut off the lights and lock the door to her office. "Nardello, may I help you?"

"Hi. How about meeting me at the Bistro at six?"

"I was locking up and about to head home. You were supposed to call around noon, Jerry. What happened?"

"I had to drive down to Danbury. An employee of Integrated Systems fell and broke his back. I left the hospital parking lot a few minutes ago. I'm calling from my cell phone."

"I'll stay here at the office for awhile longer. Call me when you get close to town and I'll walk over to the Bistro. What's the prognosis for the poor fellow that broke his back?"

"I'm not sure. I expect it will take time to get the man back on his feet. A banister broke on a walkway above the production floor, and he landed on the concrete floor."

"Ouch! I'll see you around six. Drive safely and don't forget to call me."

Jerry Nichols was an independent insurance broker who specialized in writing workmen's compensation coverage for large industrial businesses. Although he worked out of an office in Riverside, he had clients all over the state. Jerry was considered a workmen's comp expert. He had a special talent for sorting through complex situations and requesting creative solutions from the company's underwriters that went beyond normal workmen's comp coverage.

Rose met Jerry Nichols a few weeks after she'd completed the training regime at City Hall. In addition to her new economic development responsibilities, Frank Mancuso had asked her to assume responsibility for administering the city's insurance coverage. He suggested that Rose meet with Nichols, a former Riverside athlete, and review the city's workmen's compensation package. Nichols had just completed his first year as an independent broker, and Frank wanted to give the young man a shot.

After graduating from Riverside High School, Nichols continued his education, earning a bachelor's degree from Western Connecticut State University. From there, he applied for, and was accepted into, a special risk management program offered by the Travelers Insurance Company. While enrolled in the program, Jerry recognized that the complexities inherent in workmen's compensation represented a business opportunity and decided to specialize in workmen's comp insurance after he earned his broker's license.

Nichols was a gregarious, outgoing young man while in high school, and that upbeat attitude continued into his adult life. He was slender and handsome. Unfortunately, he was also prematurely bald. What was left of his hair was confined to the back one third of his head, and he kept that in the form of a brush cut, a style that had been popular in the 1950s. Rose jokingly told him that if he allowed his beard to grow for three or four days, it would end up longer than the hair on his head.

Everyone who met Nichols liked him immediately, including Rose. Soon after their first meeting at Riverside City Hall, the two became friends. Rose enjoyed Jerry's company: he was intelligent and possessed a great sense of humor. Rose seemed to relax whenever she was in his company. They never became romantically involved, however: neither of them wanted to upset their special "best friends" relationship by introducing the subject of marriage and family.

Their collective attitude toward marriage was challenged one spring afternoon, however. Jerry and Rose had driven to Pawtucket to spend a weekend visiting with Rose's parents and with Rita Fernandez and her children. As they were departing Pawtucket, Rose said, "I love Rita's kids. They're a lot of fun to be around. It makes me want to have one of my own."

Jerry took his eyes off the road for a moment to determine if Rose was serious or was just joking. Realizing she was serious, he said, "I have to admit that I feel the same way, Rose. Rita's lucky to have such great kids. They'll probably end up being her best friends when they grow up. The love they share was hard to ignore. I was a little envious when we left last night."

Both remained silent as they recalled the pleasant evening with the Fernandez family. Rose said, "On the other hand, I wouldn't want to go through what Bill and Ethyl Rado are experiencing. They are really hurting. Little Bobby was admitted to New Haven Hospital two weeks ago and his condition is deteriorating. I met the specialist who's treating him while I was at that medical equipment conference last weekend." Rose turned and looked at her friend. "The physician who's handling his case wasn't very optimistic about the boy's chances. It sounds like the boy is going to die.

"On the other hand, Jerry, I don't want to end up an old maid with no family to love and care for. I'd like to have a child of my own." Their eyes met momentarily. "You know my biological clock is ticking, Jerry. The older I get, the less chance I have of getting pregnant."

He turned toward her and smiled, "Was that a marriage proposal, Miss Nardello?"

Rose sat quietly for a moment before answering. "I guess it was a half-hearted proposal. All I know is that I care for you, and I think you care for me. You're my best friend. What else matters? Do you think we could make it work?"

With a broad smile on his face, Jerry said, "You're getting sentimental on me. We could make marriage work, but I don't think either one of us believes it would be a good idea at this time. No question…we have a special relationship. But, marriage could change everything." Jerry took a deep breath and added, "Have no fear, you'll find a romantic interest. When that happens, we'll have to work harder to remain friends."

10

The city of Riverside straddled the Housatonic River in western Connecticut. The city evolved as a major copper and brass products fabrication center during the late 19th and 20th centuries because of an abundance of river water. Following WW II, however, demand for brass products began to decline. Connecticut firms began to move their fabrication facilities to southern states where labor costs were lower. Unlike other cities within the Housatonic Valley, Riverside was spared the traumatic experience of losing its largest employer.

Riverside knew that it was just a matter of time, however, before the Delta Brass Works, Riverside's largest employer, would announce that it was moving its remaining Riverside operations to the south. When the announcement finally came in 1988, it caused a major jolt to the economy. To make matters worse, Delta said that it could only afford to transfer a few of its managerial employees. With Delta gone, the city's economy slowly sputtered to a crawl.

Rose Nardello, the city's newly-appointed economic development director, was charged with the responsibility of providing the moribund economy with a shot in the arm. She worked diligently for over four years to attract a business with job growth potential, but to no avail. Her persistence finally paid off when the management of International Technologies of Bridgeport announced that it would locate its start-up fuel cell development group called HydroCell, to Riverside.

In order to attract HydoCell, Rose structured a financially attractive package of incentives that included tax breaks and utility subsidies. Although Delta left a decaying infrastructure behind, a consultant retained by Rose determined that the buildings were still usable, given extensive renovation.

Rose was able to convince the City Council to allocate redevelopment monies to pay for the renovation.

The gifted Rose Nardello became the city's favorite citizen, the darling of the local media, and a star within the city administration. She had proven that Frank Mancuso's decision to promote her and to give her the job of Economic Development Director had been correct.

A first time visitor to Riverside City Center would be stimulated by the bold geometric design created by Connecticut's foremost architect, William Howell. His unique design featured three geometrically different buildings. A large circular building at the center that housed the council chambers and council member offices; a triangular building provided space for the city's administrative services, public lobby and conference rooms; and a square building housed the Fire and Police Departments, and the D.A.'s offices. The furnishings and artifacts in all three buildings reinforced the basic geometric design of the building: sculptured works in the lobby and paintings by local artists.

Howell's unique City Center design was in stark contrast to the city itself. Riverside was an old, blue-collar industrial town. Before and just after World War II, the city's very existence depended on a large copper and brass production base. Residents affectionately referred to the entire valley as the "Brass Center of the World." Through his City Center design, William Howell attempted to dispel the "old economy" image and create a new Riverside: a progressive community determined to make its mark as a leader in the development of new technologies not tied to an obsolete industry with old, run down buildings.

The central section of Riverside hadn't changed much since the 1890s. The focal point of the city, and its most appealing feature, was the city's central park: a 20-acre rectangular plot affectionately called the Green by Riverside citizens. The Green remained an inviting scene, no matter from which direction you approached.

While Howell's creative architecture served as the focal point at the north end of the Green, three traditional buildings comprised the area to the east of the Green: the Riverside Inn, a 100-year-old, red brick, three-story hotel, one of the first hotels built within the Housatonic River Valley, at one end; a new Performing Arts Center was at the other end; and a four story parking garage separated the two. Buildings on the west side of the Green had been the beneficiary of redevelopment funds. The city upgraded a two-block retail district and created a new downtown: boutiques, specialty shops, bistros, upscale restaurants, art dealers, and offices for professionals.

Rose shifted in the side chair in front of Frank Mancuso's desk, crossed her legs, and sighed, "I can't imagine how Ethyl and Bill are feeling right now. They must be devastated. They're in seclusion, so I haven't been able to talk with Ethyl. When did Bobby die?"

Frank reached for a paper clip on his desk and rubbed it like he would a genie bottle. "Bobby died about 8:00 this morning. Bill's brother Ernie called me around 9:00." Both fell silent for a few moments as they dealt with their own thoughts. Frank continued, "Dr. Bernstein told Ernie that the boy's breathing was so labored that his heart just gave out." Frank sat quietly looking at nothing in particular, and mumbled, "Bill and Ethyl went through hell, Rose. They tried everything, but nothing seemed to work. Their family doctor wasn't able to do anything, and the respiratory specialist in New Haven wasn't able to do anything."

"I know. The doctor's name is Sydney Bernstein. I met him at the conference I attended a few weeks ago."

"I remember you telling me about him." Frank stood and moved from behind his desk to a window facing the parking lot. He was keenly aware that Los Angeles-like smog was beginning to creep into Riverside air, and that it seemed to be getting worse. He'd even begun to follow the data supplied by Los Angeles that showed the number of smog alert days declared and wondered when Riverside, although a fraction of L.A.'s size with only 70,000 residents, might have to start the same practice. During the hot summer months the year before, the smog had begun to obscure visibility.

He turned around and with a scowl on his face, said, "I don't want you to repeat what I'm about to tell you, Rose. This is just between the two of us, okay?" Rose nodded. "Dr. Bernstein told Ernie that he suspected that the exhaust from diesel trucks could have been the major cause of Bobby's death."

"Dr. Bernstein told me the same thing, Frank."

"I wasn't aware of that. Bernstein must be pretty sure of his facts, or he wouldn't be willing to talk with you and Ernie about it. He must be confident that the post mortem will confirm his suspicions." Frank looked up at the ceiling and sighed. "Here I am, city manager of Riverside, Connecticut, and I have done nothing to protect our children from the poison spewed out night and day by those damn trucks. How many more kids will get sick before I do something?" Frank slumped back down into his chair and looked at Rose pleadingly, like the look of a dog with its ears back. He said, "I feel powerless, Rose." Raising his voice and smacking his desk, he added, "I've got to do something. But, damn it, I don't know what."

Rose could only frown at Frank's outburst. She felt as impotent as he did. "I wish I could help, Frank, but I'm at a loss. I don't know what to suggest."

"That's okay, Rose. It's my problem, and I'm going to have to deal with it." Frank lowered his eyes and looked at his hands. "I'm between a rock and a hard place. If I try to reduce the volume of truck traffic through the city, the business community will crucify me. If, on the other hand, I don't do something to alleviate the pollution, parents and senior citizens will crucify me. Not only that, I won't be able to live with myself."

Rose straightened and her facial expression changed from concern to resolve. Even with a frown on her face, Rose was an exceptionally beautiful woman. Although he was 15 years older than Rose, Frank enjoyed watching her every move. He thought Rose could have been a model. He wasn't the only male member of the City Administration that considered Rose Nardello beautiful. Her well-proportioned body, face, and legs seemed to be accentuated by her attire: Rose was a clotheshorse, always dressed to the nines, whether at work or attending a social gathering. Men couldn't help but look at her when she was nearby. Frank smiled within himself when he realized what he was thinking. He recalled reading somewhere about the marvels of the human mind: how it could concentrate on two or three things simultaneously, like driving a car while listening to a book on tape.

In contrast to the beautiful Rose Nardello, Frank Mancuso was unattractive. While Rose tipped the scales at less than 120 pounds, Frank weighed over 200 pounds. He was about the same height as Rose, 5' 6", with a receding hairline. No matter how often he shaved, he had a perpetual five o'clock shadow. Meeting him for the first time, a casual observer would describe Frank Mancuso as being overweight and out of shape. On the contrary, Frank Mancuso was not out of shape: he worked out three times a week at a local gym and could still bench-press over 200 pounds.

After a prolonged silence, Rose said. "I don't have a solution to the smog problem, Frank, but I do have an idea." Frank Mancuso leaned back in his chair, placed his hands behind his head and assumed the roll of an attentive listener. Rose had earned his respect for her incisive reasoning, intelligence, and creativity. Her economic development proposals were practical and well thought out. He'd given her most of the credit for attracting HydroCell, a new division of International Technologies, to the city a few months earlier.

"What's your idea? I'm primed and ready."

Rose sat back and crossed her legs. "Let's back up and look at what we've learned during the last few weeks. It's interesting when you think about it. First, the day I met Dr. Bernstein, we discussed Riverside's smog problem. He obviously was already aware of what we've been experiencing. Second, he responded immediately when I told him about your concerns. Within days, he sent us valuable information about diesel emissions, stuff that we didn't know just a few weeks ago. Third, he took the time to tell me about the results of the research going on at New Haven Hospital; research that shows a direct correlation between respiratory diseases and diesel emissions. Without saying it directly, Bernstein seemed to be saying that the inhalation of pollutants emitted from diesel trucks was the root cause of Bobby Rado's emphysema."

Rose hesitated for a moment, and then slapped her hands together. "I'm beginning to believe that Dr. Bernstein has been feeding us information for a reason. Maybe he wants the city to stop talking about our smog problem and do something about it."

"I'm not sure I'm following you, Rose. What do you think he wants us to do?"

"Have patience. I'm leading up to that." Rose stood and began to pace. She took a deep breath. "Let's look at the situation. Both State Route 10 and Interstate 64 go through the center of Riverside. Route 10 is the main north/south transportation corridor through the Housatonic River Valley. It runs from Long Island Sound, through western Connecticut, western Massachusetts all the way to the Canadian border. Interstate 64 is the main east/west route through Connecticut. That means that long-haul, diesel-powered trucks crisscross our city day and night, spewing pollutants into the air." Rose stopped pacing. "To make matters worse, there's an incline on both highways just before they cross. I'll bet if we analyzed it we'd find that the hills to the west of Route 10 near the Rado home form an air pocket and trap vehicle emissions. My Dad used to tell me that the black stuff we see coming out of the exhaust pipes of diesel trucks intensifies when the drivers downshift, especially when the trucks are carrying heavy loads." Rose sat back down. "People living near that intersection, or in the hills surrounding the intersection, must be subjected to serious pollution every day, and there isn't a damn thing they can do about it." Rose took a deep breath, "I propose we sue one of the diesel engine manufacturers."

Mancuso's body snapped forward. "What did you day? Sue who?"

Rose turned, leaned forward and placed her hands on Frank's desk. She said in a confidential tone, "The engine manufacturers, Frank. I'm thinking of a class action against the Diesel Engine Corporation, a suit similar to the one some of the State's Attorneys General in this country brought against the tobacco industry a few years ago. If we could muster enough support from some of the other valley cities along I-64 and State Route 10, like Terryville and West Chester, we'd have a powerful voice. Admittedly, their truck traffic isn't as much as ours, but I know they have a smog problem, too. Maybe we could set an example and initiate an attitude change in this state."

"Where the hell would we find the money to retain an attorney to prepare a class action, Rose?"

"I don't know, Frank. Maybe we could get a large law firm to put it together on a contingency basis. Just think, if we could get the cities along Route 10 and the Interstate to commit, we'd wield a hell of a hammer."

Mancuso sat quietly thinking through what Rose had just proposed. Then he leaned forward and said, more to himself than to Rose, "It sounds far fetched, but—maybe it'd work. Let's see, who could we talk to about this? Call Sydney Bernstein and get his reaction to the idea."

11

Rose burst into Frank Mancuso's office in the Administration Building unannounced. Frank frowned and placed a hand over the mouthpiece and nodded for Rose to take a seat. Rose fidgeted while Frank continued with the telephone conversation. "I need the road repair schedule and a cost estimate before this afternoon's Council meeting, Jack. You should attend, just in case they want details." Mancuso paused, undoubtedly listening to Jack Dillon's response. "How about after lunch, say one o'clock? Good. See you then." As he hung up the phone Mancuso looked at Rose and asked, "What's the problem? You exploded in here like a wild animal."

"Sorry, Frank." Rose attempted to compose herself and moved forward in the chair. "I'm furious. Those people in South Warwick and Waterville have decided not to join our class action lawsuit against D.E.C. They're afraid it will backfire. They think the trucking industry and the Teamsters would seek political retribution in Hartford if they join in the suit against D.E.C. They also question the information you got from the state."

"You mean the data that shows that 62 percent of the heavy trucks registered in Connecticut are powered by D.E.C. engines?"

"That's it, Frank. They're not accusing anyone of inflating the numbers. They just think the state is wrong." Rose sat back in her chair and in a more controlled voice added, "I think the real problem here is that both cities are afraid of the Teamsters. They think the Teamsters would cause trouble with their public employee unions. Read this letter South Warwick received from the President of Teamsters Local 1640."

Frank read aloud, "'Teamsters Local 1640 strongly opposes any legal action that the city of South Warwick might bring against diesel engine manufacturers. Such a lawsuit could limit the development of new, more efficient and cleaner diesel technologies, which in turn, could increase the cost of shipping goods throughout the U.S. Such an action would have a devastating effect on the economy of Connecticut, New England, and the United States. The development of new, environmentally friendly technologies could also be adversely affected. Engine manufacturers would undoubtedly divert funds away from research and development to fight the proposed legal action. The Teamsters cannot, and will not, stand on the sidelines and allow the diesel engine manufacturers to be saddled with production restrictions placed on them by the courts.'"

"Damn! This is a veiled threat. If Riverside gets a letter like this, Mike Fusco will jump on it."

Rose said, "If we can't get those two cities, Frank, we probably won't get Terryville or West Chester."

Mancuso banged his fist on the desk. "Have you told Sandler?"

"No. I thought I should tell you first." Rose speculated, "Sandler may advise us to abort." Barry Sandler, Riverside city attorney, wore two hats: he served as managing partner of his own firm, Young and Sandler; and served Riverside as its city attorney.

"Maybe Barry can talk with the Council and persuade them not to change their minds. I'd better call him right now." Mancuso buzzed his secretary. "Marie, please call Barry Sandler for me. If he's not there, leave a message. Ask him to call me A.S.A.P."

Less than a minute later, Marie buzzed Frank, "I have Mr. Sandler on line one."

"Thanks, Marie." Mancuso pressed the button for line one, "Barry, it's Frank Mancuso. Thanks for taking my call. Rose Nardello is here with me. I'll put us on the speaker phone."

Rose reacted by saying in a voice that Sandler could hear, "Hello, Barry."

"Good morning, Rose. What's up, Frank?"

"South Warwick and Waterville decided against joining the class action against Diesel Engine Corporation. They're concerned the Teamsters and the trucking industry will initiate some form of retribution. They may be right, Barry. The Teamsters in particular could cause all kinds of trouble with our public employee unions. And then there's D.E.C.: they have powerful lobbyists." Frank sighed before continuing, "Mike Fusco has already voiced concern about a union backlash. I'll have to present this latest development to the Council this afternoon. I'm concerned that they will throw in the towel. Would you come to the meeting and help me persuade them not to quit, and if necessary, that we should move forward on our own?"

"Hold on a minute, Frank. Let's look at the facts. What can the diesel engine industry do, try to exert political pressure in Hartford? Let them try! Riverside has solid representation in Hartford with Jerry Burns in the Senate, and Joe Como in the Legislature. If D.E.C. were to attempt some form of retribution because of a lawsuit, the media would crucify them. The negative publicity would damage their corporate image." Sandler chuckled, "And, Frank, we could help that happen."

"Now the Teamsters threat, that's a different issue." Barry paused. "I'll bet we can package this in such a way that the Teamsters will support the lawsuit. I'll have to think about that. Hold a second while I check with Doris to see if I'm free this afternoon." Barry buzzed his secretary, "Doris, am I free this afternoon?"

"You arranged to have an early dinner with Mrs. Sandler. Do you want me to call her and postpone until later?"

"Yes. Tell her I'll probably be tied up all afternoon and maybe this evening with the City Council." Sandler pressed line one again and said, "I'm okay for the afternoon, Frank. You take the lead, and I'll support you. Don't worry. I've got a surprise for you and the Council. I think we've got the situation under control."

Frank hung up the phone and said, "You heard that, Rose. I wonder what he has up his sleeve." Frank thought for a moment. "I think you should attend the work session, Rose." He stood up. "I'd better go talk with the Mayor and make sure she puts me on the agenda. I'll talk with you later."

Frank stopped at Mayor Barbara O'Connor's office and peeked in. "May I have a word with you, Barbara?"

"Certainly, Frank. Come in and sit. What's up?"

"I've invited Barry Sandler to join us at the working session this afternoon. Do you have any objections?"

"Can you tell my why?"

"It'd be premature if I tried to explain. I'd rather wait until this afternoon to talk about it. Trust me."

"Okay, Frank. I guess I can wait. How much time do you need?"

"Fifteen minutes, maybe."

"Oops! Should we revise the agenda?"

"I don't think so. If it's okay with you, I'll reduce my regular report to the Council by a few minutes. That should give us enough time."

Riverside's City Council met in closed working session every other Thursday at 2:00 p.m. in a conference room contiguous to Council chambers. The conference room had two entrances. One opened to a back hallway near the mayor's office. A second connected the conference room to the Council Chambers. The conference room was sparsely decorated, highlighted by a large chrome and wood table, and matching chairs. A full-length tapestry hung on the wall opposite the entry doors. A large window ran the length of one wall, and provided a view of a small, enclosed garden resplendent with blooming roses and ferns.

All five councilpersons, Mayor Barbara O'Connor, Florence Laguna, Kendall Williams, Sheila Bernard, and Serafino "Mike" Fusco, were present for the afternoon session. Following brief opening remarks by Mayor O'Connor, Frank Mancuso reported that the cities of West Warwick and Waterville had declined Riverside's invitation to join in the pending class action lawsuit against Diesel Engine Corporation. He explained that both cities were concerned that lobbyists working for the trucking industry could cause problems in Hartford. "But, that's not their only concern, Madam Mayor. South Warwick received a letter from the President of Teamsters Local 1640. Unless you have an objection, I'd like to read part of it."

When Frank finished reading the Teamsters' letter, he recommended the city ignore the threats and go it alone. All five Councilpersons reacted with dismay. Fusco was the first to speak. "That changes everything as far as I'm concerned. If we proceed on our own, we'll be bare-ass naked. I'll have to vote against proceeding when it comes to a vote tonight."

Rose Nardello fidgeted, frowned, and stared at Councilman Fusco. *What a pompous ass!*

Barry Sandler spoke. "Madam Mayor, members of the Council, may I say a few words?"

The Mayor smiled. "You may, Barry, but only if you have good news."

"I do have good news, Madam Mayor. An old-line New York firm, Roberts and Spencer, has agreed to represent the city and the city's children on a contingency basis." All five councilpersons stared at Sandler in disbelief. "Jason Roberts, the firm's managing general partner, told me that the city's proposed class action against a diesel engine manufacturer is of great interest to his firm. If the city is successful, they see an opportunity to open up litigation against all diesel engine manufacturers, both domestic and foreign, light duty as well as heavy-duty engines. They believe the potential awards could be as big, or bigger, than tobacco. The fact that West Warwick and Waterville backed away from the class action at this time won't mean much to Jason. I'm sure he can convince those rebellious cities to join the action later."

Sandler checked his notes. "Jason is suggesting that the city pursue a double barrel strategy: file a wrongful death claim against D.E.C. in the name of the Rado family, as well as a class action. He cited only one condition: Riverside must agree to retain a qualified consultant to prepare a report that supports the city's class action and the wrongful death charge." Sandler paused and looked into the faces of each of the five councilpersons. "Jason wants to see a direct correlation between emphysema and diesel emissions. He suggested we contact the California Environmental Protection Agency and ask for referrals. I believe West Warwick and Waterville will be sorry they didn't participate when they hear this news." He sat back in his chair, looked around the table. "Are there any questions?"

"Yes, I have a question, Barry." Fusco leaned forward. "Can we expect a counter suit? If so, where are we going to find the money to defend ourselves?" Fusco leaned back in his chair and declared, "I don't like the whole idea."

"Under normal conditions, your concern would be well-founded, Mike. However, the arrangement with Roberts and Spencer is different. Please understand that once Roberts and Spencer agrees to represent the Rados, the city, and the children of Riverside, they will represent them all the way. They'll defend the city as long as the countersuit is directly related to either the class action or the wrongful death claim."

Florence Laguna asked, "What about possible political retribution in Hartford?"

"Roberts and Spencer can't defend the city against politically motivated decisions in Hartford, Florence. It appears to me, however, that the city has excellent representation in Hartford. I'm sure our representatives will provide unconditional help if and when we ask for it. They'll fight tooth and nail to defend the children of Riverside and the city once they are briefed and understand why the city is filing the charges."

Frank Mancuso remarked, "I'll vouch for that, Florence. Let me give you an example. I called Representative Jerry Burns's office a few weeks ago and asked for data about truck registrations. He told me he was very supportive of our proposed action. He called back the same day with the information. He checked with the Department of Transportation and was informed that 62 percent of the diesel trucks registered in Connecticut are powered by D.E.C. engines."

Florence exclaimed, "My God, it sounds like those people have a monopoly."

Mike Fusco waved his hand again. "I have another question, Barry. What about the Teamsters? What's the downside if we have to battle them?"

"That's the $64,000 question, Mike. I've given the subject a great deal of thought. I believe we can gain the support of the Teamsters if we become proactive; provide the union leadership with reports that show the negative health effects of diesel emissions on children. Once the Teamsters understand our position, they'll see that it is in their best interests to support our claims, not fight them. It could be a public relations windfall for the Teamsters if the public believes they're protecting children.

"We're not trying to create a problem for the Teamsters or anyone else, for that matter. We just want change. Remember, our legal initiatives have one major objective: we want to force diesel engine manufacturers to reduce harmful emissions by incorporating what some experts believe is state-of-the-art technology."

Fusco said, "Okay, I can see that, but what about Joe Panullo? Joe's one of our leading citizens. He's been a D.E.C. dealer for many years." Looking around the conference table, Mike said, "We all know Joe and his son Joe, Jr. The Panullos are good people. Have we considered how lawsuits against D.E.C. would affect Joe's family and his business?"

Sandler responded. "As I see it, an action against D.E.C. could be a double-edged sword for Joe Panullo. Over the short term, he might experience a decrease in sales. But, remember, Joe doesn't manufacture D.E.C. engines, nor does he have to honor the engine warranty. That's D.E.C.'s responsibility. On the other hand, if we can force D.E.C. to retrofit engines currently in service, that would be a huge boost to the service end of his business, which, as I understand it, is the most profitable anyway."

Looking around the table again, Sandler asked, "Any other questions?" Not hearing any he said, "In summary, filing a class action against the Diesel Engine Corporation on behalf of the children of the city and a wrongful death claim on behalf of the Rado family won't cost the city anything. On the other hand, it could boost the credibility and reputation of this Council. Think about that before you vote this evening. I recommend you move forward and comply with the request of Roberts and Spencer. Find and retain the services of a qualified, competent consultant as soon as possible. If you want, I will attend the Council meeting tonight, and answer questions that you put to me."

Mayor O'Connor replied, "Yes, Barry, I think that would be wise."

"I guess that does it for me. Unless you have further questions, I will take my leave." Sandler gathered his documents, inserted them in a brief case, shook hands all around, and left.

Mayor O'Connor remarked. "Well, that was certainly succinct and positive. Barry appears to have done his homework. I can't see any downside."

Fusco answered in a voice not much louder than a whisper, "I can't either, and that's what troubles me. Something is bound to go wrong."

"What do you think, Frank?"

Mancuso leaned forward. "I believe Barry Sandler has gone beyond what I expected. He obviously believes the city should go forward and aggressively represent the children of Riverside. But more importantly, his announcement that Roberts and Spencer is convinced that we are heading in the right direction is very exciting news. With one of the most respected law firms in the nation behind us, I believe we must take a stand against a business that is poisoning our children. If the city stands up for what is right and just, we will gain stature in Connecticut, as well as the rest of the country. How do you feel, Rose?"

"If we are proactive as Barry suggests, the media will say good things about the city. This Council will be admired for its environmental activism." Rose smiled and jokingly added, "That might make my job as point person for economic development a lot easier. Seriously, a proactive stance by the Council will send a signal to the private sector that this is an environmentally sensitive community. That reputation may cause some businesses to turn away from Riverside. But, we probably don't want those businesses anyway. I see this as an opportunity for Riverside to become more than a sleepy ex-brass center of the world. It can become a leader in the fight to clean up our environment. In my opinion, filing those two lawsuits against D.E.C. is the right thing to do."

12

Architect William Howell's rotunda design for the Riverside City Council Chambers was the most striking and recognizable feature of the City Center complex. Howell's design placed the rotunda between the administrative and public safety buildings and was tied to both by connecting breezeways. A series of elaborately-designed glass doors near the center of the structure provided access to Council Chambers from a beautifully landscaped courtyard and garden area. The Chamber lobby featured a high ceiling, a large crystal chandelier, and two sets of stairs leading down from both left and right to a recessed area that Riverside residents had affectionately nicknamed "the pit." The pit provided 65 comfortable theater chairs for the public. A raised semi-circular, elevated section faced the pit to accommodate a 30-foot semi circular table/desk with high back, black leather executive chairs for five Council members, the city attorney, the city manager and a few department heads. When in session, the Council faced a single lectern on the floor level directly in front of the public seating.

Every chair in the pit was occupied when Mayor O'Connor gaveled the Council meeting to order at 7:05 p.m. An overflow crowd stood behind the chairs. "We have a full agenda tonight and I intend to be home by eleven o'clock, so let's get started." The first five agenda items dealt with routine zoning variances, and were disposed of quickly. Mayor O'Connor then asked the city clerk to read item six.

"'The city of Riverside shall retain the law firm of Roberts and Spencer, New York, New York, to prepare and proffer a class complaint against the Diesel Engine Corporation of Pawtucket, Rhode Island, for contaminating the air in and around the city of Riverside, Connecticut, thereby causing serious respiratory problems for the city's most vulnerable citizens, seniors and children. The city's action is in response to the recent death of Robert

Anderson Rado, age five, from chronic obstructive pulmonary disease. The city will show that the disease that afflicted Rado was the direct result of the involuntary inhalation of harmful poisons in the particulate matter emitted from diesel engines.'"

As the clerk read, Frank Mancuso noted a change in the audience. Those that were seated slid forward, and those standing seemed to shuffle their feet and stand taller. The clerk continued to read, "'The city shall authorize Roberts and Spencer to petition the court to certify the city's complaint against the Diesel Engine Corporation as a Class Action on behalf of the children and seniors of Riverside. The suit will claim that Riverside children and seniors are the most vulnerable to toxins, carcinogens, and particulates emitted from diesel engines manufactured by the Diesel Engine Corporation, and therefore is liable for the respiratory problems of it's most vulnerable citizens under several theories, including negligence, gross negligence, and product liability for defective design, failure to warn, conspiracy, and fraud.

"'The city will show that engines manufactured by the Diesel Engine Corporation are the major source of harmful smog hanging over the city of Riverside. A month-long survey conducted by the city at two data collection points, one on Interstate 64 and the other on State Route 10, separated by approximately only two miles, showed that over 82 percent of the trucks that pass through that intersection are heavy-duty trucks powered by diesel engines. Data supplied by the Connecticut Motor Vehicle Department show that 62 percent of those heavy duty trucks are powered by diesel engines manufactured by the Diesel Engine Corporation.'"

The clerk hesitated, scanned the faces of a few people sitting in the first row, and then looked at the five Councilpersons to judge their response to that charge. It was obvious that everyone was listening intently, and was in agreement. She continued, "'If the William Rado family elects to file a wrongful death claim against the Diesel Engine Corporation for the death of their son, Robert Anderson Rado, the city would also support such an action.'"

The clerk looked up and declared, "That's it, Madam Mayor."

"Thank you, Agnes. We'll open the meeting to allow comments from residents. Please state your name and address clearly for the record. You have three minutes to present your thoughts. You may petition the Council for an additional three minutes. However, I want to be clear, your request may be denied.

"I see that Mr. and Mrs. Rado are present, and unless I hear an objection from a member of the Council, I invite them to speak first." Hearing no objections, Bill Rado stood and walked to the podium. He reached into his pocket and pulled out two sheets of yellow-lined notepaper. He smoothed the paper on the podium and said, "Thank you, Madam Mayor and members of the Council." He hesitated a moment. "I prepared a statement, but I've decided not to read it." He deliberately refolded the sheets of paper. Bill spoke slowly and softly. "To say that the weeks following our son's death were rough would be an understatement. Losing a child is bad enough, but not understanding why is doubly difficult. Dr. Bernstein of New Haven Hospital, the specialist who was treating Bobby at the time of his death, met with Ethyl and me a few days ago and told us that the post-mortem confirmed his diagnosis that Bobby suffered from emphysema. His breathing difficulties put a lot of strain on his heart. Dr. Bernstein also said that Bobby's emphysema was the result of ingesting harmful pollutants found in diesel truck exhaust. I want to make sure I've got this straight." Bill unfolded his notes again and spread them out on the podium.

"The medical examiner's report said, and I quote, 'The same harmful chemicals normally found impregnated in diesel exhaust particles were found in the Rado boy's lung tissue.'

"After meeting with Dr. Bernstein and reading the post-mortem report, Ethyl and I went from sadness to anger. We're convinced diesel emissions from heavy-duty diesel trucks caused our son's death. To make matters worse, most of those damn trucks have nothing to do with Riverside. They're just passing through! They're from other cities in Connecticut, or they're from out of state, for God's sake! Now, the state is saying that a high percentage of those trucks are powered by D.E.C. engines. I'd venture to say, Madam Mayor, that D.E.C. doesn't give a damn about the children or the seniors of Riverside or anyone in Riverside, for that matter." Bill lowered his head and paused. The room was quiet. If someone had coughed, it would have sounded like thunder. Bill raised his head slowly, and with tears forming in his eyes looked into the eyes of the Council, and exclaimed loudly, "Damn it, somebody should pay for our son's death!"

He began to sob as he tried to continue but couldn't. Ethyl rushed to his side and put her arm around his trembling shoulders. Bill regained his composure. "I'm not sure what else to say, except that Ethyl and I support the Council's proposed class action." Bill looked at Ethyl. She nodded. "We've decided to ask the New York law firm to help us prepare a wrongful death claim."

The audience erupted into a sustained applause. Bill and Ethyl turned and walked back to their seats. Ethyl wrapped her arms around his shoulders again and kissed him on the cheek. Mayor O'Connor gently gaveled the meeting back to order. "Thank you for those eloquent remarks, Mr. Rado. Does anyone else wish to speak?"

Sarah Allen rose and moved to the podium. "I agree with Bill Rado. Something needs to be done to bring these people to task, but I have to ask a question. Does the city have enough money to pay for what I can only imagine will be significant legal fees?"

Mayor O'Connor said, "Mr. Sandler, would you please answer that question?"

Barry Sandler detailed the arrangement he'd negotiated with Roberts and Spencer. "The senior partner's only stipulation is that a respected, competent consultant be retained to prepare the information his firm needs to support the legal action. I can't imagine that cost would exceed $30,000."

"Thank you, Barry. Does anyone else wish to speak?"

Jack Burgess, a grizzled senior citizen who attended City Council meetings on a regular basis, stood and walked to the podium. "Madam Mayor, members of the Council, I have been coming to Council meetings for many years and I've never attended a meeting where there's been general agreement on anything. This is different. I sense widespread community support for this legal action. Someone has to blow the whistle before more of our children are struck down with lung cancer or respiratory diseases. In my opinion, if you just attempted to recoup the health care costs that diesel emissions cause, you'd be right on. But that doesn't go far enough! How long are we gonna let trucks pass through our city irresponsibly and make our kids sick?" Burgess turned and looked into the faces of the audience. "How many more kids are in the hospital with breathing problems? I've been told it's four, just at Riverside Hospital alone, and two of those are pretty bad off." He turned back to face the Council. "We should set an example for the rest of the country and take action now. I'll bet everyone in this room would agree: go for it, Riverside!" Again, the room erupted in applause, and a few whistles were heard. Before leaving the podium, Burgess said, "It sounds like I've spoken for the others, Madam Mayor." Rose Nardello, standing in the back of the room caught Frank Mancuso's eye and smiled. He held up his right hand with the thumb extended upward and returned the smile.

In spite of his deep concern that the Teamsters might retaliate in some form and cause problems with the local that represented most of the city employees, Mike Fusco sat on his hands. He realized he'd be a lone voice in the wilderness if he were to say anything against initiating a class action lawsuit against D.E.C. It was obvious that the citizens of Riverside wanted blood. They wanted the Council to move forward, and being the astute politician that he was, he realized a unanimous vote in favor would dramatize the action and increase media attention.

Mayor O'Connor asked, "Any further citizen comments?" Not seeing any movement toward the lectern, the Mayor announced, "I will close public comments and open discussion within the Council."

Councilman Fusco, seated in the last chair on the left side of the dais, leaned forward and looked into the faces of the other Council members. He smiled, and declared, "Madam Mayor, I think the Council has made up its mind and is ready to vote."

"Okay. We can bypass Council discussion and call for a vote if you want. Council, please vote up or down on this action." Five green lights lit up the voting board. For the third time in less than 15 minutes, the audience erupted in applause.

13

The Diesel Engine Corporation, a closely held, family-controlled New England manufacturer, pioneered the development of the diesel engine. Three out of the five major truck manufacturers in the United States were using D.E.C. engines in their vehicles by the mid 1990s. D.E.C. built diesel engines at its main plant in Pawtucket, Rhode Island, and at its west coast plant in Medford, Oregon.

In 1995 Winston Alfred Osborne, III, and his younger sister, Beatrice, inherited over 90 percent of the outstanding shares of the corporation from their father, Winston, II, who succumbed to colon cancer. Buoyed by his sister's unconditional support, Winston, III, assumed the day-to-day managerial control of the corporation and declared himself President and C.E.O. immediately after his father's death.

In spite of the father's efforts to prepare and train his son, Winston, III, was not ready to assume the presidency, and it didn't take long for D.E.C.'s middle management to recognize his deficiencies. He was not like his father: he was an inconsiderate, arrogant snob and impossible to work for. They soon discovered that he was also unreliable, unpredictable, and incompetent. His employees saddled him with the disparaging nickname "the 3rd." When "the 3rd" walked through the lobby first thing every morning, the expression on his face would signal whether this would be another bad day at D.E.C., or that the employees would be allowed to do their jobs without his interference.

It took less than one month after assuming control of the business that Winston, III, showed his true colors: he discontinued funding all grants to non-profit civic and humanitarian organizations within the city of Pawtucket, and he announced the company would not award any year-end bonuses, in spite of forecasted increases in the company's revenues and profits.

D.E.C.'s employees were not alone in their dislike for their boss. He was ridiculed and scorned by his peers within the truck engine industry for his seemingly endless proposals, most of which were related to avoiding or circumventing government regulations. Industry executives believed D.E.C.'s successful 1996 was the work of D.E.C.'s Vice President of Marketing, Daniel Abbott, not Winston Osborne, III.

At 5' 5" (5' 6" when he wore his elevator shoes), Winston had the short man's complex: always seeking to dominate people he came in contact with, regardless of their age. Winston's arrogance was certainly not founded on his good looks or his physique. The man looked like a character actor from a B-movie, someone who always played the role of a gangster's sidekick: long face; big nose; partially-bald head; and skinny, weighing no more than 150 pounds soaking wet.

In addition to gaining control of the Diesel Engine Corporation, Winston, III, and his sister inherited title to a large home near the campus of Brown University in Providence, as well as a waterfront home in Newport, Rhode Island, built by their grandfather in 1890. Beatrice moved into the Providence mansion, while Winston took up residency in Newport. The Newport mansion was "the 3rd's" pride and joy. Grandfather Osborne, the original Winston, called his 6,000 square-foot mansion Lowell Manor in honor of his English father, Lord Lowell Osborne. While not as large or as distinctive as the Astor's Beechwood, or the Bellmont's Belcourt Castle, Lowell Manor established itself early on as one of Newport's most recognizable waterfront mansions. The most distinctive and striking feature of Lowell Manor was its front entrance: a columniation based on Greek architecture that surrounded a marble porch and framed large carved double doors. The hall just inside the front doors was an equally impressive marble showcase: a marble floor, marble trim, and marble tables that enhanced the magnificence of a 30-foot ceiling and a huge imported chandelier from France dating back to the early 1800s. A broad marble staircase that gradually narrowed as it ascended to the upper floors dominated the center of the hall.

A combination Osborne family museum and library was off to the left of the hall. It was the pride and joy of Winston, II. Stacks of books and trophies graced every wall, including many books chronicling the Osborne family history from the 1600s to the present day. A receiving room to the right of the stairs was another of Winston, II's, favorite rooms: he used it when guests visited the mansion. He'd personally chosen each item of furniture while on vacation in France.

Within days of the senior Osborne's funeral, however, Winston, III's, equally snobbish and arrogant wife Olivia removed all vestiges of her father-in-law's painstaking acquisitions. She redecorated and refurnished that receiving room and many of the other rooms in the mansion.

Winston Osborne's arrogance stemmed more from being identified as the owner of Lowell Manor, rather than the owner and C.E.O. of Diesel Engine Corporation. He viewed managing D.E.C. as merely something he had to do to maintain his standard of living. He'd leave Lowell Manor for work reluctantly each weekday morning. His whole demeanor would change when he exited Interstate 95 and drove east on Division Street past McCoy Stadium to the D.E.C. headquarters building on Bacon Street, because he despised industrial Pawtucket: it was a blue-color town, not fit for the likes of an Osborne.

The agreement that established Mario Nardello's Trucking Company as D.E.C.'s official test facility was forged in the early 1980s while Winston Osborne senior was still alive and managing D.E.C. The agreement evolved from a chance meeting between D.E.C.'s Vice President and Chief Financial Officer George Stevens and Mario Nardello at a Pawtucket Planning Commission hearing. Winston, II, had been informed by one of his influential friends within the Pawtucket city administration that the school district planned to close an old, outdated elementary school strategically located between D.E.C.'s main production facility and Nardello Trucking's warehouse and transfer yard. Osborne, II, had been coveting the land for years: he saw it as an ideal location to build a research and development facility.

Osborne submitted an unsolicited, but generous purchase offer to the district. The parties negotiated a contract of sale, contingent on the approval of D.E.C.'s application to re-zone the property. A hearing was set and Osborne, II, sent George Stevens to the hearing as his representative. The Planning Commission invited the school's other next-door neighbor, Nardello Trucking, to comment on the re-zoning request. Believing that a research and development facility would make a good neighbor, Mario Nardello supported D.E.C.'s application. Following the hearing, Stevens thanked Nardello for his positive remarks and offered to buy him a cup of coffee.

Mario was delighted to have an opportunity to talk with a key D.E.C. management person: he was anxious to tell someone about a new horsepower enhancement system his people had recently developed. Mario was so impressed with the system's effectiveness, he envisioned incorporating it into every D.E.C. engine in his fleet. When he discovered that Steven's expertise was finance, not engineering, he decided to tread lightly on the subject of horsepower: he'd only discuss the system if he were given an opportunity. The opening came when Stevens asked who Mario used to maintain his trucks.

"We're self-sufficient, George. We do our own maintenance and repair."

"That's interesting. Does it pencil out for you?"

"Yes. I check every six months or so to see if I could save a few bucks by farming out the work." Mario smiled. "I haven't seen an advantage yet." Adopting a more serious tone, Mario added, "There's really more to it than money, George. There are intangibles, like scheduling. I have a much better handle on truck availability because I'm confident my people are giving me accurate estimates of the time it takes to repair something. I'm also confident I'm getting realistic repair cost estimates."

"Sounds like you have a competent crew. You must pay your mechanics pretty well."

"We do, and you're correct, they are a knowledge group. They are constantly experimenting with devices and systems to increase operating efficiencies and mileage. A few months ago our lead mechanic developed a horsepower enhancement system. We added the new system to three of our truck engines and found that we could pull heavier loads. By the way, the system works especially well with D.E.C. engines."

"I'll have to tell Mr. Osborne. If I can convince him to come over here, would you be willing to demonstrate the system?"

"You bet. Whenever it's convenient for him."

The next morning, Stevens briefed Winston, II, on the action taken at the Planning Commission meeting and then told him about Mario's horsepower enhancement system. Osborne was impressed and asked Stevens to arrange a meeting.

"Welcome to Nardello Trucking, Mr. Osborne, and a good morning to you, George"

George responded, "Morning, Mario."

"Thank you for meeting with George and me this morning, Mr. Nardello. I'm sorry that I only have one hour, so can we get started?"

"Certainly. Our maintenance and repair building is at the far end of the yard. Let's walk outside so you can see how we operate."

Mario led Osborne and Stevens through his office, to a back door, and entered the transfer yard. As the three men walked past a two-story warehouse structure, Osborne noticed that all five loading docks on the ground level were occupied with backed-in semi-trailers, and rows of four tractor trucks and five trailers were lined up along the fence on the left side of the yard.

"How many trucks do you have in your fleet, Mr. Nardello?"

"Please call me Mario, Mr. Osborne. We have 19 truck cabs: 15 are powered by D.E.C. engines, 4 by Cummins engines."

"Call me Winston, Mario." Mario turned and smiled.

After witnessing an impressive demonstration of the new horsepower enhancement system by Mario's lead mechanic, and after a discussion of the system's benefits, Winston Osborne complimented Mario. "I'm impressed. You run a clean and efficient operation, Mario. I'd like you to show your system to our Director of Engineering, Bob Prescott." Osborne thought for a moment, and then asked, "While Bob is over here, would you be agreeable to talk with him about testing some of our prototype engines and retrofits?"

"I'd be delighted, Winston."

"I'll ask Bob to call you within the next few days." Looking at his watch, Osborne said, "Well, I have to leave now. I have a luncheon appointment. Thank you for your time and for the demonstration." He shook hands with the mechanic and with Mario and exited the yard.

A subsequent meeting between Bob Prescott and Mario spawned a series of demonstrations and negotiating sessions that resulted in Nardello Trucking being designated as D.E.C.'s test facility for new engines and engine retrofits.

The day following his successful meeting with Mario Nardello, Bob Prescott received some shocking information: a report released by the California Air Resources Board claimed that the particulates found in the exhaust of diesel engines represented a serious health risk. He phoned Mario Nardello immediately and faxed over a copy of the report. During a subsequent telephone conversation, Prescott asked Mario to research the problem to see if his engineers could come up with a technological solution. The technological review lasted over six months, and after a series of tests of various engineering options, Mario's engineers came up with a promising technology that involved adding a particulate trap to the engine fashioned out of a ceramic material coupled to an electronic timing device.

Unfortunately, the senior Osborne was never able to witness a demonstration of the Nardello ceramic trap system. His colon cancer spread and took his life before Mario's engineers completed their work. Prescott, however, wouldn't let the tragedy of the senior Osborne's death slow down development of the new technology, and asked Mario to begin extensive tests without delay. When further tests confirmed the legitimacy of the concept, Prescott notified the director of the Diesel Engine Manufacturers Association and suggested that D.E.C. host a meeting of industry engineering managers with the goal of standardizing an industry approved emission control system based on the Nardello technology.

Within a few weeks of his father's death, however, Winston Osborne, III, ordered the cancellation of the planned meeting and the termination of Mario's development work on the ceramic trap. He said that he was not impressed with the Nardello system. As far as he was concerned, the ceramic system was too expensive and would result in higher production costs and lower profits. He also was opposed to Prescott's idea of making the "costly" ceramic system an industry standard. In his mind, the ceramic system was nothing more than a cave-in to regulators. He abhorred government regulation of any kind and was determined to ignore them, especially if the regulations interfered with the bottom line.

Instead of financing the development of a ceramic trap, young Osborne ordered his own engineering staff to come up with a less expensive alternative to the ceramic trap. The engineering staff, however, was unable to satisfy Winston's timetable, and his dissatisfaction boiled over.

Winston shouted in a contemptuous tone of voice, "I don't want any more damn excuses, Prescott. I don't think you understand the severity of the situation. The Industry Association is already on my ass. They're telling me to either start using the ceramic trap or provide them with an alternative supported by meaningful in-house test data."

Bob Prescott, seated in a straight back chair in front of Winston's desk, bit his lip. He wanted to tell his new boss to shove it, but he was not prepared to resign, not yet, anyway.

Winston continued, "Your boys out back have been going around in circles for weeks. You'd better tell them they have until the end of the month to come up with an alternative, or I'll find someone else who can."

14

After a particularly busy day, Dr. Julius Simpkins telephoned his wife Thalia at her Sacramento office and suggested they have dinner at Desmond's, a downtown Sacramento restaurant. "Good idea, honey. I'm too tired to even think about preparing a meal. I can leave here in about 30 minutes."

"Perfect. I'll call and make a reservation. I'll meet you there. Did you see the latest newsletter from the American Cancer Society?"

"No. We don't get that newsletter. What about it?"

"I'll make a copy and bring it to dinner. It's powerful stuff, Thal. See you in 30."

Julius Simpkins, M.D., inherited the physical characteristics of his mother, a small African-American woman weighing less than 110 pounds, more brown than black. When he entered high school, Julius weighed just 135 pounds and had already reached his maximum height of 5' 8." His face featured high, sculptured cheekbones; a prominent chin; and well-shaped lips. His slight build didn't, however, limit his athletic achievements. He lettered in track each of his four years at Sacramento's Central High.

Julius may have been a physical lightweight, but he was an intellectual heavy weight. Julius was an outstanding student at all levels of his education. However, it wasn't until he entered medical school at the University of California that his true potential became evident. He led his class in every category and, as a result, was able to practically handpick locations for his internship and residency. Simpkins was aware that a resident's wages were meager at best, so he chose Sacramento General Hospital, only seven miles from his parent's home.

Thalia Washington met Julius at a spring meeting of the N.A.A.C.P. in Oakland. Julius was in the final year of residency at Sacramento General and Thalia was a graduate student at University of California at Berkeley when they met. An African-American female with a 3.9 grade point average, Thalia was heavily recruited by businesses in northern California. It didn't hurt that she was also an attractive young lady with the figure, face, and complexion of a model. A week before her graduation, Thalia accepted an offer from the Sacramento Gas and Electric Company to enter its management trainee program.

Five years into their marriage, Julius and Thalia reluctantly accepted the medical consensus that Thalia was sterile: children would not be part of their future. Thalia redirected her boundless energy toward supporting her husband's career and building one of her own. Within a relatively short ten-year period, she was promoted to the number two position in S.G.E.'s Planning Department. When her boss retired in the mid-1980s, Thalia assumed his position and quickly became the driving force behind a S.G.E. decision to evaluate and test various alternatives to traditional energy sources. Management encouraged her to expand her research beyond stationary power plants and investigate the potential represented by new transportation technologies.

An unusual sequence of events resulted in Dr. Julius Simpkins joining the newly-created Department of Safety. The new department head, Jack Walsh, was fixing a flat on U.S. Highway 99, just south of Sacramento, when a car plowed into the rear end of his vehicle, propelling Walsh over the shoulder and into a ditch. A passing motorist saw the impact, slammed on the brakes, and tried to pull over to help but his car's momentum took him about 50 yards past the accident. While he was running back toward Walsh's vehicle, he watched helplessly as the offending driver exited her car, examined the front end of her vehicle, looked into the ditch at the unconscious Walsh, and made a hasty escape from the scene. The action happened so fast the "good Samaritan" didn't think to look at the license plate as the driver fled the scene. He was, however, able to flag down a truck and ask the driver to call for an ambulance and the police.

Jack Walsh was a broken man when he was wheeled into the emergency room of Sacramento General at 7:00 a.m. Resident physician Dr. Julius Simpkins was on E.R. duty that evening and was credited with saving Walsh's life. Jack Walsh never forgot what Dr. Simpkins did that evening.

Within a year of the accident, he recruited Julius Simpkins to join his new organization and serve as his assistant director for citizen safety. Julius was reluctant at first because he didn't feel he was qualified. He dragged his feet until Walsh convinced the governor to allow Julius to staff his group with the brightest young scientists he could find within the University of California system.

Jack Walsh's definition of citizen safety went beyond traditional concerns like occupational safety: he had strong environmental concerns as well. Supplied with mounting evidence that the emissions from diesel engines was having a negative effect on the health of California citizens, especially its children and senior citizens, Walsh decided it was time for the state to be proactive. He directed Dr. Simpkins to organize a study team to determine why diesel emissions had been identified as a health risk and prepare a response plan.

While Julius's team was studying the health risks associated with diesel fuel and engines, Thalia Simpkins department at S.G.E. began to search for a technology to replace the internal combustion engine. Julius was delighted. It meant that he and his wife would be working toward a common goal.

"May I serve drinks while you look over the menu?" asked the waiter.

Julius looked at Thalia, and she nodded. "Two glasses of your house chardonnay, please."

"Yes, sir."

Thalia asked, "Would you like to split a pasta dish?"

"Sure. Go ahead and pick one. I'm game for anything." Julius reached into the inside pocket of his sport coat and retrieved the American Cancer Society newsletter. As he unfolded the document he said, "I want to read from the A.C.S. newsletter I mentioned on the telephone. The article seems to refute the belief that breast cancer is the major cancer killer. Listen to this. 'After an extensive, five year study, the American Cancer Society has determined that lung cancer is the leading cause of cancer deaths. Deaths from lung cancer are four times higher than breast cancer deaths and are rising. For the year ending in December, the study found that lung cancer caused 160,000 deaths, whereas 60,000 died from colon cancer, 40,000 from breast cancer, and 30,000 from prostate cancer.'

"That death rate from lung cancer is bad, Thal, but listen to this next statement. 'The A.C.S. found a strong correlation between heavy-duty truck traffic and increases in respiratory diseases and cancer.'" Julius placed the document on the table. "I found that last sentence to be the most alarming and distressing part of the report. I guess it will probably take some kind of tragedy involving school children before our politicians insist on regulating an industry that produces those incredibly dirty diesel engines."

15

A report published in the Los Angeles Journal about a class action filed by a group of parents against elected members of the Sunnymead, California, school board spread throughout the diesel engine industry like a wildfire. The complaint alleged that the school board ignored warnings from the California Air Resources Board about the health risk from exhaust fumes emitted by older diesel powered school buses. The warning said that tests showed that fumes from diesel engines were polluting the interior of the school buses as well as the outside, ambient air. The C.A.R.B. statement read: "The general public doesn't understand or isn't aware of the health risks from older diesel school buses. Harmful fumes seep into the interior of older school buses because the exhaust systems are so inefficient. Toxic pollutants are emitted inside as well as outside these older buses and can cause serious respiratory problems for some children."

A consultant retained by the parents found that the level of particulate matter in the exhaust of Sunnymead school buses was five to ten times higher than average levels measured at fixed-site monitoring stations. He also discovered that the levels of fine particles and black carbon were even higher when the buses were idling, even when the doors and windows were open. The highest pollution occurred when the buses queued to load or unload students and the engines were allowed to idle. He found that pollutants tended to accumulate inside the vehicles, which meant that the students were exposed to the pollution buildup during the trip home.

Attorney Richard McCoy, president of the Sunnymead P.T.A. and the father of five schoolchildren, was appalled and angry when he read the consultant's report. He convinced his fellow P.T.A. members to fight back. By ignoring the C.A.R.B. warning, he said the board failed to protect the health of their children. The parents agreed and filed the class action charging the school board with negligence.

The parent's complaint also claimed that the school board reneged on an earlier commitment that it made to the local Parent/Teachers organization. The board pledged that it would purchase four new compressed natural gas buses if the public approved a bond issue specifically earmarked for that purpose. After the bond was approved, however, the board elected to purchase four used diesel buses from Los Angeles County instead of the new natural gas buses.

Although it wasn't the primary reason behind the class action, the intransigence of the Diesel Engine Corporation contributed to the parent's action. Attorney McCoy heard a rumor that D.E.C. had been circumventing a directive from the California Air Resources Board to retrofit all D.E.C. engines already in service with a new ceramic particulate trap system. McCoy contacted C.A.R.B. and found that, yes the rumor was true: D.E.C. attempted to rig test data by retrofitting its engines with an inferior system that produced one set of test results at the factory and another set of results when operating under normal highway conditions.

Another unrelated development reinforced the parent's class action. The federal E.P.A. announced with little fanfare that it had underestimated the level of toxins found in the air from gasoline and diesel fuels by as much as 50 percent.

A local tabloid heard of the parent's complaint and reported it in a brief, factual account with little amplification. Consequently, it received minimal attention outside the local communities affected. An enterprising reporter from the Los Angeles Journal, however, was intrigued by the story and investigated further. She interviewed parents and school officials, researched the internet, and made numerous phone calls to school districts across the country. She found that most school districts in the U.S. employed older buses, some as old as to 20 to 30 years, to transport students.

The more she dug, the more she realized that the story could have national implications: children riding to school in polluted school buses could become a huge issue. If the Sunnymead parents were successful with their action and the school board was found to be negligent, the result would turn school busing on its ear. She speculated that the parent's complaint might very well become a class action against all California school boards, and if that happened, it could be unparalleled in the annals of environmental law.

Although the Sunnymead complaint hadn't charged diesel engine manufacturers directly, it did underscore and describe in considerable detail the harmful health effects of diesel engine emissions. The journal report speculated that the industry itself could be charged with negligence at a later date, fined, and be sued for substantial sums of money. The executive director of the Association of Diesel Engine Manufacturers was invited to appear on a network news magazine to defend the industry. The interview was a disaster. The director's glib assurances that diesel engines were pollution free and that diesel trucks represented the lifeline of the economy were perceived by most viewers as being insensitive to health issues, especially issues relating to the health of seniors and children.

16

Winston Osborne, III, stomped around his office like a little by who'd been denied a toy when he heard what the director of the industry association said during the television interview. Then, when he saw a replay of portions of the interview on the news, he became irate again. He threw a stapler across the room and yelled obscenities. His hatred of the press was exceeded only by his hatred of government bureaucrats. Aware of Winston's occasional tantrums, D.E.C. employees knew enough to stay out of his way when he was ranting and raving. The following morning, Winston was still seething.

Soon after his arrival his secretary buzzed him and announced, "Mr. Osborne, Mario Nardello is on the phone. He insists it's important. Should I put him through?"

Winston frowned, and mumbled, "Damn it, Susan, I don't have time for his bullshit. But, yes, go ahead and put him through." Winston was uncomfortable talking with Mario Nardello: he felt that having any contact with the man was beneath him. One of the goals that he'd established for himself when he'd assumed management control of D.E.C. was to sever all ties with Nardello Trucking as soon as possible. However, he needed Nardello for a few more months, at least until D.E.C.'s new research and development center was up and operating.

Winston asked in a bored, impatient voice, "What is it, Nardello?"

"Winston, I'm afraid I have some news you're not going to like. My daughter phoned last night and told me the city of Riverside plans to file a class action lawsuit against D.E.C. for poisoning its air."

"What?" Osborne jumped out of his chair and shouted, "Poisoning its air? What the hell are you talking about?"

"Apparently, a five-year-old boy died a few weeks ago from respiratory problems, and the city is blaming his death on emissions from D.E.C.

engines. The city is also encouraging the boy's family to file a wrongful death complaint."

"I hope you're not jerking me around, Mario. This isn't funny."

"It's on the up and up, Winston. The Riverside City Council has engaged a respected law firm in New York, Roberts and Spencer, to prepare both lawsuits. I didn't ask a lot of questions because my daughter doesn't know about the testing arrangement I have with D.E.C."

"Damn!" Osborne fell back down into his chair. "I'd better look into this. Call me later." Winston disconnected without further fanfare and dialed the number for D.E.C.'s legal counsel, Peterson and Foster.

"This is Winston Osborne. I want to speak to Jim Foster."

"Mr. Foster has someone in his…"

"Interrupt him. This is important."

The secretary put Osborne on hold and buzzed Foster. "Sorry to interrupt, Mr. Foster. Mr. Osborne is on the phone and insists on speaking with you. Can you take the call?"

Foster looked over at his partner, Phillip Peterson. "Osborne is on the line. Do you mind?"

"No, go ahead. That guy has to be the biggest pain in the ass this side of Boston!"

"Winston, how…"

"Forget the pleasantries, Foster. I was just informed that the city of Riverside, Connecticut, intends to file a class action lawsuit against us." Winston went on to repeat what Mario Nardello had just told him. "I want to crush this thing before the media gets on it. See what you can find out from attorneys in Riverside, and then check on D.E.C.'s liability exposure. Call me." Without another word, Winston hung up.

Jim Foster was stunned. He remained seated, holding the phone in his hand. He turned and looked at Peterson, and said, "You won't believe this, Phil, but a Connecticut city is about to file a class action complaint against D.E.C. for poisoning its air!"

Osborne leaned forward on his elbows and placed his right hand on his forehead. He sat for a moment and contemplated his response to this very negative news. He buzzed his secretary and asked that she locate D.E.C.'s Marketing Director, Daniel Abbott. "Tell Dan I need to talk with him in my office, now!" Winston sat fidgeting while he waited. A few minutes passed before Dan Abbott walked in. Without saying as much as a hello, Winston asked, "Don't we have a dealer in Riverside, Connecticut?"

"That's right, Winston: Richard Panullo and Sons. They've been a dealer for over 20 years. Why?"

"It looks like we may have a legal problem in Riverside. Sit down, Dan, and I'll fill you in." Dan sat quietly as Osborne proceeded to tell him about the Nardello phone call. "I want you to drive over there and find out what the hell is going on." Before Dan could respond, Winston continued. "We need to take defensive action, Dan. But since I don't know the details, I'm not sure what I should do. I just talked with Jim Foster and asked him to investigate the legal side." Winston mumbled, "If the media gets wind of this, we could have a problem."

Abbott stood up to leave. "I can drive over to Riverside tomorrow. I'll call and set up an appointment with Dick or his son." He placed both hands on the back of the chair he'd been sitting in, and said, "I'm afraid we already have a problem. We just received a demand letter from the California Air Resources Board. They want us to provide all factory and field test records that relate to our trap system."

"Damn it!" Standing as a gesture of dismissal, Osborne said, "Call me from Riverside." Once Dan exited the office, Winston repeatedly slapped his desk with an open hand.

17

Rose Nardello telephoned Dr. Sydney Bernstein the morning following the Riverside City Council's decision to file a class action complaint against the Diesel Engine Corporation. Dr. Bernstein was pleased and asked Rose to congratulate the Council for him. Rose explained that a prominent New York law firm, Roberts and Spencer, had agreed to accept the case on a contingency basis if the city retained the services of a competent, well-respected consultant to help prepare the complaint. "Roberts and Spencer wants emissions data that will unequivocally tie the Rado boy's death to the Diesel Engine Corporation. That's a tough challenge. Can you recommend someone who can do that?"

Sydney thought for a few moments and then, without further hesitation, suggested Dr. Julius Simpkins, the recently retired associate director of the California Air Resources Board. He explained. "Four years ago, Julius helped establish the Department of Safety within California Air Resources Board. His major accomplishment was the release of a controversial report that detailed the negative health effects on humans from the exhaust of trucks, transit buses, and school buses. His team compiled a significant body of information, especially linking diesel exhaust to respiratory illnesses and cancer. The most damaging data linked respiratory illnesses in children directly to the inhalation of fumes seeping into the interior of older school buses.

"Julius submitted his report to the governor detailing his team's findings, accompanied by a recommendation encouraging the governor to recommend legislation to regulate diesel exhaust. The governor decided to accept Julius's recommendation and went ahead and released the Simpkins' report to the media. That's when everything hit the fan. Julius and the governor had to duck: the trucking industry, diesel engine manufacturers, and the oil industry came down on everyone. They demanded that the governor ignore the report, claiming the findings were exaggerated and unproven. They claimed that if diesel engine emissions were restricted, operating costs of heavy-duty trucks would skyrocket, and the economy of California would be adversely affected. Julius was denounced as an incompetent medical doctor who couldn't make it in private practice and that he was out of his element.

"Julius knew that he'd face an uphill battle if he took on industry lobbyists, but he fought back. He was persistent. He tried to convince the governor and key legislators that his report was accurate and defensible, but his arguments were deflected by the lobbyists. He was stalled at every turn. The governor flinched and backed down. Julius became extremely frustrated and bitter and considered retiring early.

"Julius was vindicated when a group of concerned parents in Sunnymead, California, filed a complaint against the local school board. The parents claimed the board violated their constitutional rights by ignoring a voter mandate to purchase compressed natural gas buses. The board purchased used diesel buses from Los Angeles instead. The parents claimed that the older diesel buses endangered the health of their children.

"The story of the parent's lawsuit appeared on page one of the Los Angeles Journal and immediately created a frenzy of activity. Commentaries critical of school districts that hadn't upgraded their school bus fleets in years commenced appearing on the editorial pages of newspapers across the country. Broadcast media from all over the country willingly joined the controversy. Syndicated columnists and "talking heads" began to defend both sides of the issue on weekly television interview programs. The California governor could no longer ignore the Simpkins' report. Instead of the ridicule he'd suffered earlier, Julius became the focal point for corrective action. He became the darling of the legislature. Unfortunately, those positive developments occurred just before Julius was scheduled to retire at the mandatory age of 65.

"There aren't many people in the world that know more about the harmful effects of diesel emissions than Dr. Julius Simpkins. In my opinion, he's the most qualified consultant you could find. The timing may be perfect, Rose. The city of Riverside might be able to lure him out of retirement."

"Your recommendation will carry a lot of weight with Frank and the City Council."

"I'll call him if you want me to."

"Yes, please, Dr. Bernstein. He might be turned off if I call him cold. If he's interested, tell him I'll initiate a conference call so we can talk with him. It might be a good idea for you to be involved in the conference call as well. Call me after you talk with him."

"I'll be persuasive, Rose. I have a selfish motive. Having Julius here in Connecticut for awhile should be helpful to our group in New Haven."

18

"Julius, Sydney Bernstein from New Haven."

"Sydney! What a pleasant surprise! How are you?" Simpkins sat up straight and smiled to himself. Other than talking infrequently on the telephone about medical matters, the men hadn't shared any significant time together for a number of years. Julius was obviously pleased to receive the call and immediately thought back to the days when he and Sydney frequently discussed national politics: Julius hadn't had the "privilege" of listening to one of Sydney's lectures for some time. He recalled one particular cocktail party just prior to the start of a weekend cardio-respiratory seminar at Chicago University. Sydney was holding a martini glass high in the air moving it back and forth while he expounded on how the United States could resolve the ongoing Israeli/Palestinian conflict. He became so agitated, he spilled most of the drink on his suit jacket.

"It's been a couple of years, hasn't it, Syd?"

"Yes, I'm embarrassed to admit. It has been a long time. It's been too long, my friend!" Taking on a more cheerful tone, Sydney asked, "Hey, I read your recent commentary about diesel emissions. Based on what I've heard from my academic friends here on the east coast, your commentary created quite a stir."

"Yeah, some people were upset with me." He laughed and admitted, "It was exciting for a few weeks. I received a few threatening telephone calls. When I reported the threats to the police, they initiated around the clock surveillance of the area near my home. Things are back to normal now. Did I say back to normal? That's not entirely true, Sydney. Normal is terrible."

"My God! I didn't know you'd been threatened."

"They were just empty threats." He sighed. "I just hope someone in government reads what I wrote and does something about it." Julius summarized his deepening concern about the growing frequency of respiratory illnesses among children living in urban communities. He said he was having difficulty understanding why state governments, other than California, were not investigating the problem. "New discoveries linking diesel emissions directly to respiratory problems are occurring frequently now, but lobbyists representing the trucking industry are just too strong. They seem to be able to fight off any attempt at the federal level to promulgate meaningful regulation of the industry."

"Julius, tell me about the lawsuit filed by a group of parents against the Sunnymead, California, school board. Does the lawsuit redress some of the aggravation you had to put up with the past few years?"

"I don't know if the parent's action redressed anything, Syd. But I have to admit it felt good to read about it." Julius described the circumstances that provoked the lawsuit. "The Sunnymead lawsuit seems to have been a wake up call for our California state legislators and bureaucrats to address the diesel problem."

Sydney said, "We may have a similar situation here in Connecticut. Five-year old Bobby Rado died from a severe case of emphysema. Four other children are sick, one in serious condition. I had a very personal interest in the Rado boy's health. He was a patient of mine. His lung capacity deteriorated before my eyes. Near the end, his breathing was so labored, his heart gave out: it couldn't handle the load any longer. The Riverside City Council is convinced that the Rado boy's respiratory problems were caused by diesel emissions. After I reviewed the medical examiner's report, I have to agree with them. The M.E. found tiny carbon particles in the boy's lungs. Here's the clincher, Julius. The lungs were replete with the same harmful particulate matter found in the exhaust of a diesel engine."

"Where did the particulate matter come from, Syd? If memory serves, isn't Riverside a fairly small city near the western side of the state?"

"That's right. However, the boy lived close to the intersection of two main highways: State Route 10 and Interstate 64. The intersection is in the heart of Riverside. In response to all the flack he was getting from residents about the quality of the air in Riverside, the city manager hired a statistics professor from the University of Connecticut to monitor the volume of heavy-duty truck traffic passing through that intersection each day. The statistician came up with an average of 8,000 trucks each day. As I recall, 8,000 per day approaches the volume of truck traffic at some intersections in southern California."

"That's correct."

"The pressure for action forced the City Council to hold a public hearing. It was a packed house. City Manager Frank Mancuso really set the meeting on its ear when he reported that 62 percent of the heavy-duty trucks registered in Connecticut have Diesel Engine Corporation engines. That information tipped the scales. The citizens pushed the Council to do something. The Council voted five to zero to investigate the feasibility of initiating a class action lawsuit against D.E.C. on behalf of the children of Riverside."

Julius said, "Do you realize the significance of Riverside's action? When a City Council gets involved on behalf of its citizens, especially children, we may be playing in a different ball game. It brings the politicos directly into the fray. When politicians become advocates for technological change and not just pawns of the business community, meaningful things happen. I know from experience."

Bernstein replied, "The City Council didn't have much of a choice. Riverside residents were madder than hell: one child dead and four more sick in the hospital." Bernstein sighed. "Come to think of it, the Rado boy didn't have a choice, either. He was a victim. He involuntarily ingested that particulate matter. As far as I'm concerned, there's a direct connection between the diesel emissions that are spewed out at that Riverside intersection, and the death of that boy."

"That's a powerful accusation, Syd. If word gets out that you're pointing a finger at the trucking industry, you'll be attacked. Does the M.E.'s report provide enough justification for your position?"

"I'm confident it does." Sydney paused. "I'd better be confident. Word of my opinion is already out. A local newspaper reported on what I told the Riverside City Council"

"What happens next? Will the City Council do something, or will they just think it was a few citizens letting off steam and wait for the problem to go away?"

"I don't think the citizen's anger will go away, Julius. I'm confidant the Council won't sit on their hands. The city attorney has already contacted a prestigious, conservative, old-line law firm in New York, and they agreed to represent the city on a contingency basis. The law firm's offer contains one major contingency: Riverside has to retain a respected, competent consultant to provide technological support for the class action. They want a solid and well-documented foundation for the class action. Otherwise, the media would have a field day. The senior partners of the law firm want to avoid any semblance of negative publicity that could tarnish the firm's reputation."

"I think I understand their position. We've had our share of embarrassing legal pronouncements here in California."

Sydney said. "The city manager asked me to recommend a consultant. I recommended you."

"I'm flattered, but I don't know anything about Riverside or a hell of lot about Connecticut, for that matter."

"I'm not worried about that. The pollution in Riverside can't be that dissimilar to the pollution in California. The city manager would like to talk with you, Julius. He suggested a conference call, but I think it would be better if you were to fly back here and talk with him and the City Council face to face. I'll ask the city manager to pick up the tab for the flight. Are you interested?"

"You bet I'm interested. Now that I'm retired, I have lots of time. Please tell the city manager that I'll come to Riverside whenever it's convenient for him."

"Okay, I'll let him know today. How about next Wednesday? You could stop on your way through New York and visit with one of the partners at Roberts and Spencer. If it's okay with you, I'd like to meet you there and also go with you to Riverside."

"That's an excellent idea!"

"That looks good to me. If you take the red eye to New York, I could take the train into the city and meet you at the law offices mid-morning. Our meeting with the Riverside City Council is scheduled for Wednesday morning. We could drive up to Riverside together Tuesday night. I'll ask Frank Mancuso to send you an official invitation. What's your fax number?"

For the first time in months, Julius Simpkins was anxious to get out of bed in the morning. His energy level appeared to be back to normal. Sydney had been very persuasive and had stroked his ego by saying that the city couldn't find a more qualified consultant. He'd told the city manager that Julius Simpkins had more knowledge and experience about the harmful emissions from diesel emissions than just about anybody.

Julius stretched, slipped on sandals, and strolled into the kitchen to make a pot of coffee. Thalia elected to sleep in: she'd stayed up late the previous night watching Nightline. He stood next to the counter, staring at nothing in particular: he was consumed by thoughts of how a panel of jurors might respond to Riverside's class action complaint, and what he'd need to convince them.

A formal invitation to meet with Riverside City officials had arrived the previous day to discuss the parameters of a study project. City Manager Frank Mancuso suggested Wednesday, May 16 at 9:00 a.m. Julius was pleased that the invitation included an offer to negotiate terms of a consulting agreement. Mancuso also sent a copy of the invitation to Jason Roberts, the senior partner at Roberts and Spencer, and suggested that Dr. Simpkins meet with him in New York before coming to Riverside. He wrote a note on the copy suggesting that Roberts attend the meeting with the City Council.

Mancuso's invitation hadn't included specifics about what the city wanted, but based on his telephone conversation with Sydney, Julius had a pretty good idea. However, specifics were important: Julius wanted a clear understanding of the City Council's expectations. Was there a hidden agenda with one or more council members that could surface later and cause a problem? Before he'd agree to work for the city, they'd have to sign a letter of understanding, a document that not only spelled out what was expected of him, but also included project objectives and a clear description of the complaint that they intended to file against Diesel Engine Corporation.

The sound of a newspaper striking the front door brought Julius back to the present. He poured a cup of coffee, retrieved the newspaper, and settled into his favorite chair for a relaxing hour of catching up with current events.

Julius called his old friend Oscar Jackson, owner of Jackson Travel, just after 9:00 a.m. to arrange his flight to New York. Oscar and Julius had been close friends at Central High School in Sacramento during the 1950s. After high school, they attended college together and eventually moved back home to the California state capitol to settle down. Oscar was an ex-basketball jock, having played professionally for the Golden State Warriors.

The Jackson Travel Agency had earned a reputation for being the travel agency of choice for Sacramento sports enthusiasts. If you were a resident of Sacramento and wanted to attend a major sporting event anywhere within the United States or Canada, you'd call Jackson Travel. Sacramento's professional basketball team, and a few of the local college teams, used Oscar's agency to arrange their travel. Julius was proud of his friend's business success. Oscar had been elected to the presidency of the Sacramento Chamber of Commerce the previous spring, the first African-American to be elected to that position. Oscar, in turn, was one of Julius's vocal supporters during the frustrating period when Julius was attempting to convince California legislators to enact meaningful restrictions on diesel engine emissions.

"What's up, Julius?"

"I need to fly to New York next Monday night. I'm scheduled to attend a meeting near Wall Street at 10:00 a.m. Tuesday morning. What options do I have?"

"Off the top of my head, I'd say not many. Northwest has a red eye leaving Sacramento at midnight that would get into LaGuardia before 6:00 a.m. You'd probably have a row of seats to yourself. You could stretch out. If you drive into Oakland, you'd have a much better selection. Tell me why you're going to New York."

"Buy my lunch and I'll tell you."

"You're on, my friend. Let's meet at 11:45 at Shirley's Place."

The sky was clear and the temperature was in the 60s when Julius's red eye flight landed at LaGuardia. He rented a car at the airport and drove into Manhattan. To avoid the usual vehicle congestion on the streets of Manhattan and the difficulty finding a suitable location to park the rental car, Julius decided to implement a strategy he'd used once before: he'd leave the car in a parking garage in upper Manhattan and take the subway to the Wall Street area. Following the meeting at Roberts and Spencer, he and Sydney would take the subway back to the parking garage, pick up the car, and drive to Riverside. With the aid of a map and directions from the car rental agent, Julius found his way to a parking garage. It was not yet 6:30 a.m., so he located a remote space on the upper level, reclined the car seat, and promptly fell asleep. He awoke refreshed and was on the subway headed for the Wall Street district by 9:00 a.m.

Drs. Julius Simpkins and Sydney Bernstein were ushered into John Dowling's office at the southeast corner of the seventeenth floor of the old Standard Oil Building exactly at 10:00 a.m. Standing to greet his visitors, John extended his hand. "Welcome to New York, Dr. Simpkins, Dr. Bernstein. Can Gretchen get you something to drink: a cup of coffee, soda, water?"

Both men declined. Julius said, "Please call us by our first names. Doctor is too formal."

"You're right. We'll be seeing a lot of each other, so let's get used to first names. Mine is John." Dowling smiled and initiated another round of handshakes. "Please have a seat, gentleman. Jason will join us in a moment."

Julius was drawn to the large windows behind Dowling's desk. He couldn't help but delight in the view: a 180 degree view of New York harbor, including the Statue of Liberty and the Verrazano Bridge.

The clothes worn by the four men seated in John Dowling's office could only be described as a mixed bag. Julius, having just arrived on an overnight flight from the Bay Area, was dressed casually: tan sweater over a white button-down shirt, tan shacks, and brown loafers with small bows attached. Sydney wore a blue blazer, a Yale University tie, gray slacks and black loafers. John, on other hand, personified the image of a Wall Street lawyer: conservative gray suit, vest, and black shoes. He could have passed for a model right out of a Brooks Brothers catalogue. Jason, on the other hand, looked like a disheveled English professor: a gray crown around a mostly baldhead, suit slightly rumpled, tie askew, and scuffed shoes.

After a few moments of friendly chatter, Jason Roberts said, "Okay, let's talk about Riverside. I'll get right to the point. How confident are both of you that we can convince a jury that diesel emissions killed the Rado boy?"

Sydney responded, "It won't be easy. We'll be casting our line in an unfamiliar pond. Ten years ago, diesel exhaust was considered a smelly nuisance. But, things have changed. Scientists in California and at prestigious institutions like Harvard, the American Cancer Society, and some European universities now recognize that harmful chemicals, and tiny, microscopic particulate matter are present in diesel exhaust. There is a growing body of evidence that links the inhalation of these particulates to chronic respiratory illnesses. That linkage can no longer be disputed. I can supply you with that information.

"I'm confident the Rado boy's heart gave out as a direct result of emphysema, and the emphysema was caused by the inhalation of these microscopic particulates. The particulates are tiny carbon specks, significantly less than the thickness of a human hair. They were just too small to be stopped by the boy's normal respiratory defenses. Combining the information contained in the medical examiner's report with the results of independent research that's going on in Europe and the U.S. for the past few years, you should have a strong case."

Jason Roberts turned in his chair and leaned his head back. Dowling looked at Simpkins and Bernstein, lifted his hand and shook his head, signaling that they should remain quiet. He knew from experience that Jason Roberts was about to say something important. The latter stood up and walked over to the window. A moment later he spun around, and said, "Gentlemen, I propose that we really shake things up. Let's broadside D.E.C. with the simultaneous filing of a class action and a wrongful death claim. We file the class action on behalf of the thousands of young children living in Riverside, and the wrongful death claim on behalf of the Rado family. That strategy would really put D.E.C. on the defensive. We should play the children card all the way by asking the court to name Robert Rado as the class representative in the class action. If the court denies that request because Robert is deceased, we might be able to list the city as the designee."

He sat down and leaned back in his chair. "I'm optimistic about successfully prosecuting a class action *and* a wrongful death claim simultaneously. My confidence, however, is contingent on providing positive answers to two questions. First, is there enough factual evidence that the particulate matter found in the Rado boy's lungs was from the exhaust of diesel engines, and second, can we tie that particulate matter directly to D.E.C. engines? We agree that the findings of scientists here in the United States and in Europe are essential, but if we are to prevail with a jury, we must prove there's a direct connection between D.E.C. engines and the Rado boy's emphysema. In other words, our challenge is to prove that the boy's emphysema and the subsequent heart failure were caused by particulate matter emitted from D.E.C. engines."

Dr. Bernstein responded. "We already made that connection. The tissue samples taken from the Rado boy's lungs were analyzed at our epidemiology lab at New Haven Hospital. The lab found that the particulate matter in the lung tissue matched the particulate matter found in the exhaust of a diesel engine. It was a clear match. It was reassuring that our lab was able to validate the linkage. Their findings have the potential to set the diesel engine industry on its ear."

Dowling asked, "What about the second question? Can we say the particulate matter inhaled by the Rado boy came from D.E.C. engines?"

Dr. Simpkins answered. "I believe we can, John. I'm confident we'll be able to borrow a new, sophisticated monitoring system from C.A.R.B. called the Laser Trail. It's designed to detect particulate matter down to 2.5 microns. Given that degree of technological sophistication, we'll be able to accurately measure the level of particulate matter emitted from each truck. I'll recommend that Riverside set up two monitoring locations, one on I-64 and one on the state highway. We'll randomly monitor the exhaust of heavy-duty diesel trucks that pass each location, 24 hours each day for 30 days. If we can confirm the state's estimate that a high percentage of the diesel engines traveling the roads of Connecticut were produced by D.E.C., you'll have a strong cause and effect relationship, and if the statistical reliability of the data is high enough, you should be able to convince a jury that the exhaust from D.E.C. engines had to be the primary cause of the boy's death.

"The Laser Trail system is fairly simple to operate: a trained operator enters the truck's license plate number into a laptop computer, and then places an adjustable cup-like device over the end of the tail pipe while the engine is running. If the exhaust is emitting excessive particulate matter, the flow of electrons in the cup will be interrupted. Instrumentation within the cup measures the extent of the interruption, sends the reading to the laptop where it is converted to a p.m. level. We should be able to complete a single test in five minutes or less. If the readings exceed predetermined guidelines we'll complete a more extensive examination of the engine."

"You'll be interested to learn that D.E.C. is considered a problem company out in California. I met with a former associate of mine yesterday to find out what he knew about D.E.C. He told me that C.A.R.B. technicians dismantled one of D.E.C.'s particulate traps a few weeks ago, and instead of finding a ceramic filter as required by current regulations, they found an asbestos filter. Apparently, D.E.C. is not only ignoring regulations, they may be breaking the law. Isn't the use of asbestos in any form illegal?"

"Yes! Who the hell is running that company?" Roberts asked.

Sydney said, "Winston Osborne, III. From what I've been told, he's an arrogant, egotistical man that hates government interference."

"If your information about D.E.C.'s use of asbestos is correct, Julius, I predict we will win both lawsuits, hands down."

20

Frank Mancuso stood, reached out, and shook the hands of Julius Simpkins and Sydney Bernstein. "Welcome to Riverside, gentlemen. Please come in and have a seat. Our meeting with the City Council will be delayed for about 20 minutes. Dr. Simpkins, I assume you met with Roberts and Spencer on your way through New York."

"Yes, Sydney and I had a productive meeting with John Dowling and Jason Roberts."

"I didn't know that Dr. Bernstein went with you. That's good news."

Julius and Sydney provided Frank and Rose with a detailed account of the meeting, emphasizing the attorney's concerns. Bernstein concluded his remarks with, "I think we both have a better appreciation for the legal challenges we face."

A discussion of the monitoring program ensued. Dr. Simpkins said, "C.A.R.B. enthusiastically supported the use of the new Laser Trail system in Riverside. As C.A.R.B. sees it, both parties will benefit: Riverside will secure the data it needs to pursue its legal goals, and C.A.R.B. will benefit because Riverside will serve as, pardon the expression, a guinea pig. C.A.R.B. anticipates that we'll sort out the bugs before the system is introduced in California."

"When do you expect to have the monitoring systems installed and operating, Doctor Simpkins?"

"The equipment was shipped yesterday. C.A.R.B. agreed to send along a former colleague of mine, Charlie Olson, to install the systems. I expect we could have them up and running within two weeks if we can iron out the logistics with the state. We could start to train operators after the equipment is thoroughly tested."

The discussion continued for another half hour with Dr. Simpkins describing the operation of the Laser Trail system in as much detail as he could recall. He also covered Olson's assessment of Winston Osborne, C.E.O. of the Diesel Engine Corporation. "The air resources people in California think Osborne is devious. He'll use every deceitful trick he can think of and battle us all the way."

Mayor Barbara O'Connor studied the faces of the people sitting with her around the conference table: Dr. Bernstein, Dr. Simpkins, Frank Mancuso, Jason Roberts, Rose Nardello, and City Attorney Barry Sandler. "Thank you for driving up to meet with us, Mr. Roberts. We are anxious to hear what you decided when you met with Dr. Simpkins and Dr. Bernstein in New York."

"It will be my pleasure, Madam Mayor." He summarized his understanding of the circumstances that existed at the time of the Rado boy's death, and his proposed strategy. "The city's class action will charge that particulate matter emitted from D.E.C. engine exhaust is impregnated with harmful chemicals, and that the children of Riverside were subjected to those harmful pollutants day and night. John Dowling and I strongly recommend that the city implement a double-barreled legal strategy: file a class action on behalf of the children of Riverside against the Diesel Engine Corporation, and encourage the Rado family to file a wrongful death claim. We also recommend that the city support the Rado's claim by filing a 'friend of the court' brief.

"The most difficult hurdles are: one, establish an irrefutable link between the particulate matter found in the exhaust emitted from D.E.C. engines and the particulate matter found in the boy's lungs; and two, compile statistically reliable data that show D.E.C. engines are the major source of that particulate matter. Aren't those the challenges, Drs. Simpkins and Bernstein?"

Julius replied, "I believe you've summarized the situation quite well, Jason. Allow me to add one important warning. D.E.C. will attempt to convince the trucking industry and the Teamsters union, in particular, to do everything under the sun to thwart our effort to collect emission data at the monitoring stations." Dr. Simpkins turned and looked at Frank Mancuso. "I expect that you'll have to play hardball, Frank."

"Don't worry, Dr. Simpkins, our police know how to play tough." Frank Mancuso sat forward in his chair and looked around the table. "Does anyone have a problem with Jason's strategy?"

Rose Nardello said. "I like the strategy, Frank, but it's been over two months since the idea of filing a class action against D.E.C. was discussed openly at a Council meeting. Because emotions were running high that evening, I think it would be prudent to give the public another opportunity to comment."

Jason Roberts jumped in, "I agree. Let's be open about this. We don't want to give the appearance we're hiding anything, and we certainly don't want D.E.C. to claim later that the people of Riverside were not behind our actions."

Mayor O'Connor said, "Alright then, it sounds like we should schedule a second hearing." Turning to Jason Roberts, the Mayor asked, "Would you prepare drafts so we can review them before the Council meeting? Assuming there aren't any problems, Barry could read them."

"I'll do better than that. I'll not only prepare the drafts for your review, I'll bring the final documents to the meeting and read them myself."

"Excellent! We'll call you as soon the hearing is scheduled."

Mayor O'Connor stood and said, "I guess that's it. Frank, I want you to serve as our information conduit. That way we can all keep in touch. Thank you all for coming this morning."

Frank and Rose escorted Drs. Simpkins and Bernstein to the parking garage. As they shook hands, Frank asked, "When will you turn on your consulting clock, Dr. Simpkins?"

"I'll start as soon as I return to California. I want to talk with my former associates at C.A.R.B. to learn more about our friend Winston Osborne, about C.A.R.B.'s relationship with D.E.C., and about their attitude toward the Diesel Engine Manufacturers Association. I also want to learn more about that asbestos trap that D.E.C. used. I should be able to return to Riverside in a few days." Sydney Bernstein volunteered to drive the rental car back to New Haven and arrange for it to be picked up at the hospital. Rose offered to drive Julius to the airport in Hartford.

As she and Dr. Simpkins exited the city limits and drove north toward the Hartford airport, Rose said, "In spite of what Frank said about being tough, I'm concerned. What happens if a driver refuses to wait when we inform him or her that we want to check the particulate trap?"

"I don't have a ready answer for your concern, Rose. Frank will have to work something out with your police chief."

"Why don't we ask the City Council to pass a temporary ordinance that would provide the Riverside police with the authority to arrest a driver if he or she refuses to allow us to dismantle the particulate trap?"

"Would your Council be receptive to that idea, and would it be legal?"

"I don't know, but we sure could try."

"Okay, check that out while I'm gone. One more thing: start thinking about where we should put the monitoring stations. Maybe we can use the weigh station on I-64 just west of the intersection. Finding a spot on the state highway will be more difficult. You and Frank may have to meet with the director of the Connecticut Department of Transportation and work something out."

21

"Hold for just one moment, Sergeant." Joan Michael buzzed Chief Walter Pierson of the Norwich, Connecticut, Police Department. "Sir, Sergeant Joe Godfrey from McAllen, Texas, is on the phone."

"Thanks, Joan, I'll take the call."

Chief Pierson sat up straight and exclaimed, "Sergeant, it's good to hear from you again! What is it...6:30 in the morning in Texas? You start work early."

"I'm not at work, Chief. I'm at home sitting in my recliner drinking my first cup of coffee."

"You must be a mind reader, Sergeant: I was planning to call you later today. My assistant told me that she ran into Martin Leary the other day at church. Martin told her that you'd solved the Acuna murder and had made an arrest. Is your case strong enough to convict?"

Sergeant Godfrey briefed Chief Pierson on the status of an investigation into the murder of Jose Acuna, a graduate student at the University of Texas in Austin. Acuna had been assassinated; he was killed when a bomb exploded while he was working at a field laboratory in Elsa, Texas. "I believe we have enough evidence to convict the alleged killer. The killer admitted that his brother-in-law paid him to kill the student. We arrested the brother-in-law a few weeks ago. He was the drug czar in Austin."

"You used the past tense, Sergeant."

"That's correct, Chief. The D.E.A. offered the brother-in-law protection if he'd provide them with information about the Texas drug cartel. He accepted their offer willingly. I guess he realized that if he were convicted of murder in Texas, he'd probably receive the death penalty. When the cartel learned of his deal with the D.E.A., they killed him."

"My God, Sergeant, how'd they do that?"

"I'm embarrassed to admit that he was picked off while he walked in the county jail exercise yard, right here in McAllen. Most of his head was blown off." Godfrey paused. "The other reason I called, Chief, is to report that we've closed the book on Martin Leary. Your recommendation that we use Martin to flush out Acuna's killer was a good one. Martin showed a great deal of courage. He put his life on the line, and it worked. We've cleared him of all charges."

"That's good news, Sergeant. I haven't talked with Martin lately. He must be relieved. What've you heard about his precious metals project?"

"Because of his help with the investigation, the Texas Railroad Commission lifted its hold on further precious metals tests and agreed to refund a portion of the fine they imposed on the project. Maybe everything will turn out okay for Martin. You said you were about to call me, Chief. Was it to get an update on the Acuna investigation?"

"No, Sergeant, I was calling about a job opening here in Connecticut. I attended a meeting of Connecticut chiefs of police over the weekend. Rocco Tarencelli, the Riverside, Connecticut, police chief, told me he's looking for a top-notch homicide detective. I told him about you. He said he'd like to talk with you. I think the pay scale would be higher than you're earning now, but it's possible a salary increase might be partially offset by a higher cost of living here in Connecticut. I don't know. You'd have to check that out. Would you be interested in relocating to Connecticut?"

"My first reaction is probably no, Chief. I'm a Texan. I'd probably have a difficult time adjusting. But I'm flattered. I'd like to give it more thought, though. Do I have time to think about it?"

"Yes, but I'll need an answer tomorrow. I'll wait a day before I call Chief Tarencelli."

"What time should I call?"

"Call me between 11:30 and noon. I'll delay leaving for lunch until I hear from you."

Joe placed the telephone in its cradle, leaned back in the recliner, and weighed the significance of Chief Pierson's information. He didn't know anything about Riverside, Connecticut, or even where it was located. He raised his 210 pound frame from the chair and walked to the hall closet to look for his copy of the Rand McNally road atlas. At 6' 2", Joe Godfrey had little difficulty rummaging through the contents on the top shelf to find the book. He retrieved the atlas, moved to the dining room table, and opened to the page showing a map of Connecticut. He was surprised to find that the distance between the city of Riverside and his cousin's home in Granby was less than 50 miles. While he maintained his focus on the map, his mind wandered back to Chief Pierson's offer. *Why did I automatically say no when Chief Pierson asked if I'd consider relocating to Connecticut? Have I become too comfortable in south Texas, maybe to settled?*

Joe stood up and went into his kitchen to refill the coffee mug. *Have I become too complacent? Maybe I'm just insecure, fearful of the unknown?* Joe returned to his recliner. "Damn it! I should be more open-minded," he mumbled. "I've got to think positive, not negative!" He frowned and snatched a yellow pad from the side table, and wrote "Pro" on the upper left hand side, and "Con" on the right.

Starting with the Pro, he listed: probably a higher wage, four seasons, lots of trees and lots of green, close to Ginny, within driving distance of Long Island Sound and the Atlantic. Joe moved to the Con column and listed: miss fishing in the Gulf with Jake; I'll miss working with Sheriff Zedillo; I'll miss the Texas weather; I don't know anyone in Connecticut, except cousin Ginny. Joe sat back in his chair and wrestled with his thoughts. *Why the hell do I want to stay in Texas? I'm in my mid-thirties and live alone in this damn apartment.* He stood and walked to a bay window that overlooked nothing but a dirty parking lot. *Damn it. I'm going to call Chief Pierson in the morning and tell him I'm interested.*

Ginny Newburg was overjoyed when her cousin told her that he was flying to Hartford at the end of the week to interview for an opening at the Riverside, Connecticut, Police Department.

Joe arrived at Hartford's Bradley Field before five, retrieved his luggage, and asked a security guard for directions to the Airport Administration offices. Dressed in tan slacks; loafers; and a sport shirt with the logo of his alma mater, the University of Houston, Joe climbed a wide staircase and entered a large lobby area. Small, glass enclosed conference rooms ringed the lobby. He walked straight ahead to a waste high reception counter and asked for Virginia Newburg. The receptionist dialed Ginny's number and announced Joe's arrival. "Miss Newburg will be with you in a few minutes. Please make yourself comfortable. Would you care for a cup of coffee?"

"No, thank you." Joe sat in a large, upholstered chair in the center of the lobby and studied a group of people seated around a conference table wondering what they were talking about. Probably they're talking about something to do with airport safety, or security, or flight schedules, or labor negotiations. Who knows? Shrugging his shoulders, he leaned forward and picked up a magazine.

Meanwhile, Joe's cousin Ginny sat nervously strumming her fingers on her desk as she attempted to conclude a phone conversation. When she finally hung up, she jumped up and rushed to the lobby area. Given the surroundings, the cousins embraced and kissed respectfully. Ginny grabbed both of his hands, leaned back and smiled. Joe returned the smile, and whispered, "You look terrific, Gin." Ginny did look terrific. To compliment her short black, pixie-like hairstyle; her attractive figure; and lovely, well-proportioned face, Ginny wore a dark blue suit with matching shoes and a white blouse.

"Gosh, it's good to see you again, Joe." Ginny considered her cousin a very special guy: a kind and thoughtful man with a great personality. "You're staying in Granby tonight, aren't you?"

"You bet. I don't have to be in Riverside until 10:00 tomorrow morning."

Ginny dropped her hold on his hands and reached for his right elbow. "Let me show you around our facility. After that, let's have dinner at the Grist Mill. I made a reservation for 7:00."

The following morning Ginny convinced Joe to drop her at her office and drive her car to the appointment in Riverside rather than incur the expense of a rental car. She located a Connecticut map and worked out the best route from Granby to Riverside.

Joe left State Route 10 at the Brooks Street exit and proceeded south toward the Riverside City Center. As he drove along Brooks Street, his eyes were drawn to the buildings on both sides of the street. Joe hadn't seen anything like them before. Most were two and three-story, wood tenements, probably built during the 1920s or 30s, separated only by a single, narrow driveway. It looked like the first floors of the buildings housed a variety of retail and service establishments, while the top floors appeared to be residential apartments. The monotony of the architecture extended for ten or more blocks, interrupted only by an old red brick hospital building that had been in that same location for so long, it hugged the sidewalk.

Joe had the sensation of coming out of a tunnel into the sunlight when he emerged from Brooks Street and encountered a beautiful rectangular park resplendent with rows of maple and elm trees. The buildings that surrounded the park were in direct contrast to what he had just seen on Brooks Street. They projected a totally different feel. He was reminded of a person who decided to shed his or her out-dated clothing for a more contemporary look.

Not knowing which way to turn, Joe circled the park once before locating the City Center. The offices of the city administration, Council Chambers, and Fire and Police Departments, plus an adjoining parking garage, were located at the north end of the park. Joe parked his vehicle in the three-story parking garage and walked across a pedestrian footbridge that connected the parking structure with the City Center complex. He followed the signs that directed him to the Police Department, and entered a bright, colorfully decorated lobby. Joe felt like he'd landed on another planet. His current employer, the Hidalgo County Sheriff's Department in McAllen, Texas, didn't even have a lobby. Visitors were forced to sit on a bench in a hallway. The Riverside P.D. lobby looked more like the lobby of large corporation, rather than a Police Department. Two matching blue sofas and a large walnut coffee table dominated the center of the room. Large photographs of Riverside, taken during all four seasons of the year, hung on beige colored walls. A large skylight created an outdoor feel, and a puzzling piece of contemporary sculpture towered over a flower filled planter.

Joe was ushered into Chief Tarencelli's office 15 minutes later. He was greeted warmly by a rotund man in a tailored police officer's uniform with epaulets on his shoulders. "Welcome to Riverside, Sergeant. Chief Pierson said you were a big man, and he sure as hell was right. How tall are you?"

Taken aback by this unusual greeting, Joe's only response was, "Six foot two, Chief."

"Well, you've got about four inches on me, Sergeant. Please have a seat. Call me Rocco, okay? I'll call you Joe. Want a cup of coffee?"

"Yes, black, please." Smiling, Joe said, "I may have difficulty with calling you by your first name, Chief, but I'll try."

"Great! Now let's get down to business. Walter had nothing but good things to say about you. How'd you accomplish that?"

"I'm not sure, Rocco. When I met Chief Pierson, I was just Detective Joe Godfrey from rural Texas, investigating a murder."

"How'd the investigation pan out?"

"We got our man: a drug dealer from Austin. He paid his brother-in-law to kill a young college student."

"Can you fill me in, Joe? Walter told me the case had some interesting twists."

Joe described Dr. Ely Gerba's precious metals technology in lay terms, the field test location, the crime scene, and the involvement of a Connecticut Realtor, Martin Leary. "For one brief period, I thought Leary might be a suspect. That's why I traveled to Norwich to meet with Chief Pierson. Leary lives in Norwich." He summarized the investigation and gave much of the credit for solving the case to Detective Jack Kelly of the Austin Police Department.

"That's interesting. I like to see cooperation between law enforcement departments. Unless the investigation is burdened with inflated egos, cooperation improves the efficiency and success rate for everybody."

Rocco picked up Joe's resume. "I've reviewed your resume, talked at length with Chief Pierson, and spoke briefly with your Sheriff Zedillo: nothing but high marks. We'd like you to join us and take over responsibility for our Homicide Division. Sheriff Zedillo told me what you make. I can give you a 50 percent increase. Given that kind of increase, what else will it take for you to move to Riverside, Joe?"

"I'm flattered and very interested, Rocco. I just need to get a better feel for the city and the cost of living. Could one of your detectives give me a cook's tour of the department and the city? Maybe I could look at a few apartments."

"Absolutely! I'll ask Pete Desmond to show you around. It'll be a good way to get to know him and talk about the job. He's the person you'll be replacing. Are you staying at the Riverside Inn?"

"No. I'm staying in Granby with a cousin."

Rocco paged his secretary. "Janis, ask Pete Desmond to come into my office." Turning back to face Joe, Rocco said, "Assuming you'll be satisfied with our fair city, let's talk about a start date. How about the Wednesday after the 4th of July? Pete will be retiring in two months. You'd have three to four weeks to work with Pete before he leaves."

"That start date sounds fine with me. But, I should check with Sheriff Zedillo. I need to give him time to find a replacement. From what you've just told me, I suspect that he's already anticipating my resignation and he's out looking for my replacement."

Pete Desmond knocked on the door and stuck his head in, "You wanted to see me, Rocco?"

"Come on in, Pete." As Desmond entered Joe noted that Chief Tarencelli stood, out of respect for the retiring homicide detective, so he followed suit. "Pete, meet Joe Godfrey."

Joe reached out and took Pete's hand. "I'm happy to meet you, Pete."

Desmond grasped Joe's hand firmly, and smiled. "Godfrey! So, you're the hotshot from Texas. Rocco was right. You are a tall son-of-a-gun." Pete smiled and added, "Oh, by the way, I'm glad to meet you."

Joe's face lit up and he answered, "I'm six feet two, Pete, and it's all muscle!" All three men laughed.

Rocco was pleased with the friendly encounter. He thought, *Good way to start, Godfrey.* "Joe's agreed to join us, Pete. His first day will be the Wednesday after the July 4th. We've got find him a decent place to live. After that he's your responsibility until you retire. Give Joe a tour of the office, and then the city." Rocco began to turn away, but remembering something, he turned back and said, "I suggest you take Joe over to Betty Ryan's office and ask her to show Joe the best apartments in her inventory." Turning to Joe, Rocco asked, "What time is your flight tomorrow?"

"Three fifteen out of Hartford."

"Good. Stop by my office about 11:00 and we'll have lunch before you leave." Turning back to Pete, he said, "Take as much time as you need." Rocco smiled at Joe and added, "Now, go find a place to live. I have work to do."

Joe called his cousin Ginny Newberg after he and Pete completed their mini-tour of the city. "It's all set, Gin. I was offered the job and I accepted. I start on July 6th."

"That's great news, Joe. I'll get to see you more often than once every 20 years. Come to think of it, maybe that was a better arrangement."

Joe exploded with laughter. "Thanks, you twerp."

"What are your moving plans?"

"I've arranged for a McAllen moving company to pick up my meager collection of home furnishings on the Friday before the 4th. I'll leave McAllen on Saturday. If I drive at a leisurely pace, it will take me four or five days to drive to Riverside."

"Have you found an apartment yet?"

"Yes. Detective Peter Desmond, the man I'm replacing, found an apartment downtown. It's a two-bedroom place with a kitchen and decent size living room. I guess it's about the same square footage as yours. It's in a great location, on the south side of town and only a five-minute walk to Police Headquarters. There's also a shopping center within walking distance.

"Peter is a good man, Ginny. I'm lucky that I'll be working with him until he retires. He'll help me get my feet on the ground." Joe hesitated. "Hey, I just had a thought. Is there any chance you could take a few days off and meet me somewhere, say Atlanta or Washington? We could enjoy a short vacation together while we drive to Connecticut."

"That's a great idea, Joe. I'll check into it and call you tomorrow."

"It's late. I guess I'd better go have something to eat. Damn, just the thought of eating reminds me of Jake's Coffee Shop. You may remember me talking about Jake and about our fishing escapades together. Jake's a great guy. In spite of the age difference, Jake's my best friend. I'm gonna miss him. Maybe I'll fly down to Texas next year and go fishing with Jake."

"Joe, you're beginning to sound nostalgic, and you haven't even left Texas yet."

"I'm sorry, Ginny. I think Jake and Sheriff Tony Zedillo are the only people I'll miss."

"Go have something to eat."

22

"Mr. Osborne, Mario Nardello is on the phone. Do you want to talk with him?"

Winston raised his eyebrows in exasperation. "No, damn it, but go ahead and put him on." Osborne picked up the phone. "I'm busy, Nardello, make it fast."

"I was just told that you're not using a ceramic material in your particulate trap. Is that true, Winston?"

"Who told you that, Nardello?"

"My daughter, Rose."

"Your daughter? What the hell are you talking about? How is your daughter involved?"

"You must have forgotten, Winston. My daughter, Rose, is the Riverside, Connecticut, economic development director. Now, let's get back on the subject of traps. You didn't answer my question. If you're not using a ceramic material in the trap, what are you using?"

Winston hesitated. "I can't answer your question now."

"I deserve to know what my people have been testing, Winston. What's the problem? You don't trust me anymore? D.E.C. trusted me long before you came on the scene. When your dad was running the company, I was always consulted during the development process."

Osborne stood up and yelled into the phone, "I don't give a damn about what happened while my father was running this company. When I think it's time to tell you about the material we're using in our trap, I'll tell you. In the meantime, it's none of your damn business. You can't seem to get it through that thick skull of yours that I'm running the company now. As far as I'm concerned, Nardello Trucking is overpaid for what it does. I'll honor the contract that my father signed two years ago. But if you expect me to sign a new contract when the current one expires, you'll have to do more to justify the $50,000 I pay you."

The blood drained from Mario's face. He could feel the skin on his scalp tighten. He depended on the D.E.C. retainer to keep his small firm afloat. In a more permissive tone of voice, Mario said, "Winston, why don't you let us do more than just test your engines? I know we could reduce your labor and equipment costs if we were more involved with the development cycle."

"We'll see. I have to go, Nardello. I have another call waiting. Work up a proposal, and we'll talk about it later." Winston hung up the phone and leaned back in his chair to think. After a few moments of reflection, he buzzed his secretary. "Find Prescott. Tell him I need to see him now!"

Robert Prescott walked into the office a few minutes later. Osborne pointed to a chair. "Take a seat." Osborne rose from his swivel chair, walked around his desk and sat down in the side chair next to Prescott. "How many of our people know that we're using asbestos in our trap?"

"Let's see. Besides you and me, there are only three others: Bill Stinson designed it, so he knows. But he retired last August. Vic Richards and his assistant would be the other two."

"I haven't visited Richards' building lately. Is it still secure?"

"Yes."

"Have you issued any additional keys?"

"No. The only people who have keys are you, me, Richards, and the assistant."

"Can those two be trusted?"

"They've all signed confidentiality agreements, Winston. They know you'd take them to court if they revealed any information you've classified as confidential. What would they gain by talking?"

"Money. Someone could bribe them."

"Why would someone try to bribe them?"

"Do I have to spell it out for you, Prescott? Using asbestos is illegal. I'm concerned that somebody might talk. If an aggressive attorney finds out that we're using asbestos, he could cause us a lot of grief. Attorneys have been known to pay people to testify in their favor, you know. If the Feds find out we're using asbestos, we could be fined big time." Winston stood and walked back behind his desk. "I want you to shred all files that even mention asbestos. That includes test data over at Nardello Trucking. Keep only files that support our tests of the ceramic material. I want you to report back to me before Friday." Osborne sat down, picked up a piece of paper and without looking at his subordinate, announced, "That's all for now, Prescott."

"Mr. Osborne, Mr. Abbott is calling from Connecticut. He's on line one. Are you free to take the call?"

"I'll take the call." Winston pressed the button for line one. "Tell me what you've learned, Dan?"

"It's not good. It looks like the city of Riverside is serious about going after us. They're promoting two lawsuits: a wrongful death action by the family of a five year old that died a few weeks ago and a class action."

"Shit!"

"They retained a consultant, a retired executive from the California Air Resources Board. He's a black dude. Julius Simpkins is his name. Dick Panullo, Jr., told me the guy's already beginning to make waves."

"Where's Panullo getting his information?"

"Young Panullo is a friend of Rose Nardello, the city's economic development director. Did you know that Rose Nardello is Mario's daughter?"

"Yeah, I know. I just found out."

"Apparently, young Dick and Rose double date occasionally. Dick said that she knows what she's talking about. She's the information link between the California consultant and the city. The City Council approved the consultant's plan to measure the amount of particulate matter in the exhaust of most diesel trucks that travel the east/west Interstate 64, and the north/south State Route 10. Look at the map I left with you: both highways run through the center of Riverside. The consultant's gonna set up two monitoring stations near the intersection, one on each highway. Every damn truck that goes through the city will be tested for particulates and nitrogen oxides. If a driver tries to avoid the monitoring stations, he'll have to take back roads and go around the city. But it sounds like the police have that covered, too. They are going to patrol the back roads. They'll ticket any truck they intercept trying to avoid the monitoring stations."

"How'll they do the monitoring without creating a serious bottleneck?"

"They're gonna use a new system that was developed in California. Apparently the system's very quick and accurate. The particulate test will only take a few minutes to complete."

"What if the driver refuses to allow the test?"

"The City Council passed a temporary ordnance to put teeth into the program. If a driver refuses to cooperate, his company will be fined. If the driver is an independent, he'll be fined individually. The fines will be substantial, Winston. I suppose a fine could be challenged, but since the testing is only expected to last a couple of months, I don't think anyone will fight it unless they want to spend a lot of money on legal fees, and then wait for months or years for the challenge to be resolved."

Winston fidgeted. "When does all this bullshit start?"

"In a few weeks."

"Did young Panullo say anything about what the city's looking for? You know what I mean, Dan, are they going to get technical?"

"That's the scary part, Winston. If a test shows that the particulate level is excessive, the city will quarantine the truck, move it to the city maintenance yard, and have trained mechanics disassemble the emission control system. It sounds like the city is very serious about building a strong case against us."

Winston pounded his desk with the flat of is hand. "Damn it!" He thought for a moment. "What happens if the driver doesn't let the city take the truck to the maintenance yard?"

"The driver will be arrested. A Riverside police officer or a Connecticut State Police trooper will be at each station."

"Do the Panullos have any ideas? Like, what the hell we can do to protect ourselves?"

"Yeah. Dick said we'd better try to neutralize this consultant right away, or he'll destroy us."

23

Winston Osborne paced back and forth in front of his desk. He stepped out of his office and instructed his secretary, in no uncertain terms, that he didn't want to be disturbed. He reentered the office and slammed the door shut. He stared at the telephone instrument on his desk for a few moments before he slowly lifted it and dialed Mario Nardello's number.

"Nardello, you complained the other day that you no longer are privy to important engineering decisions at D.E.C. Well, I'm going to give you a chance to regain your position as an integral part of our testing program."

"I'm pleased you've reconsidered, Winston. What do you want me to do?"

"It looks like I'm gonna have to get tough with a competitor. I want you to help me find an enforcer type person. You know what I mean, a tough guy, someone who knows how to intimidate. This competitor person is beginning to bother me, Nardello. I'm concerned his actions may adversely affect D.E.C.'s bottom line. I just want to scare the guy a little so he'll mind his own business. All I need from you, Nardello, is a contact, someone from the Providence underworld…"

"Hold it, Winston! Where'd you get the idea that I know people in the Providence underworld? I don't deal with anyone in the mob."

"Nardello, don't insult my intelligence. I know you're brother-in-law is attorney Mark Aquavia. From what I've heard and read, Aquavia has strong ties to the local crime organization. He's even served as defense attorney for a few of Providence's more notable mob figures. I'm not asking that you do anything illegal. All I want is a contact and an introduction. In return for this favor, I'll renegotiate your services contract and increase Nardello Trucking's retainer to $75,000 a year."

Mario was stunned. He was speechless for a few moments.

"Nardello, are you there? Did you hear me?"

"Yeah, I heard you, Winston. I guess I don't know what to say."

"It's a simple favor, but the rewards could be substantial. We both have a lot riding on this, Nardello. Yes or no."

"It's against my better judgment, Winston, but I'll do what I can."

At the end of a combative telephone conversation Mario's brother-in-law attorney Mark Aquavia reluctantly agreed to help. "I'll help you, Mario, but only because of Teresa. I want to make it perfectly clear that I don't want my sister to know anything about this conversation. Paul DeCurcio is the only one I know of who can deliver what you want. Paul is the treasurer of Teamsters Local 2900 and knows everyone with clout in Rhode Island from the governor on down, especially people involved with, let's say, questionable endeavors. As a favor to me, I'll ask him to help you. But understand, Mario, if he does, you're gonna owe him big time."

Every driver employed by Nardello Trucking was a member of the Teamsters. Since Mario's only contact with Paul DeCurcio had been during bi-annual contract negotiations, his nerves were on edge as he drove to DeCurcio's office in Cranston. DeCurcio joined the Teamsters during the 1960s and was currently serving as the union's treasurer.

Paul DeCurcio's office was located in an old union warehouse building that no longer served as an active warehouse: it was used primarily for storing important union files and financial records, strike related equipment, personal items, and a few antique cars. The only access to his office was a narrow, circular metal staircase from the warehouse floor to a loft on the second level. Paul was a stickler for security. His office was the first in a line of five at the top of the stairs, each of which featured a large picture window. If he chose to stand next to the window, Paul had a panorama view of the interior of the warehouse. He'd even arranged his furniture so that he had a clear view of the warehouse entrance from his desk chair. He was able to see most of the parking lot without moving from his desk: he'd placed a video monitor that he wired to a camera mounted above the warehouse entrance.

Mario had to wait in the hallway outside Paul's office while he completed a telephone call. DeCurcio hadn't bothered to provide amenities for his guests. There were no magazines: just one straight back, wooden chair that looked like it had been transplanted from someone's kitchen. After a ten minute wait, DeCurcio opened his door and asked, "Coffee, Mario?"

"Yeah, I could use a cup." Paul beckoned and the two men descended the circular staircase and walked over to a table with a coffee urn, condiments, Styrofoam cups, and napkins. Mario wondered why he hadn't noticed the man's limp before. Paul's right leg appeared to be shorter than his left. Mario speculated that he was probably injured during a physical confrontation with strikebreakers much earlier in his career. Paul was not an imposing man: he was thin, of average height, and probably didn't weigh over 175 pounds. Except for sideburns that ran down below his ears and a ring of hair that encircled the back of his head, the man was bald. In contrast, his eyebrows were so thick Mario thought he might pass for an Irishman. It was his dark brown eyes that defined him as Italian. Those eyes seemed to stab at you like a dagger. Paul motioned toward the stairs, and said, "Let's go back up to the office to talk."

Following Paul up the stairs, Mario asked, "Are you still negotiating with the waste haulers, Paul?"

"Yeah, but I expect a breakthrough within a few days." He laughed. "The public is beginning to be a little upset with the garbage that's accumulating on the sidewalks."

A light and friendly conversation ensued after they returned to the office: Paul briefed Mario on the status of the waste hauler negotiations, and Mario talked about his business.

"How's that lovely daughter of yours, Mario?"

"Thanks for asking Paul. Rose is doing great. She's the director of economic development for the city of Riverside, Connecticut. She reports directly to the city manager."

"Impressive!"

"I assume Mark called you, Paul. Did he tell you why I wanted to talk with you?"

"Yeah, he said you needed help. Mark was a bit secretive about it, so it must be important. All he said was that it would be a special favor to him to meet with you and do whatever you wanted. Should I put my business hat on?"

Mario sighed. He decided the direct approach would be the best. "I know you're busy, so I'll get right to the point. I'm not sure how else to describe what I need, Paul, except to say that a business associate of mine needs an enforcer, a man who would be willing and able to put the fear of God into another person."

DeCurcio's facial expression changed. What had been a happy, smiling face turned into a frown. He didn't say anything for a few moments. He just stared at Mario with those penetrating brown eyes. "On a scale of one to ten, ten being the highest, what level of enforcement are you talking about?"

"From what I've told, it's a ten, Paul."

Paul stood up and closed his office door. "If Mark weren't involved, I'd throw your ass out of this office, Mario." He pounded the desk with his fist and then turned his back on Mario and looked at the monitor on the wall. "Damn it, Mario!" Turning back, he said, "I'll have to call around. Don't call me. I'll call you. What's your number?"

Later that evening, Teresa Nardello answered the phone. "Teresa, it's Paul DeCurcio. I'd like to talk with Mario."

Teresa said, "Hello, Paul. I haven't heard your voice in ages. Hold on, I'll get Mario." She shouted, "Mario, Paul DeCurcio is on the phone."

"Okay. I'll take it in the office."

"I want to be very clear, Mario. I don't like this kind of a deal. I'm pissed at Mark for contacting me. I'm being used because of my position. You'll both owe me big time when this is over. Call this number at 4:00 tomorrow: 555-5867. It's an unlisted number. Tear if up after you call. Ask for Tony Summa." Without saying another word, Paul disconnected. Mario lowered the phone from his ear, and, holding it with both hands, stared into space thinking, *What the hell have I started?*

"Mario Nardello calling. I'd like to speak with Tony."

"I'm Tony. Paul DeCurcio said you'd be calling. He said you needed help."

"A friend of mine needs help. Can we meet and talk?"

"I'll meet you at the front entrance to the Railroad Station at 6:00 a.m. tomorrow. Wear something red: shirt, sweater, or jacket. Don't be late. I won't wait."

Following Tony's instructions, Mario arrived at the railroad station 15 minutes early wearing a red sweater as instructed. His nerves were like a taut violin string. He began to pace back and forth in front of the main entrance. He practically jumped out of his shoes when Summa approached stealthily from behind and tapped him on the shoulder. Mario spun around and was taken aback by what he saw: the tall man facing him looked like a misshapen cartoon character with arms that were too short for his torso. Summa couldn't reach down far enough to put his hands in his pockets. He had a pronounced overbite, and his head appeared to have been squeezed by a vise. His shirt and trousers were mismatched plaid fabrics, and he wore an old pair of sneakers. If Mario hadn't been so nervous, he might have smiled.

Mario reached out to shake Summa's hand, but Summa ignored the gesture and said, "You've got ten minutes, Nardello."

Mario nervously detailed the legal problems facing the Diesel Engine Corporation and explained why he'd been forced, reluctantly, into representing Winston Osborne. Summa listened for a few minutes, and then raised his hand as a signal to stop. He reached out and pushed his finger into Mario's chest. "Listen, and listen carefully, Nardello. I'm not doing this for you. I don't understand this shit about diesel exhaust, and I don't give a rat's ass about how you're involved. If it weren't for your brother-in-law, I wouldn't be here. Just give me the name and address of this Osborne character. We'll get the details from him."

24

Robert Alphonse "the Phonz" Cicci's 18-year career with the Federal Bureau of Investigation ended abruptly when his supervisor, Elliot Dirksen, "encouraged" him to apply for early retirement. Dirksen and Cicci disliked each other passionately. Cicci believed Dirksen was the worst supervisor he'd ever worked for and dishonest, to boot. Dirksen believed Cicci was a loose cannon, a dangerous and unreliable agent with a mean streak that could erupt at any time, especially during an arrest. Dirksen feared that it was just a matter of time before Cicci would do something that would reflect badly on his unit. Dirksen was convinced that Cicci's arrest record proved that he was a sadist: the man enjoyed inflicting physical punishment on a suspect as soon as his partner turned his or her back.

The contentious relationship came to a head when the Phonz sent a whistle blower letter to Congressman Ian Parker, a Democrat from Massachusetts, complaining that Dirksen discriminated against women. Cicci correctly surmised that a trumped up charge involving the discrimination of women on the job would elicit an immediate reaction from the congressman. Cicci didn't give a damn about women's rights, nor did he care about his career with the F.B.I. any longer: he just wanted to create a hornet's nest for Dirksen and then watch the bastard squirm.

A more accurate charge would have been that Dirksen was a pawn of organized crime: Cicci was aware of Dirksen's relationship with Anthony "Tony" Summa, the undisputed boss of the Providence mafia. In return for handsome kickbacks, Dirksen ignored Summa's drug business and his practice of skimming monies from Rhode Island's only dog track. Cicci knew what was happening, but he couldn't prove it.

However, things changed when a prominent Providence real estate developer announced his intention of building a competing dog track, and then disappeared mysteriously while sailing in Narragansett Bay. His body was never found. Law enforcement officials, including Robert Cicci, were convinced that Summa's people killed the man. But, as usual, evidence implicating Tony Summa was in short supply. Taking advantage of an opportunity to help his business partner, Dirksen stepped in and provided Providence law enforcement with enough circumstantial evidence to charge an innocent relative of one of Summa's crime world competitors with the murder. It was at that point that Cicci decided to write his letter to the congressman.

Dirksen yelled, "Cicci! Get in my office, now!" All heads in the open area of the office turned toward Dirksen, the source of the outburst, and then turned toward Cicci to see how he'd react. Cicci rose from his desk chair and strolled slowly toward Dirksen's office. Dirksen waited by the door with his arms folded across his chest. When Cicci passed, Dirksen followed and slammed the door.

"I knew you were a dumb shit, Cicci, but..." grabbing a copy of Cicci's letter from the top of his desk, he waved it in Cicci's face, "this takes the cake. You wrote this letter to Congressman Parker just to create a problem for me, you bastard." Dirksen slammed the letter on the desk and began to stomp around his office shouting obscenities. "The Civil Rights Commission filed a complaint against me yesterday! Washington told me that I'm required to respond immediately." A slight grin formed around Cicci's mouth, but he didn't respond. The letter was having the desired effect: the man was practically hyperventilating. Dirksen continued ranting, "I knew you were a liberal tree hugger, but I didn't know you were a supporter of the National Organization of Women." Pointing a finger at Cicci, Dirksen said, "You're a no good son-of-a-bitch! As far as I'm concerned, this letter ends your career with the Bureau. As long as you work for me, I'm gonna make your life miserable. I advise you to apply for an early retirement. Now, get out of my office!"

Without saying a word, Cicci whirled and returned to his desk with a look of satisfaction on his face. He'd chosen the subject of the letter well: claiming that women employees within Dirksen's Boston Field Office were not receiving equal consideration when job promotion opportunities arose had ignited a firestorm. Anticipating Dirksen's outburst, Cicci had his early retirement request typed and ready to submit. He returned to Dirksen's office, walked past the man with chin high and with broad grin on his face, and delicately placed the request on Dirksen's desk. He waved goodbye and walked out of the department.

Lacking a severance package or any obvious job prospects, Cicci contacted a number of his law enforcement friends in the Boston area seeking employment leads and suggestions. One of the friends, a detective in the Boston Police Department, suggested he contact Patrick Leahy, a Boston real estate tycoon. The friend reminded Phonz that Leahy owed him a huge debt of gratitude for recovering the man's nine-year old son from the clutches of a kidnapper.

The boy had been snatched while walking home from school. A few hours after the abduction, a distraught Leahy received a phone call from a male kidnapper demanding a million-dollar ransom. Leahy was instructed to put the money in a large manila envelop and place it on the floor of the only public phone booth in a village 20 miles west of Boston precisely at 9:00 the following night. In spite of being warned not to contact law enforcement, he called the F.B.I. Robert Cicci and his partner were assigned to the case and were ordered to covertly follow Leahy to the drop spot, apprehend the suspect, and recover the boy. The two agents drove to the village and hid in the bushes near the telephone booth. When the inept kidnapper arrived to retrieve the money, Cicci and his partner converged from different directions and apprehended him. They checked the kidnapper's car, and found the Leahy boy in the trunk, tied and gagged.

Patrick Leahy was pleased that Cicci asked for help. "I'll find you a job, Phonz. It won't be in law enforcement, but the pay will be good." The job he had in mind would provide Cicci with more than an adequate income, at least until he found something more closely allied with his F.B.I. experience. Leahy called his old friend Tony Summa, in Providence. He cajoled and convinced Summa that, in spite of Cicci's F.B.I. background, he'd make an excellent bodyguard and enforcer. Summa reluctantly acquiesced and Cicci went to work for the Providence mobster. Cicci recognized that Leahy's offer to help was not totally altruistic: he was cynical enough to realize that Leahy probably wanted to put one of his own in Summa's organization to keep an eye on the man.

It was a difficult transition for Cicci: one day he was a respected agent of the F.B.I. and one of the Agency's front line sharp shooters and the next, he was an enforcer and bodyguard for a Rhode Island mobster. The initial humiliation that he felt didn't last long, however. Cicci admitted to himself that when push came to shove, it really didn't matter whether he was working for the F.B.I. or Tony Summa, as long as he had a decent income and could occasionally bust a few heads.

25

Cicci decided to take a few days off between jobs and drive down to his old stomping grounds, Cape Cod. But, before he left for the Cape, he met with Tony Summa to discuss his new job responsibilities. Leahy had assured Cicci that the responsibilities of his new job would be consistent with his F.B.I. training, but Cicci wanted to hear an explanation directly from Tony Summa. F.B.I. records showed that Summa gained control of the Providence mob and the lucrative drug business, by "eliminating" his two biggest rivals in one week: one with a car bomb and the other from a shot through the back of his head while he was getting a hair cut. Once he'd gained control of the mob, Summa maintained his dominance with a cadre of enforcers like Robert Cicci.

At the conclusion of their cordial meeting, Summa asked Cicci to complete one, minor assignment while he was on the Cape: collect an unpaid gambling debt. A Providence realtor by the name of Jack O'Brien refused Summa's polite request to satisfy the debt, claiming he'd been cheated by Summa. Calling Tony Summa a cheat was not a wise decision on O'Brien's part. "This is not the first time Jack O'Brien refused to pay a gambling debt, Phonz. I want you to teach him a little fiscal responsibility, understand? I want you to come back to Providence with my money and an apology."

It was late in September when Cicci arrived at the motel near Chatham. The weather was warm: New Englander's called it Indian Summer. Built in the '50s, the motel was small by Cape standards, just twelve separate cabins, but all were spacious and well-appointed. Cicci parked his BMW next to the cabin he'd been assigned and unloaded his bag. He was looking forward to lying on a beach towel within a few feet of the ocean, savoring the sound of the surf, enjoying a few hours of uninterrupted sleep, and then walking to a nearby seafood restaurant to enjoy a leisurely dinner.

Although he'd just turned 40, Cicci had the build of a National Football League halfback: 6' 1", broad shoulders, narrow waist, and muscular legs and arms. His penetrating gray/blue eyes contrasted with his dark, Sicilian skin. He'd initiated a genealogy search a few years earlier but never was able to uncover how he'd ended up with gray/blue eyes. In spite of his well-conditioned body and handsome facial features, the Phonz was beginning to feel somewhat self-conscious about the traces of gray in his sideburns.

Returning to his cabin after spending a leisurely day on the beach, Cicci showered, dressed in a sport shirt and slacks, and drove up the coast to the home of Jack O'Brien. O'Brien responded quickly to the ringing doorbell. *He must have been standing by the window watching me drive up,* Cicci thought. Cicci introduced himself and quietly informed Mr. O'Brien that he'd come to collect an unpaid gambling debt owed Tony Summa. O'Brien became belligerent, called Summa a few unpleasant names, cursed, and ordered Cicci off his property. Cicci smiled within himself: *I'm going to enjoy this.* He grabbed O'Brien's arm, twisted it up and behind the man's back, lifting him off his feet, and pushed him into the house past a screaming Mrs. O'Brien. He practically dragged O'Brien into the living room; seized a poker from the fireplace; and with one vicious swing, broke O'Brien's left kneecap. Jack O'Brien didn't need additional convincing. The following day he called his brother from a hospital bed and persuaded the latter to satisfy the debt immediately.

Phonz took advantage of an unseasonably warm fall day on the beach, reading, sleeping, and swimming. When he returned to his cabin to shower and dress for dinner, he noticed that the red message light was lit. He called the front desk and was informed that a Mr. Tony Summa called and requested Mr. Cicci return the call as soon as possible.

"Tony, it's Phonz."

"How's my good friend O'Brien?"

"I'm sorry to report that he's not feeling well. He's in the local hospital recuperating from an accident. The poor man broke his left kneecap."

Summa erupted in laughter. "I'll have to send the bastard a get well card."

"I'm meeting O'Brien's brother tomorrow morning to pick up your money."

"It sounds like you're enjoying yourself. Get much beach time?"

"It's a great place. I've been here a little over a day, but I can tell you this: I love the Cape. I'd like to come back again soon and spend more time. You should buy a beach house down here, Tony."

"Yeah, maybe I'll do that."

"What's up?"

"I've got another job for you. This one's a little more interesting. After you collect the money, cut short your visit and come back to Providence tomorrow afternoon. We'll talk about it then."

"Okay. What time?"

"Let's meet at my condo in East Providence, say five o'clock?"

Although Summa had only suggested that he return to Providence the following day, Cicci wisely took it as a direct order. "That'll work. I'll call if I get hung up in traffic."

Tony Summa lived in a large condominium in East Providence, only a few miles from the Brown University campus. The complex was a landmark in East Providence, built in the days when land was cheap and building materials were of the highest quality. It resembled an English country estate, featuring a u-shaped, tree-lined drive that ran through well-maintained grounds to an ornate front entrance. He'd acquired the four-story building in the mid-nineties with laundered funds from his numerous mob related businesses and by threatening the previous owner with an offer he couldn't refuse.

To avoid a direct connection to the ownership, Summa recorded the title in the name of a wholly-owned shell company. Unaware that Tony Summa was their landlord, long-term residents of the condominium complex wondered how a gangster, with seemingly no previous association with the owner or any other resident, was able to gain access to the largest unit, when their requests for larger quarters had been denied for years.

Cicci arrived at Summa's condo just before 5:00 p.m. He was ushered into the study by a maid and asked if he wanted anything to drink. "Yes, a soft drink. A Coke if you have one."

Summa walked into the study a few moments later. "How about you and me have a smoke while we talk. You're a cigar smoker, ain't ya'?"

"Yeah, sounds good."

Summa opened a humidor on the coffee table. He held one up. "See that cigar band? They're Sinatras. They're my favorite brand." He laughed. "I smoke 'um because I liked Frankie. The man was one hell-of-a singer."

After completing the ritual of clipping the ends of the cigars, lighting them, and savoring the taste of the first drag, they made small talk about recent happenings in and around Providence until the maid returned with a Coke. After she left, Summa leaned forward in his chair placing his elbows on his knees. Cicci unconsciously did the same. Summa said, "A man that I trust contacted me a few days ago looking for a hit man. Are you interested?"

Cicci was stunned. He leaned back in the chair and stared at his boss. He wasn't sure how he should respond to a blunt question like that. "Shit, Tony, you don't beat around the bush."

"I don't like to beat around the bush. Yes or no." While Cicci fidgeted, Summa demanded, "Well, what's your answer, Phonz?"

"Yeah, I'm interested, but I've got to know the details before I commit."

"Okay. Here's what I know, which ain't much. Yesterday, I met with a Pawtucket guy that owns a trucking company. Mario Nardello. Do you know him?"

"No, but I've heard of him. Isn't Mark Aquavia his brother-in-law?"

"That's the guy." Tony summarized what he'd been told about the pending lawsuit against Diesel Engine Corporation, about Nardello's relationship with the company president, Winston Osborne, and why the city of Riverside decided to retain a consultant from California.

"This guy Osborne is willing to pay big bucks to scare the consultant so he'll high-tail it back to California. But, I don't think just scaring this guy will work. The guy's got to be eliminated. So here's the deal that I want you to take to Osborne. Give him a choice: either we eliminate the consultant for $50,000, or no deal. If he goes for my plan, thirty-five goes to you, five to my contact, and ten to me.

"The target is supposed to be in Connecticut in about two weeks. You need to drive down to Newport tomorrow and make contact with Osborne. Get this, his full name is Winston Osborne, III." Tony slapped his knee, leaned back and laughed uproariously. "Son-of-a-bitch, that's a first for me. I've never heard of a third before, have you?" He wiped his eyes with a handkerchief. "Sorry, I got carried away."

He leaned forward again. "Nardello told me Osborne should be easy to find. He's one of them wealthy, arrogant bastards with a home on the waterfront. After you find him, he's supposed to give you the name of the target. It's up to you how and where you do it. That's all I can tell you. You want the job?"

Cicci smiled. He thought about his pride and joy stored in his bedroom closet, the old reliable Weber and Walther rifle with a telescopic sight. "The job sounds interesting, Tony. Yeah, I'll do it. I expect I'll be gone for at least a couple of weeks checking things out. Is that gonna be okay?"

"Not a problem." Tony laughed again. "Make sure you get a picture of the guy, so you don't knock off the wrong one." In a more serious tone of voice, Tony added, "Nardello said that this Osborne character wants to finish the job A.S.A.P., so you'd better get your ass down to Newport tomorrow."

26

Winston Osborne, III, slowed his step as he approached the intersection of Broadway and Rhode Island Avenue in downtown Newport. He looked both ways before crossing and was about to step off the curb when he felt a jab in the back. He spun around and looked angrily into the eyes of a homeless man dressed in a navy pea coat, knitted hat, sunglasses, and sporting a beard. "Mr. Osborne, I understand you wish to terminate a pest. Is that correct?"

Winston frowned and tried to sort out what the homeless man meant by that question. It finally dawned on him: this could be the contact he'd been promised. Winston's frown disappeared and his mouth dropped open. He was speechless for a moment. He'd expected a telephone call, not a face-to-face encounter in broad daylight on a major street in downtown Newport. The stranger began to turn around to walk away when Osborne grabbed him by the sleeve and whispered, "Are you nuts contacting me like this?"

Standing next to Osborne, but looking the other way, Cicci said, "Let's just say I'm fulfilling your request to meet with someone capable of fulfilling your wish. I don't have a lot of time, Osborne. I suggest you get off your high horse and give me an answer. Do you want to contract for my services?"

"Yes, I want your services. Don't leave."

Cicci turned and faced Osborne with a smile of satisfaction on his face. He enjoyed putting people on the defensive "That's better, Osborne. Meet me at the Middletown Bowling Center on South Ocean in two hours. I'll find you." He turned and walked away.

Winston's scalp tightened and he began to perspire. He looked around to see if anyone he knew had witnessed the encounter. *No. Thank God for that.* He stepped off the curb and continued to walk across the intersection, his mind working overtime. Without realizing it, he found that he'd walked past his original destination, Atkinson's Men's Wear. When he realized what he'd done, he turned around to retrace his steps, but decided he couldn't enter the store now. Reginald Atkinson would think he was sick and start asking a lot of questions. Winston leaned against the building next door to Atkinson's to settle his nerves. *I don't know where this bowling alley is. Shit, I never even heard of the damn place.* He looked at his watch. *It could take me at least 15 minutes to find it. I'll have to ask for directions. I'd better head back to the car now.*

Winston entered the bowling center guardedly. He stood next to a bowling ball rack, watched a young couple bowl for a few moments and then scanned the interior of the center for anyone that looked familiar. He turned repeatedly both to the left and the right in search of the man. After several minutes, he felt a tap on the shoulder. Osborne turned to find a person very different from the homeless man he'd encountered earlier. This time the stranger was clean-shaven, wore a bowling shirt with the name of a local company embossed on the back, bowling shoes, and khaki pants. He moved to within inches of Winston's face and said, "Let's grab a beer."

Making sure they were beyond earshot of patrons and employees, they sat on bar stools at the very end of the lounge, sipping a beer. Cicci said. "I'll ask the questions, you provide the answers. Are you prepared to pay $50,000: $25,000 in advance and $25,000 after the job?"

The normally self-assured Winston Osborne could only nod in the affirmative.

"Okay. Who do you want eliminated?"

Winston tried to answer, but his voice box just wouldn't work. He tried again, this time he heard himself mutter, "Dr. Julius Simpkins."

"Do you have a picture of this Dr. Simpkins?"

"No."

Cicci quietly stared at Osborne wondering how he'd identify his target. "Where will I find this Dr. Simpkins?"

"He'll be staying in a hotel in Riverside, Connecticut."

"What hotel?"

"I don't know."

Cicci frowned. His cold, steely eyes remained riveted on Osborne and seemed to further shrink the man. "That's very helpful, Osborne. You don't have a picture of the man, and you don't know where he'll be staying." Cicci turned, took another sip from his glass of beer, and then turned back toward Osborne. "You don't seem to know very much, Osborne. Can you at least tell me when Dr. Simpkins is supposed to arrive in Riverside?"

"He's supposed to arrive in about a week."

"Why is Dr. Simpkins coming to Riverside?"

"He's a consultant. The city of Riverside hired him."

"Okay, Osborne, we have a contract, but since you can't give me the information I need, I'm adding $10,000 to the price. The job will cost you $60,000. Take it or leave it."

Osborne nodded his assent.

"Be ready to pay me the first $30,000 in cash on Friday. I'll call you on Thursday and tell you where to leave the money. Give me one of your business cards."

After pocketing the card, Cicci slid off the stool smiled, and with a flourish, consumed his glass of beer in two gulps. He smacked the glass of the table and asked, "Can you at least give me a description of this Simpkins?"

"No. I never met the man."

Cicci moved his head from side to side, turned and walked out of the bowling center leaving Winston alone, scared, and bewildered. He smiled as he unlocked the door to his car, relishing the pleasure he derived from tormenting someone. He muttered to himself, "I hope he shits his pants, the rich bastard."

Cicci drove west across the Jamestown Bridge toward Interstate 95 and then north toward Pawtucket. His first stop was Mike's Tobacco Shop. Mike's was part of a new strip mall on Division Street just off Interstate 95 and only a few blocks from McCoy Stadium where the Boston Red Sox farm team played baseball. Cicci entered Mike's with a flourish with a broad smile on his face. "Mike, you old bastard, how ya' doing?" If he'd been asked, Cicci would have listed only a few close friends, and Mike Capaldo would have been on that list. Mike was a short, stout, perpetually happy man with an infectious laugh. Cicci enjoyed his company, in spite of the age difference.

"Phonz! Good to see you again. I can't kick. Old age is creeping up on me, but outside of that, I'm okay. How about yourself?"

"I'm doing good, Mike. I need a box of Johnson's." Cicci expected the assignment in Riverside would keep him away from home for one to two weeks, and his supply of Johnson cigars was running low.

"Which brand, the Pinatas?"

"I think I'll try the Sinatras for a change."

"Tired of Pinatas?"

"No. A friend of mine gave me a Sinatra yesterday and I liked the taste. If I still like 'em after a few weeks, I may switch."

"How are things out in the country? Don't you get kind of lonely? "

"I like being by myself, Mike. Besides, I've been real busy. I didn't even plant a garden this year." Over the next half-hour, the friends shared experiences since Cicci's last visit and talked about their next trip to Narragansett Park.

"One of these days, I'm gonna buy me a horse, Phonz. Those owners make a lot of money."

"I wouldn't be too hasty. Owning a horse can be very expensive." Smiling, he added, "More than a wife, Mike."

Mike laughed and said, "You're right about that! What are you doing this Sunday? Want to go to the races?"

"I can't. I'm going out of town for a few days."

"You headed down to the Cape again?"

"No. I've got a job over in Connecticut. I should be back in a week or two. I'm leaving tomorrow, so I need to head home and pack."

"Okay, a box of Sinatras coming up." Mike retreated to a back room to grab a box. Cicci paid for the cigars, and shook Mike's hand.

"You take care, old man. Don't do anything I wouldn't do."

"Unfortunately, I won't. I probably couldn't even I wanted to."

27

"Come on in and have a seat, Rita. Just give me a minute, okay? I've got to check with the dock foreman on the status of the I.T.T. shipment."

Rita Fernandez sat down at a small round game table that Nardello used for small conferences and laid out the financial reports that she and her boss were scheduled to discuss. While she waited for him to complete his telephone call, she looked around the office at the familiar pictures, all of which were expressions of the man's personality. Framed pictures of Rose and Teresa were prominently displayed on the desk. Directly behind the desk, Mario had hung a large photo of Rose in her cap and gown the day she received her master's degree. Numerous photos of Mario in his high school football uniform were grouped together on one sidewall. The other sidewall featured the largest framed picture in the office. It showed the Mayor of Pawtucket presenting Mario with the 1994 "Businessman of the Year" award.

Rita's eyes moved from the pictures to the familiar furnishings: beige carpeting, crimson draperies, Mario's large oil walnut desk, a low-back leather swivel chair, and two matching arm chairs in front of the desk.

Mario closed the telephone conversation. "Good. Let me know when the truck leaves, Dick. I want to call I.T.T. and let them know that it's on the way." He hung up the phone. "Okay, young lady, it's time to concentrate on financials."

Rita asked, "Have you heard from Rose lately?"

"Last week. She called and talked with Teresa. Teresa said she talked about being impressed with a new detective from Texas that joined the Riverside police force recently. Rose doesn't talk with Teresa about men very often, so this new guy must be something special." As he moved from behind the desk to sit next to Rita at the conference table, he smiled. "Okay, let's see what you came up with." Rita placed the financial statements in front of Mario and commenced explaining the problem she'd uncovered.

Winston Osborne fretted about the encounter in Newport all weekend: he had trouble sleeping and his appetite was nonexistent. On Monday morning, he drove to Pawtucket and parked his car next to the entrance to D.E.C. headquarters in the space reserved for the C.E.O. Instead of entering the headquarters building, Winston turned toward the sidewalk, walked out of the parking lot and down the street to the offices of Nardello Trucking. Not waiting to be announced, he barged through the lobby and walked down the narrow hallway to Nardello's office. He bolted past Mario's discombobulated secretary, and without knocking, opened the office door, walked in, and slammed the door behind him.

A startled Rita Fernandez jumped to her feet, scattering her financial records in the process, and moved back against the wall. Mario yelled, "Hey, you can't just barge in here like that!"

"Like hell I can't. Throw me out if you want, Nardello. But if you do, I'll cut your balls off. You won't do another day's business with D.E.C." Not hearing any response to his threat, Winston continued, "Now that we understand one another…"

Mario's concerned secretary opened the door. "Mr. Nardello, are you all right? Should I get some of the drivers to throw this man out?"

"No, Agnes. We're okay. It's Mr. Osborne. He's a little upset." Mario turned toward Rita. "Rita, would you please excuse us? We'll meet again later today. You can leave your documents here. Please close the door on your way out."

Rita hustled out of the office without a word, closing the door behind her. She stopped next to Agnes's desk. "So, that's the infamous Winston Osborne. What a rude man! What's he so upset about?"

Shaking her head and lifting her shoulders, Agnes answered, "I haven't the slightest idea, Rita."

Osborne stood in front of Mario's desk, leaned over and placed both hands on the desk top. "Who was that animal that contacted me last Saturday?"

Puzzled, Mario asked, "I don't know what you're talking about, Winston."

"Bullshit you don't. You sent him."

"Calm down, Winston." Thinking for a moment, Mario asked, "Are you talking about what I think you're talking about, the termination of a pest?"

"Yes, damn it."

"Now I'm beginning to understand. Did the person offend you in some way? Is that why you're upset?"

"No. It was the way he contacted me. He scared the living shit out of me. I didn't expect to be approached on a downtown street corner in broad daylight." Winston calmed and sat down in an armchair in front of Mario's desk. He sighed and related the story in every scary detail.

"I have just one question, Winston. Did you make the deal?"

"Yes."

"Okay. The ball's in your court, now. I don't want to talk about this again, ever! And I don't want you frightening my employees ever again, either." Mario stood up and pointed toward the door. "Either we confine out conversation to the business of diesel engine testing, or you can take your sorry ass and get out of here."

28

Before he'd unpacked his bag, Julius Simpkins called Chuck Olson, Senior Emissions Engineer with the California Air Resources Board. "Chuck, I just returned from Connecticut. I've got some interesting things to tell you. Can we meet later this afternoon?"

"Sure. How about 4:00?"

"That's good for me. While I'm over there, could you arrange for me to see a demonstration of the new Laser Trail emissions monitoring system?"

"Not a problem. We'll set it up and test it before you get here."

Following the demonstration, Chuck and Julius adjourned to the lunchroom for a cup of coffee. Julius recounted the essential outcomes of the meetings he had in New York and Riverside. "I was impressed with both the Riverside city manager and the attorneys in New York. The attorneys were adamant that we tie the particulates found in the Rado boy's lungs directly to D.E.C. engines. They were pleased when Syd Bernstein reported that the composition of chemicals extracted from the black carbon particulates found in the boy's lungs matched those taken from a diesel engine. Add that to the information the city manager obtained from the Connecticut Department of Motor Vehicles: something in the neighborhood of 62 percent of the long haul trucks registered in the state are powered by D.E.C. engines.

"From what I've seen today, it looks like the Laser Trail system is sensitive to particulates even smaller than 2.5 microns. If we can achieve the same results at the monitoring stations in Connecticut, we'll generate the kind of meaningful data the attorneys need to tie the Rado boy's of death to D.E.C. engines." Julius thought for a moment. "I'm going to have to describe the system in lay terms when I go back. If I say the system as similar to an electric eye, would I be oversimplifying?"

Chuck said, "Yes, but it's not a bad analogy. Electron beams are directed at each other from two cup like devices. The cups are small, only about two inches in diameter. When particulate matter from the exhaust interrupts the electron flow, the system's sensitive instruments will measure the magnitude of the interruption. The instrument readings are then matched against a predetermined conversion table to tell us the volume of particulates in the exhaust. You're correct, once the system is fine-tuned, we should be able to measure particulates smaller than 2.5, and do it within a matter of seconds. I believe the system will provide the accuracy and consistency you're looking for.

"The timing of the Connecticut project couldn't be better, Julius. Yesterday, the Science Foundation released the results a two-year study about the causes of global warming. They claim that diesel truck engines emit 25 to 400 times more black carbon particulates per kilometer than gasoline powered vehicles. And last week, the E.P.A. announced that their air toxic assessment model has been under-predicting the level of pollution caused by toxic metals. It's been a long hard road, Julius, but I think we may be finally seeing the light at the end of the tunnel."

"I guess the next step is to meet with Director Bemis and get his permission to use the Laser Trail system," said Julius.

"I anticipated your request, Julius. I already talked with the Director. He believes using the Laser Trail in Connecticut will provide us with needed data to show that the system is reliable. He also approved my suggestion that I deliver the two systems in person, and supervise set-up."

"That's fantastic. I was concerned about that."

"The system shouldn't be too difficult to install. The challenge will come after I leave. You may have to train the operators yourself," said Chuck.

"I'm not concerned about that. Given the city's commitment, we shouldn't have a problem recruiting competent people."

"Have you planned the test regime?"

"I'll have three teams. I'll stagger the testing between the three: one hour on and one hour off, around the clock. That way we may be able to measure the exhausts of approximately 200 trucks each day and still provide rejuvenation time for the people operating the systems."

"What happens if the test shows that the readings exceed E.P.A. standards?"

"The City Council passed a temporary ordinance that gives the police authority to slap a $500 fine on the owner of the truck if the readings exceed the standards. We'll record the truck's license plate number, truck model, engine manufacturer, engine serial number, and the name of the operator of the truck. The police will arrest the driver if he gives us a hard time. We may take the truck to the city maintenance yard and dismantle the filter trap."

"Julius, your project gets more interesting every time I talk with you. I'm beginning to look forward to visiting Riverside."

As the men disposed of their Styrofoam cups, Julius asked, "What's your opinion of Diesel Engines' C.E.O. I believe his name is Winston Osborne?"

"He's a royal pain in the ass, Julius. Under his leadership, D.E.C. has become a pariah within the industry. D.E.C. continually tries to circumvent state and federal regulations. D.E.C. was the primary reason C.A.R.B. fined the diesel engine industry $1.2 million last year for manipulating electronic fuel control test results. "

"What's the latest on the parents' lawsuit against the Sunnymead School Board?"

"Attorneys representing the parents submitted a motion for class action certification, but the motion was rejected. Apparently the complaint was not inclusive enough to warrant certification. I expect that will change, however. Before Riverside applies to the court for certification as a class, I suggest you convince them to enlist a few other Connecticut cities to join in their action."

Julius called the Riverside Inn from his home to make a reservation before heading to the Sacramento Airport for his return flight to Connecticut. When the reservation clerk at the Inn learned that he'd be working with Riverside City Manager Frank Mancuso on a special project related to Bobby Rado's death, he was given a suite for the regular room rate.

Julius was looking forward to his return to Riverside: he was impressed with the many specialty shops and restaurants in the downtown area during his last visit, all of which were within walking distance of the Inn. The Inn's proximity to City Hall was also a plus.

Julius checked his watch and decided he had enough time to call Rose Nardello. "Rose, it's Dr. Simpkins. I'm about to leave for the airport. Thought I'd give you a call to see how things are progressing at your end."

"Good afternoon, Dr. Simpkins. No snags here, at least not that I'm aware of. It looks like Frank convinced the city of Sheridan to join our complaint against D.E.C. Sheridan's city manager will meet with Frank this week and discuss the details."

"Good! I think it might be helpful to have a few more cities join the action. I suspect that the more children represented by the lawsuit, the easier it will be to obtain certification as a class action. Check with Jason Roberts to see exactly what's needed.

"You're not the only one with good news, Rose. I was given permission to bring the Laser Trail system to Connecticut. It's a simple system: just two lasers pointed at each other, like an electric eye. It appears to be very reliable. Training operators should be a snap. The next step is to get the approval of the Connecticut Transportation Department to let us install a system at the weigh station on Interstate 64. Ask Frank to contact the Director's office and see if he can set up a meeting for this Friday, or sometime early next week. It might be helpful if he could convince the assemblyman from the Riverside area to attend, and maybe the State Senator as well."

"I doubt we'll have any difficulty. Frank talked with the Director yesterday. The Director understands that the city's effort to control diesel emissions is a watershed initiative. He said he'd do what he could to support us." Rose paused. "I'm more concerned about the media, Doctor. I may have spilled the beans, inadvertently. I told my father that the city retained you, but I failed to tell him to keep the information confidential. Apparently word is out. The media is beginning to ask questions."

"Don't worry about that, Rose. It was just a matter of time anyway. I suggest Frank meet with the publisher of the Riverside Journal and ask him not to report on our activities until the monitoring tests begin. If the trucking companies find out what we're up to, they'll try to bypass the monitoring stations. Truckers talk with each other all the time at truck stops and on their radios. The fact that we're setting up monitoring stations will be old news in a matter of days, but the test schedule is the thing that must remain confidential, at least until we actually start testing. Try to keep the location of the monitoring stations and the testing regime confidential. Only people with a need to know should be told about our plan.

"I'd like to stagger the testing: one hour on, and one hour off during a full 24 hour period, 28 straight days. That'll put a lot of pressure on local law enforcement. Has Frank talked with Chief Tarencelli about a police presence while we're testing? If he hasn't, ask him to arrange a meeting in the next couple of days. We should also brief the State Police. Maybe Frank should call the Superintendent and arrange to have a deputy at each monitoring station for a few hours each day. I've got to go, Rose. I don't want to miss my flight."

29

Robert Cicci was faced with a difficult challenge: the only information he had was the target's name. He needed more, much more. He had to find out who the man was, why he was coming to Riverside, and where and how long he'd stay. Cicci expected that it'd take him two or three days to obtain the answers to those questions. He'd return to Providence at the end of the week to collect the first half of his fee.

Believing it wouldn't be prudent for him to stay at a motel in the city, Cicci registered at a Holiday Inn outside of town just off the Interstate. He spent the next hour creating an elaborate disguise: a blond mustache, blond wig with matching goatee, and eyeglasses. Cicci wanted to convey the image of a successful businessman, a man on a mission. He returned to the motel lobby and obtained directions to Riverside City Hall.

Cicci entered the lobby of City Hall and strode toward the reception desk dressed in a dark blue three-piece suit and carrying a briefcase. Suspecting that Simpkins had not yet arrived in Riverside, Cicci confidently approached the City Hall receptionist and asked to see Dr. Simpkins. He instructed the lady to inform Dr. Simpkins that Jeffrey Ambrose was here to see him. "I'm sorry, sir. I don't know of a Dr. Simpkins working here at City Hall."

"There must be some mistake, miss. I was told he'd be here."

The receptionist referred to the City Hall directory. "He's not listed in our directory, sir. Maybe he's a guest of someone here at City Hall. I'll check with the city manager's secretary."

"Mr. Mancuso's secretary said that Dr. Simpkins is a consultant who will be working on a special project for the city, but he isn't scheduled to arrive from California until tomorrow."

"I'll come back tomorrow. Thank you, miss."

Cicci found a pay phone just outside the entrance to City Hall and placed a call to the Riverside city manager. "I'm sorry, sir, Mr. Mancuso is out of the office today."

"Maybe you can help me. I was told that my old friend, Dr. Julius Simpkins, is arriving in Riverside tomorrow to work on a special project for the city. Do you know where he'll be staying?"

"I don't know where Dr. Simpkins plans to stay. I think your best bet is to call Dr. Simpkins' home in California and talk directly with him."

"I tried that, miss, but all I got was his voice mail saying that he'd be out of town for a few days. Could you venture a guess about his lodging plans?"

"We suggested he stay at the Riverside Inn, just down the street from City Hall. You might try there."

"Thank you, miss. You've saved me a lot of time." Cicci decided not to ask any more questions for fear she'd remember him.

The following afternoon, Cicci entered the Riverside Inn through a side entrance that led into the lobby of the hotel's Conference Center, a remote area that served as a gathering place for people attending business meetings and conferences. The space was equipped with pay phones and comfortable seating. He wrote down the telephone number of one of the pay phones on a slip of paper, placed the note in his pocket, and continued on toward the main lobby.

Although the Riverside Inn was over 100 years old, it was in excellent condition. It'd been renovated with great care just ten years earlier. The owner, Eastern States Inns, tried hard to preserve the Inn's unique New England charm, both the inside décor as well as the outside grounds. Cicci was far from being an expert, but it appeared to him that every piece of furniture in the lobby was an expensive antique. The fabric colors in the draperies seemed to compliment the furniture. The wood floor under the oriental rugs glistened from repeated applications of wax. He couldn't resist the temptation to walk over to a large window next to the entrance and look at the beautiful grounds. The flower beds that bordered the walkway from the street to an expansive entrance appeared to be meticulously cared for. He turned away from the window and strolled to the front desk.

"Good afternoon. My name is Jeffrey Ambrose. I'm an associate of Dr. Julius Simpkins. Can you tell me when he is scheduled to check in?"

"Good afternoon, Mr. Ambrose. If you'll wait a moment, I'll check." While the clerk searched for the reservation information in the computer,

Cicci studied the young man. *That kid's overweight, soft and effeminate. He'd have a hell of a time trying out for the F.B.I. He'd never make it.*

"Dr. Simpkins will be a late check-in, Mr. Ambrose. He'll be arriving sometime after six." Acting as though he was privy to confidential information, the clerk leaned forward and added, "He's coming in from California."

Cicci looked at the clock on the wall behind the clerk and muttered, "Let's see. It's 5:30 now." "If I give you a phone number," looking at the young man's name tag, "James, would you give me a call when he checks in?"

James smiled and cocked his head. "I can do that, Mr. Ambrose. What number do you want me to call?"

Cicci thought, *The little shit is flirting with me.* He retrieved the piece of paper from his pocket and gave the clerk the telephone number. "I appreciate your help, James, but please don't tell Dr. Simpkins that I was inquiring about his arrival. I want to surprise him. We were friends in college and haven't seen each other in years."

"I understand, Mr. Ambrose. I'll keep our little secret."

Smiling, Cicci said, "Make sure you give my friend the best room in the hotel."

"Oh, we intend to, Mr. Ambrose. He'll be working with our friends over at City Hall for a few weeks. The city manager's secretary called this morning. She asked if Dr. Simpkins had made a reservation. When I told her that he had, she asked that we assign him the Chase Suite. She said the city would pay."

"That's excellent, James. Thanks again. I'll talk with you later." Cicci made his way across the lobby and approached the desk occupied by the hotel concierge. "Good afternoon, miss. Can you tell me the quickest way to get to the Chase Suite?"

"It's easy, sir. Take the elevator to the third floor and turn left. It's room number 306 at the end of the hallway."

Exiting the elevator, Cicci cautiously surveyed the hallway in both directions. He estimated that room 306 was approximately 40 feet from the elevator. He found an alcove that contained an ice machine, only a few feet form the elevator. *This looks like a good spot to watch for our friend,* he thought. Satisfied, he made his way back to the to the small lobby in the Conference Area by way of a rear staircase, removed a newspaper from the briefcase he was carrying, selected a comfortable chair near the pay phone, and settled in to await the phone call from the front desk clerk. Waiting was not a problem for Cicci: as an F.B.I. agent, he'd been trained to be patient.

Cicci awoke with a start in response to the ringing telephone. The newspaper slid off his lap to the floor as he stood and rapidly moved to the pay phone. "Hello, Jeffrey Ambrose here."

"Mr. Ambrose. Dr. Simpkins checked in a few moments ago. He went to his room, but I expect he'll come back down to the lobby shortly. He said he hadn't eaten since breakfast and wanted to have dinner in the hotel restaurant."

"What time does the restaurant close, James?"

"Eight p.m., Mr. Ambrose."

"Thank you, James," and hung up. He hurried to the staircase, navigated the stairs two steps at a time, and reached the third floor hallway in a matter of seconds. He slid into the alcove next to the ice maker and waited.

Cicci's eyes opened wide in astonishment when he saw Simpkins exit Room 306 and walk toward the elevator. *Holy shit, the guy's black.* Satisfied that he'd identified his target, Cicci retreated to the lobby of the Conference Area, and exited the Inn through the same side door he'd entered less than three hours earlier.

Walking toward the car, he was reminded of an incident that occurred a few years earlier while he was assigned to the F.B.I.'s Boston Field Office. He'd tracked an African-American man who'd robbed a federally-chartered Boston bank, shot a teller during the robbery, and then tried to escape detection by hiding out in a barn just outside the small town of Acton. Cicci smiled as he recalled dispensing his own form of justice that afternoon: he never did trust the federal judicial system. He shot the fugitive in the head from a distance of about 50 yards with his trusted Weber and Walther rifle.

He drove back to the Holiday Inn, ordered his dinner from room service, and requested a wake up call for 5:30 a.m. He felt that if he returned to the Inn before seven in the morning he'd have ample time to continue his surveillance of Dr. Simpkins activities.

30

The clock on the wall behind the registration desk read 7:00 a.m. when Cicci walked through the main entrance to the Inn wearing an entirely new disguise. He was dressed as a hotel guest who'd just completed an early morning jog: warm-up suit, baseball cap, tennis shoes, and carried a newspaper under his arm that he'd purchased from a vending machine just outside the front entrance. He poured a cup of coffee from an urn on a lobby sideboard (a daily service provided by the hotel for its guests), sat in an upholstered chair facing the elevator, unfolded his newspaper, and waited. At 8:15, Dr. Simpkins exited the elevator and walked past his chair toward an attractive young woman standing by the reception desk. When the woman saw Simpkins, she brightened, smiled, and enthusiastically shook his hand. After a brief conversation, the two advanced toward the revolving door and exited the hotel.

Cicci moved quickly. He placed the newspaper under his arm and scooted over toward the revolving door. He watched as the pair moved down the winding concrete walkway to the street and stop next to the curb. Cicci slid through the revolving door and sidled off to the side, acting as though he'd forgotten something.

It was a magnificent spring day: the sky clear and the air smelled fresh. Dr. Simpkins was momentarily spellbound by the view of the Green across Elm Street. It was obvious to him that the 20-acre park was a special place. It was meticulously cared for: the grass was a dark green and the flower beds were filled with row after row of blooming mountain laurel. Elm and maple trees lined a series of concrete sidewalks that originated in the four corners of the park and crossed each other at the center. Julius could envisage people relaxing on blankets on the grass, napping, or enjoying their lunch during the noon hour. Pointing toward the park, Simpkins said, "Years ago, someone with considerable vision planned that beautiful park, Rose."

"I wish I could tell you who deserves the credit, Doctor. I just don't know. Our city manager, Frank Mancuso, may know. We'll ask him when we get to City Hall. We have time to walk around the Green this morning if you wish. Our first appointment isn't until 9:00. I could point out a few of the important landmarks, retail establishments, and restaurants that you might like to visit while you're in town."

"I'd like that, Rose. Lead the way."

Cicci watched Rose and Dr. Simpkins turn and walk south, away from City Center. Although puzzled, he decided that he had to follow, regardless of where they were headed. He really didn't have a choice. He hurried down the winding entry path to the Elm Street sidewalk and watched the pair for a few moments before concluding that they must have decided to take a leisurely stroll around the Green before proceeding to City Center.

As Rose and Dr. Simpkins strolled south on Elm Street toward the old Episcopal Church, he asked, "How old is Riverside, Rose?"

"The city was founded sometime in the late 1700s but wasn't incorporated as a city until 1808. The church in front of us is an Episcopal Church, the second oldest in Connecticut. The original building is gone, but as you can see, the church elders made sure the old cemetery wasn't disturbed when they built the existing structure. I've walked through the cemetery and looked at the gravestones. Some of them predate the Revolutionary War."

Cicci crossed Elm Street and cut across the grass to a park bench on the Maple Street side and sat down. He speculated that if the couple intended to stroll around the perimeter of the Green before entering City Hall, they'd have to pass directly in front of the park bench he'd selected. He unfolded the newspaper and lifted it in front of his face. From this vantage, he believed he'd be close enough to study his target carefully: he didn't want to make a mistake when it came time to perform.

The strolling duo turned the corner onto Church Street and walked west along the southern edge of the Green. Rose pointed. "See that building straight ahead? Believe it or not, it's a house. It's the home of Jack Adams, one of Connecticut's foremost commercial developers. Five years ago, Jack bought the building for a song, gutted the interior, created space for upscale retail shops on the first floor and converted the second story into a 4,000 square foot apartment for himself and his wife. I haven't been invited to see the interior yet, but I understand it's spectacular."

Turning the next corner, the two headed north on Maple Street. Rose identified retail establishments and restaurants that she believed Julius might find interesting during his stay in Riverside. She stressed the quality of food at the Boston Bistro as they walked past. "The Bistro is owned by Frank Mancuso's brother, Charlie. In my opinion, Charlie serves the best food in town. I'll make sure he's aware of your visit. If you're alone when you go in there, don't be surprised if Charlie pulls up a chair and talks with you for awhile.

"See that bandstand at the north end of the Green? Weekly concerts are scheduled to end this week. I think the last group to appear will be a local high school jazz band. Even though they're a bunch of kids, I understand that they're excellent. The large building on the other side of the Green, beyond the bandstand, is the Performing Arts Center. I'll get you a schedule of events when we get to City Hall. You probably didn't see the P.A.C. when you checked in last night. That ugly four-level parking structure separates the P.A.C. from the Inn."

Cicci could hear snippets of Rose's comments about the quality of the food at the Boston Bistro and her remarks about the Performing Arts Center as they passed by the park bench. He stood up when they reached the next corner, placed the newspaper on the bench, and followed at a safe distance until Rose and Dr. Simpkins crossed City Center Drive and entered the Administration Building. He walked past the Administration Building, keeping his eyes on the ground and head facing forward. He circled the Green a second time searching for a candidate location from which he could fulfill his contractual obligation. Two locations seemed to fit his needs. If Simpkins were to make a habit of strolling around the Green every morning on his way to the City Hall, the roof of the professional building at the corner of Maple Street and City Center Drive would suffice. If, on the other hand, Simpkins decided to turn right after leaving the Inn and walk north on Elm Street, the roof of the four-level parking garage between the Inn and the Performing Arts Center would be the best location. After circling the Green a third time, Cicci decided it would be prudent to observe Simpkins' routine for a second day before making a final decision.

Further conversation came to an end as Rose and Dr. Simpkins entered the Administration Building. Rose greeted the receptionist and led Julius through a maze of paneled enclosures to Frank Mancuso's office. She introduced Dr. Simpkins to Frank's secretary and asked if Frank were free.

"He's expecting you Rose. Just knock and go right in."

Rose knocked, stuck her head in and asked, "Frank, I have Dr. Simpkins with me, may we come in?"

Cicci drove into the Elm Street parking garage the next morning dressed in Levi's; a light blue, long-sleeve shirt; a baseball cap; hard toe construction shoes; and a tool belt. He parked his BMW on the first level, inserted two quarters in a parking meter, and climbed three flights of stairs. He walked slowly around the edge of the top level, inspecting every detail. He was especially relieved that the exterior wall was only waste high. When he reached the west end of the structure, he leaned over the edge and looked down at the Elm Street sidewalk. He removed a cigar from his breast pocket, lit it, and remained standing by the wall for a few minutes studying the situation. A tall tree in front of the garage blocked his preferred line of sight. *I won't have a clear shot until he passes the garage,* he thought. *I'll have to wait until he's in front of the Performing Arts Center.* Slowly, a smile began to crease his face. *Why fret, Cicci? All you need is one shot.* He turned away from the street and focused on a small building located at the center of the top level. He walked over, and without any difficulty, picked the lock. He looked inside and found that there was enough space to hide his rifle and a new disguise if he packed them together in canvas bag.

The next two mornings, Cicci patiently sat in his truck and counted the number of cars that ascended to the fourth level to park. He counted only eight cars the first full day and six the next, and most of those arrived during the lunch hour. He was especially relieved that no cars parked on the top level between 7 a.m. and 11 a.m. He concluded that the top level was rarely used, except for events at the Performing Arts Center. Satisfied with his plan, Cicci drove to the motel and checked out. He departed Riverside and returned to Providence to pick up the first of his two $30,000 cash payments.

31

Joe Godfrey was nervous: beginning a new public service job in a community he knew little about wouldn't be easy. He parked his car in the designated area for city employees and checked his watch: 7:45 a.m. He was early, but he thought it was best to be early on the first day. He took a deep breath and walked across the footbridge toward the front entrance of the Riverside Police Station. The anxiety he was feeling evaporated when he walked into the lobby. Attached to the wall behind the reception desk was a large sign that read, "Welcome, Joe Godfrey." He smiled. *That's great. Makes me feel important.* Pointing to the sign, Joe said to the receptionist, "I'm Joe Godfrey. I'm the guy you're welcoming today. Please call Chief Tarencelli and let him know that I'm here." Joe sat down in one of the upholstered chairs and surveyed the surroundings again. He couldn't get over the difference between the décor of this lobby and the dingy confines of the Hidalgo County Sheriff's Department in McAllen, Texas.

Police Chief Tarencelli arrived a few minutes later, and extended his hand. "Welcome to Riverside, Joe. Did you have a safe trip?"

"No problems, Rocco. Everything went smoothly. Kind of like a mini-vacation. My cousin joined me in Atlanta. We had a great time together. Lots of laughs."

"Having a relative in Connecticut will make living here a lot easier. Well, let's get you settled. I'm supposed to take you over to Human Resources and have you fill out a bunch of forms, but I'm going to modify that plan this morning. I want you to meet our city manager, Frank Mancuso, before we do anything else."

Rocco introduced Joe to Mancuso's secretary, Marie Lombardo, and asked if Frank was busy. "Mr. Mancuso is just finishing up a meeting with

Rose and Dr. Simpkins. I think it'd be okay if you interrupted. Go ahead and knock."

"Thanks, Marie." Rocco turned and whispered, "You'll meet Frank's economic development director, Rose Nardello. She's a beauty, Joe, and as smart as a whip!" Rocco knocked and stuck his head around the edge of the door. "Frank, got a minute?"

"Come on in, Rocco. We were just finishing up." As Rocco led Joe into the office, he announced, "Frank, I want you to meet Joe Godfrey. Joe is taking over the Homicide Division. Pete Desmond is retiring in a month."

Frank extended his hand and said, "Welcome to Riverside, Joe. Allow me to introduce Economic Development Director Rose Nardello, and Dr. Julius Simpkins, a consultant from California."

Joe grasped Frank's hand energetically and then Dr. Simpkin's. He reached out and gently took Rose's hand. Joe said in his thick Texas accent, "I'm pleased to meet you all."

Rose thought, *Handsome man.*

"Sorry to have interrupted your meeting, Frank, but I wanted you to meet Joe before he gets tied up with those bureaucrats in Human Resources." Rocco placed his hand on Joe's upper arm. "This big guy is from south Texas. If he looks confused in his new surroundings, help him out. Well, I'd best get him processed before I get in trouble with HR. We'll talk with you later when we have more time."

After Frank's secretary closed the office door again, he looked at Rose and said, "Godfrey appears to be nice enough fellow, don't you think, Rose?"

Smiling, she answered, "I'll reserve judgment until I get to know him. He sure towers over everyone. How tall would you say, six two, three?"

Frank said, "At least." Looking at his watch, he added, "We'd better head for the Conference Room to meet with the Council. We can continue our talk later."

The last time Joe was in Rocco's spacious office, he had other things on his mind: he was being interviewed for a job and hadn't paid much attention to the office décor. Now, sitting in a plush side chair in front of Rocco's desk, he allowed his eyes to take it all in. *Rocco must like green,* he thought. A large oriental rug, featuring numerous shades of green, dominated the floor. Dark green draperies framed a large window behind Rocco's desk. Even the fabric on the side chair Joe was sitting in was a shade of green.

DIESEL DEATH

Rocco watched Joe's eyes move from one wall to the other, and then take in the furniture. "I think you've already discovered that someone likes the color green. Actually, I don't like green, but my wife does. She decorated the office."

Joe smiled as his eyes refocused on Rocco. "I like a man that knows what his wife wants."

Rocco returned the smile and suggested, "Would you like to have my wife decorate your space?" Both men chuckled. Rocco changed the subject. "We're very pleased you elected to join us, Joe. We have a great bunch of people. You'll be happy here." He buzzed his secretary. "Janis, please let Peter know that Joe Godfrey is in my office. Ask him to join us in about five minutes." Rocco settled against the back of his chair and said, "While we're waiting, Joe, do you have any questions?"

"I'd like to know more about the city."

"That reminds me. I asked Janis to pull together an information packet for you." He buzzed her again. "Please bring me the stuff about Riverside, Janis."

Janis Elder appeared and extended her hand. "Glad you could join us, Sergeant. Let's see, I've got detailed maps of the city and the state, and a Chamber publication that lists everything; retail stores, theaters, churches, and a calendar of events scheduled over the next few months."

"Great! I'm sure I'll use these many times. Thanks, Janis."

As Janis was leaving, Peter Desmond entered and looked at Joe. "You may not be able to sit around and twiddle your thumbs, Joe." Pete turned toward Rocco and added, "We just got a phone call from Betsy Wilson. You remember her, Rocco. She's involved with United Way. Betsy claims her neighbor Ann Gibson, is missing. She thinks it may be more than a missing person case. No one has seen Ann for four days. I checked around and it's true. Nobody in the neighborhood has seen or heard from Ann since last Thursday. Betsy suspects that her friend may be the victim of domestic violence. She could be overreacting, Rocco, but I don't think so. Betsy's intelligent and usually level-headed."

"Well, it sounds like you two have work to do. There's nothing like jumping in with both feet, huh, Joe? We can go over the training program later this afternoon. You'd better go see Judge O'Brien, Pete. Get a warrant to search the house and dig a few holes in the back yard. Call me later."

Peter led Joe down the hallway to the third door on the left. A navy blue sign with Homicide Division printed in white hung next to the door. When he entered, Joe was again struck by the brightness of the space: windows along the outside wall seemed to capture the sunlight. The walls had been painted an off white and were adorned with colorful artwork. Multi-colored office paneling separated the personnel. Pete's space was the largest of four cubicles that ran side by side along an outside wall next to the windows. A secretary/receptionist station was just inside the door, directly in front of Pete's cubicle. Two enclosed, soundproofed interrogation rooms with built in one-way mirrors were next to the receptionist's space.

"I know it's not much Joe, but it's going to be your home for awhile."

"You have no idea how wrong you are, Pete. This is a real office, not like my old accommodations at the Hidalgo County Sheriff's Department. I'm sure you've seen old movies that show the chaos and clutter of old newspaper offices. Well, my office in McAllen was a lot worse."

"You go ahead and take the desk chair, Joe. It's yours now."

"I understand, Pete, but I'll feel uncomfortable for awhile."

"Don't. You won't hurt my feelings. Before we head out to talk with Betsy, I want you to meet Dom DeCarlo. Like you, he's new to Homicide." Pete leaned into DeCarlo's cubicle and said, "Come on in and meet Joe Godfrey, Dom. He's the Texas Longhorn that Rocco has been telling us about. He's taking over for me, effective immediately."

Joe reached out and shook Dom's hand. "I'm glad to meet you, Dom. I guess we'll be seeing a lot of each other. When I get settled, you and I should talk."

"I look forward to it, Joe."

While Pete was on the phone calling Riverside Hospital to see if Mrs. Gibson might have been the victim of an accident, Joe observed the man he was replacing. *Pete looks younger than 59. He's still a good-looking man for his age. I'll bet the ladies still give him a look. Let's see, he reminds me of someone. That's it, actor Ed Harris, but with more hair.*

A close inspection of the Gibson backyard produced nothing unusual: there were no fresh piles of dirt or sod patches anywhere. Nor did a thorough search of the house produce anything meaningful. The husband of the missing lady was no help: he'd had a nervous breakdown, was constrained, and taken to the psychiatric ward at Riverside Hospital.

Joe and Pete huddled in the Gibson's kitchen with the two uniformed officers who'd conducted a search of the house. "Like we told you earlier, detectives, everything appears to be normal. When we went through the house we found an unmade bed in the master bedroom, clothes casually tossed over a chair, a few dishes drying in the sink, and a three-day-old newspaper on an end table in the living room. We found two newspapers by the front door, and a few pieces of mail in the box. My guess is that Mrs. Gibson left about three days ago."

The other patrolman added, "The only thing that appeared to be a little out of the ordinary was a broken vase on the living room floor. It looked like it might have been thrown against a wall."

Pete was beginning to question his initial belief that Ann Gibson was the victim of foul play. "I may have been off base on this, Joe. Maybe the lady is really missing and just didn't tell anyone where she was going. Betsy said she'd become absentminded lately. On the other hand, maybe she just got tired of her husband's bullshit and split."

Joe asked, "What about the attic? Were there any trunks up there or anything else large enough to contain a body?"

"No, I didn't see anything that large, Sergeant."

The second patrolman raised his hand and slapped the side of his head. "Damn! We didn't check the trunk of the car that's in the garage."

Pete said, "Look on the wall next to the door leading to the garage. See if you can find a key hanging on a hook somewhere."

"There're two sets of keys here, Pete. One is for a Ford product. Isn't that a Ford in the garage?"

"Yeah. Let's try it."

Joe inserted the key and the trunk snapped open. There, in a fetal position with her legs against her chest and her back to the opening, was the missing wife. All four men stared at the body for a few moments without saying anything. Finally, Joe broke the silence. "Damn, Pete, you were right!"

"Yeah, but I'm real sorry I was."

32

Early in the 20th century, Providence, Rhode Island, was a key stop on the old New York, New Haven, and Hartford Railroad system, providing residents of Rhode Island with a convenient link to and from Boston or New York. Situated on a knoll near the center of the city, the railroad station was a constant reminder of the glory years of railroad transportation in the United States. One hundred years later, the same station served passengers that used the high speed northeast rail corridor from Boston to Washington.

Robert Cicci strolled through the front entrance to the station as if he owned the place. He carried a briefcase and wore the casual attire of a weekend traveler. Without the lightest hesitation, he crossed the cavernous waiting area to the storage lockers, stopped at number 55, and unlocked it with a key that he'd picked up from a registration clerk at the front desk of the Marriott Hotel across the street. Cicci had given Winston Osborne specific instructions to leave the locker key in a padded envelope at the front desk with a note, "Hold for a Mr. Jeffrey Ambrose, scheduled to arrive on Friday."

Not generally a trusting a soul, especially when it came to a pompous ass like Winston Osborne, Cicci stood close to the locker so that no one could see him, and patiently counted the $30,000 in cash. Satisfied all the money was there, he placed the piles of bills in a canvas bag and inserted the bag in his briefcase. He walked out of the station and hurried across the street to the Marriott parking lot.

He drove west toward his country home in Quaddick, Connecticut, to spend a long weekend of relaxation, contemplation, and disguise creation. His primary objective was to create a disguise that would enable him to move around the fourth level of the parking garage without attracting attention. After considerable thought, he decided he'd be a building inspector and wear a bright red shirt, black suspenders, kneepads, cap with a visor, heavy shoes, and a dark wig. He decided that he'd better have a second disguise. After he completed his assignment, he'd become the casually-attired hotel guest again, who'd just completed his morning walk. He'd wear warm-ups, sneakers, eyeglasses, a blond wig, and carry a newspaper.

Cicci left his BMW in the garage and drove back to Riverside in his ten year old pick-up truck. Again, he elected not to stay in the city: he didn't want any record of having visited Riverside, nor did he want any part of the investigative frenzy that would certainly result from the completion of his assignment. He chose, instead, to stay at a Day's Inn five miles to the south, in the community of Rockford. After checking in, Cicci requested a 5:00 a.m. wake up call.

Dressed as a building inspector and carrying a canvas bag that contained his second disguise and his disassembled rifle, Cicci entered the parking garage before 7:00 a.m. He parked at the west-end on the fourth level and remained in the cab until he felt comfortable that he was alone. He walked over to the small elevator equipment shack and was relieved to find that no one had attempted to fix the lock he'd picked during his earlier visit.

Satisfied, he returned to the truck and opened the passenger door. Pressing his body against the seat and with his back facing out, he removed the disassembled rifle from the canvas bag piece by piece and patiently put it together. When the major components were assembled, he added a telescopic lens and a silencer, and placed the rifle on the floor of the truck so he could retrieve it quickly. He returned to the elevator shack and placed the bag containing his second disguise in a dark corner.

At 7:30, Cicci called the Riverside Inn on his cell phone and asked for Room 306. After six futile rings, the operator asked Cicci if he'd like to leave a message. "Before I do that, miss, please check the restaurant for me. Dr. Simpkins might be having breakfast." The operator put Cicci on hold, and checked with the restaurant hostess. She confirmed that Dr. Simpkins was indeed having breakfast. "Do you want him to come to the phone, sir?"

"No. I'll meet him in the lobby. Thank you for checking." Satisfied that his timing was on track, Cicci climbed out of the cab, removed a cigar from his shirt pocket, and lit it. He tossed the band aside and leaned his back against the truck. He wasn't concerned about being seen from another building: a person would have to be on the roof of the Performing Arts Center or on the roof of the Riverside Inn to see him on the fourth level of the parking garage. He doubted that either situation was likely at that hour of the morning. He also felt secure that his laborer disguise would reduce any chance that someone might think his presence on the roof was suspicious or see enough of him to identify him later.

He began to move up and down the exterior wall stopping every so often to act as though he was inspecting the drains. Every time he'd stop, he'd look over at the entrance to the Inn to check to see if Simpkins had exited early. Satisfied that Simpkins was still inside the hotel, Cicci turned his attention to the Green across the street. Three people were jogging on a perimeter sidewalk. A young couple was walking toward the entrance to the Inn on one of the diagonal sidewalks. An elderly man was sitting on a park bench on the outer edge of the Green, facing in the direction of the parking garage. Although tree branches prevented Cicci from seeing the man on the bench clearly, it looked as though he was holding a newspaper in one hand and a pen or a pencil in the other. Cicci guessed that he was probably working on a crossword puzzle. Cicci reasoned that unless the old timer had extraordinary eyesight, he'd have trouble seeing him through the limbs of the tree. Even if the man could see that far, Cicci doubted he'd see him clear enough to be able to stipulate whether it was a man or a woman on the roof.

Cicci leaned over the wall and looked up and down Elm Street a few more times to make sure no law enforcement personnel were anywhere in sight and then returned his attention to the front entrance of the Inn. At 8:05, he crushed the cigar against the wall, tossed the stub over the side, and fixed his attention on the front entrance to the Inn. At 8:15, a familiar face exited the Inn, followed by another familiar face. He muttered, "Shit!" He recognized the woman that walked around the Green with Simpkins the previous week. Cicci watched the couple stop at the curb and converse for a moment. *What do I do if they may decide to circle the park in the opposite direction again?* He let out a sigh of relief as they turned north and began to walk toward City Center. Like the gentleman that he was, Simpkins automatically moved to the outside position near the curb and Rose stepped to the inside.

Cicci mumbled, "Okay, Phonz. This is it." He quickly pulled on a pair of surgical gloves, retrieved the rifle from the front seat of the truck and returned to the wall. He leaned on the wall with both elbows and located Simpkins in the cross hairs. He continued to concentrate on the target until Rose and Julius walked clear of the one tree that was obstructing his line of sight.

The elderly gentleman looked up from his crossword and observed that the person on the roof had stopped pacing, and was leaning far out over the wall to look in the direction of the Riverside Inn. Intrigued, he decided to watch. He placed the newspaper on the bench next to him. The person on the roof suddenly stepped back away from the wall and disappeared. Believing the activity may have ended, the elderly gentleman retrieved the newspaper and returned his attention to the crossword. His peripheral vision, however, caught sight of the person returning to the wall, so he changed his mind. He watched the person place what looked like a rifle on the top of the wall and take aim. Realizing what was about to happen, he jumped up off the bench and yelled, "No!"

As soon as his target was clear of the tree, Cicci waited until Dr. Simpkins leaned slightly to his left and then he pulled the trigger.

The elderly gentleman saw the burst of smoke discharge from the front of the rifle. He turned his head to his left in the direction he thought the rifle was pointed and saw a man fall to the ground. He cried, "Oh, God. No!"

Cicci kept his target in the cross hairs for a few seconds and watched Simpkins slump to the sidewalk. It looked like the bullet had destroyed the man's head, just as he'd planned. Satisfied the assignment was now complete, Cicci rushed to the small elevator shack to dispose of the rifle. Cicci wasn't concerned that the rifle would be found: he'd already removed the serial number. He placed the rifle in a remote corner of the shack, grabbed the bag holding his new disguise, and rushed back to the truck. He threw the bag into the cab, drove slowly down the ramp to the first level, and parked in a space reserved for hotel guests. Cicci entered the hotel through the same side entrance he'd used before and walked to the nearest men's room to change his clothes.

He purchased a newspaper at the gift shop and casually walked into the hotel restaurant to have breakfast. He smiled when he heard sirens wailing: he could picture the chaos he'd caused only a short distance away. He touched the elbow of a waitress as she walked by and asked, "What's all that commotion outside?"

"I'm not sure, sir, but I'll try to find out." The waitress returned a few minutes later with news that a shooting had occurred in front of the Performing Arts Center. "The front desk clerk thinks the victim was killed."

Cicci responded indignantly, "My goodness! What's happening to this town? Crime is all around us."

Police Chief Rocco Tarencelli rushed down the hallway and into the Homicide Division. "Joe, there was a shooting in front of the Elm Street Parking Garage. The dispatcher said that one man's dead, and a woman maybe wounded. Get over there and take command."

Pete Desmond heard Rocco's outburst and rushed over.

"I'm on my way, Rocco. Do you know who was hit?"

"No. The dispatcher could only tell me that it was a man."

"I think you send a few extra uniforms, Rocco. We'll need all the help we can get to keep the curious away." Joe turned toward Pete and said, "Pete, let's go." The two detectives rushed out of the building.

The scene in front of the Performing Arts Center was indeed chaotic. A growing assemblage of the curious began to gather on the sidewalk and spill over into the street, blocking traffic. Uniformed patrolmen tried to cordon off the area with yellow tape, but the public ignored the restriction.

Following a gallant, but unsuccessful, effort to revive Dr. Simpkins, paramedics pronounced him dead and covered the body. A paramedic told Joe that the victim probably died instantly: the bullet having entered his scull just behind the right ear, exiting through the lower jaw on the left side of the face. Joe squatted, bent over the body and raised the sheet to see for himself. He let out a low whistle, and commented, "Look at this, Pete. The bullet practically destroyed the guy's face." Joe studied the face for a moment. "I think I met this guy in Mancuso's office the day I started work. Isn't he the consultant the city just hired?"

"I can't say, Joe. I didn't meet the man."

Joe located a uniformed sergeant and requested he dispatch his men to search each level of the garage, starting with the fourth level. "Tell the men to be very careful. The shooter may still be up there hiding somewhere, and he's obviously well armed."

The two detectives agreed to split up and circulate among on-lookers to determine if anyone had witnessed the shooting. A patrolman walked over to Joe and whispered in his ear. "We may have a witness to the shooting, Sergeant." Pointing to an elderly gentleman holding a newspaper under his arm, the patrolman said, "That older guy said he saw a man on the top level of the parking garage before the shooting. You may want to talk with him." Joe thanked the patrolman and approached the man.

Pointing to the police officer, Joe inquired, "The officer over there said you saw someone on the top level of the garage. Is that correct?"

"Yes, sir. Someone wearing a bright red shirt was walking back and forth, looking over the edge every now and then. At first, I thought the person was inspecting something. After awhile, the individual stopped pacing and kept looking toward the Riverside Inn as though he was expecting something to happen. Next thing I know, the person set what looked like a rifle on the wall and shot at this here fella," he said, pointing to the body of Julius Simpkins.

"What's your name, sir?"

"McCarthy. John McCarthy." Joe pulled a small notebook out of his pocket and wrote the man's name, address, and phone number. He thanked Mr. McCarthy and asked him to stay around the area a little longer so he could talk with him again. McCarthy said he'd go across the street and wait on one of the park benches.

33

The Nardello home was situated near the top of one of the hills that encircled the downtown district of Pawtucket. The design of the two-story structure was vintage 1920s: slopping roof, dormers on the second level in both the front and back of the house. It was painted white with dark gray trim and shutters.

Mario stepped out onto his spacious front porch, stopped, and looked into a cloudless sky. *Gonna be a beautiful spring day,* he thought. He lowered his gaze and looked over the roof of the house across the street. The view of downtown Pawtucket was clear: the rainstorm that passed through Rhode Island the previous evening had washed the industrial pollution from the air. Mario descended the concrete stairs to the sidewalk to retrieve the morning newspaper. He greeted a neighbor who was in the process of picking up his paper, then turned around to climb the stairs. He reentered the house. "Teresa, is the coffee ready?"

"Not yet: another few minutes. I'll bring you a cup."

"Thanks." Mario sat down and began scanning the front page. His eyes focused on an item in the lower left hand corner. "Mother of God, he yelled! Teresa, come here and read this!"

Teresa Nardello bolted from the kitchen. "What is it, Mario?"

Looking up into the eyes of his wife, Mario said, "Rose was nearly killed."

Teresa collapsed into the chair next to Mario, and asked, "What are you talking about?"

"I'll read the article to you. 'Riverside, CT...A retired executive from California was assassinated yesterday in broad daylight on a major downtown street in the center of Riverside. A single bullet, apparently shot by an assailant hiding on the roof of a parking garage, killed Dr. Julius Simpkins, Ph.D., instantly. Why Dr. Simpkins, the highest-ranking African-

American in the California state administration before he retired, was shot is not known at this time.

"'Riverside City Manager Frank Mancuso told the Associated Press that Dr. Simpkins was walking to City Hall with a city employee, Rose Nardello, when he was shot. Miss Nardello was not injured, but went into shock after the incident, and is currently under the care of a physician.'"

Teresa stood up and announced, "We've got to call Rose."

Mario reached for the telephone on the table next to him and dialed Rose's apartment. After six rings, a voice mail message kicked in. Mario hung up without leaving a message. "Do you have the number for the Riverside City Hall?"

"Yes." Teresa rushed back to the kitchen and within seconds yelled back to her husband, "The number is 203-555-1234."

Mario introduced himself to the lady who answered the phone, and asked to speak to Rose. "I'm sorry, Mr. Nardello, Rose is not in today."

"May I speak with the city manager then?"

"He's not in either, sir. I think you should talk with Mr. Mancuso's secretary. Hold on while I transfer you."

"Thank you."

"Good morning, Mr. Nardello. My name is Marie Lombardo. I'm Mr. Mancuso's secretary. Rose is fine. Mr. Mancuso thinks it's best for her to stay away from the office for a few days. The media has inundated City Hall. Rose will be staying with Mr. Mancuso's family until things settle down. Would you like to have his unlisted number so you can talk with her?"

"Yes, please."

The Nardellos were relieved after talking with Rose. She seemed to have her emotions under control.

"How long do you plan to stay with the Mancuso family?" Mario asked.

"Frank suggested I stay here until the media gets tired of asking questions and leaves: probably another day or two."

"Who was the victim, Rose?"

"Dr. Julius Simpkins, Dad. Remember, I told you about a class action lawsuit we planned to file next month against your neighbor in Pawtucket, the Diesel Engine Corporation. Dr. Simpkins was retained to help the city prepare the lawsuit."

The skin on Mario's scalp tightened and began to perspire. He mumbled something into the phone that sounded like, "Your mother wants to talk with you." Without looking at Teresa, Mario reached out and practically forced the instrument into his wife's hand.

"What's wrong, Mario?" she asked.

"Just take the damn phone." Mario rose and left the room.

His daughter heard the exchange and became concerned. "What happened, Mom? Is Dad okay?"

"I don't know what happened, honey." She sighed and said, "We're so relieved you're okay. Would you like me to drive over and stay a few days?"

"Yes, I would Mom. This weekend would be good. I could use your shoulder to lean on until this tragedy is behind me."

"I'll drive over tomorrow. I'll call when I'm ready to leave."

Teresa called to her husband after she hung up, but he didn't answer. She looked for him in the kitchen and then in the office, but he wasn't in either room. She found him lying face down on their bed. "Why didn't you answer me, Mario?" He lifted his hand, and in a gesture of dismissal, tried to wave her off.

Teresa was becoming concerned. She was familiar with Mario's emotional swings, but this was different: she had never seen him act like this before. She sat on the edge of the bed and placed her hand on his shoulder. She felt his shoulder begin to move up and down and realized he was sobbing. Her heart ached for her husband, even though she didn't know why. Teresa gently placed her head on his back and remained there until he stopped sobbing. When she stood up, Mario rolled over on his side. He stood up and hugged Teresa so tight he began to hurt her. "Easy, Mario, you're hurting me." Mario let go, grabbed Teresa's hand and led her into the living room.

34

The next morning, Joe Godfrey and Pete Desmond met with Chief Tarencelli to go over the results of a search of the parking garage the previous day and to discuss what should be done next. Joe said, "A search of all four levels of the Elm Street parking garage turned up little in the way of substantive evidence, Rocco. We closed the garage to vehicle traffic so we can go back and conduct a more intensive search today. Both Pete and I feel the shooter may have left some small item behind. I recommend we send our best forensics people to scour the place, especially the fourth level."

Rocco agreed immediately and made a phone call. Within minutes, a two man forensics team entered his office. "I think it might be a good idea if you went with them, Pete. Take DeCarlo with you. He needs the experience. Joe, stick around awhile. I want to talk about the investigation."

Following a habit he'd developed whenever he needed to concentrate, Rocco stood up and looked through the window at the well-manicured garden behind Police Headquarters. Joe waited patiently. After a few moments, Rocco turned around. "I see two possible scenarios, Joe. First, Simpkins may have had an enemy, and the enemy decided to terminate him here in Riverside. If that's the case, his being in Riverside had nothing to do with his death. Or, and this scenario could be very troublesome, Simpkins was killed because he was in Riverside working for the city. This may sound strange, but maybe someone didn't want Simpkins to find something."

Rocco sat down. "Joe, I want you to take the lead on this. Talk with Frank Mancuso and Rose Nardello. Find out why Simpkins was hired by the city and what he was working on."

Pete Desmond and Detective Dominic "Dom" DeCarlo knocked on the outside panel of Joe Godfrey's cubicle, stepped in and sat down. Pete said, "We found the weapon, a Weber and Walther rifle with a silencer."

Dom added, "It was stashed in a small shack on the top level. The building contains elevator equipment. The shooter jimmied the lock. After he whacked the guy, he just left the rifle right there for everyone to see. He made no attempt to hide it, Joe."

Pete said, "The shooter must be a marksman. He needed only one shot at maybe 20, 30 yards."

"Any prints?"

Dom crossed his legs. "Not yet, and I doubt that we'll find any. The guy probably used surgical gloves, like the ones hospital people use, or he wiped down the weapon before he stashed it. Or," he chuckled, "the bastard doesn't have any fingers."

Joe laughed. "I think we can forget that last one, Dom. He needed at least one finger to pull the trigger." Joe felt comfortable and relaxed with Dom DeCarlo. The man seemed to be happy all the time. He was the kind of person that enjoyed his own jokes. His laugh was so infectious it was hard not to laugh along with him. In spite of Dom's jolly disposition, Joe suspected the young man could be tough as nails when the situation required it.

"What else did you find?"

Dom answered, "The perp could be a cigar smoker, Joe. One of the forensics guys found a half-smoked cigar in the bushes near the sidewalk on Elm Street. We think the perp crushed it against the wall on the fourth level and then tossed the butt off the roof." Dom chuckled again. "He probably flattened Simpkins between puffs."

Joe smiled. "Anything else?"

"Yeah, I found a cigar band and a match book cover next to the wall on the fourth level."

"Was there any identification on the band?"

Dom smiled. "This'll really grab you, Joe. The name on the band is Sinatra. Can you believe that? I didn't know that Frank made cigars."

Joe looked at Pete for any sign that the name meant anything to him other than a crooning baritone but saw none. "What about the match book cover?"

Pete answered, "I doubt the match book cover has any connection to the shooter, but I could be wrong. This one's from a diner in North Attleboro, Massachusetts. Any smoker could have dropped it on the roof. Smokers tend to pick-up matches wherever they go just in case they need a light later."

Joe said, "We should send the cigar butt, the band, and the match book cover up to the state forensics lab in Hartford for analysis. I'm not very hopeful, but cigar smokers generally leave saliva on the butts of their cigars. Maybe we can recover some D.N.A. from the saliva and then run the results through the F.B.I. database."

Pete responded, "That seems to be our best hope. What about the rifle? Let's send that up to the lab folks, too. Maybe they can recover the serial number."

"Was there anything else?"

Dom looked over at Pete. Pete said, "That's all for now."

Joe stood. "Good job." Reaching out to shake DeCarlo's hand, Joe said, "Thanks, Dom. I'll talk with you later. Pete and I have a few things to discuss."

After Dom left, Joe sat down and leaned back in his chair. "I've been thinking, Pete. Rocco may be right. We need to learn more about why Dr. Simpkins was retained by the city. He asked me to talk with Frank and Rose. Since you've known them for years, maybe it would be better if you talked with them."

"I'll get right on it, Joe."

"I may drive up to North Attleboro and check out Sam's Diner. I want to find out if the place has any cigar smoking customers."

Later that same day, Pete Desmond briefed Rocco and Joe on his meeting with Frank Mancuso and Rose Nardello, and on his telephone conversations with Dr. Sydney Bernstein in New Haven and Dr. Charles Olson in California. "All of them spoke well of Dr. Simpkins. Before his retirement, Dr. Simpkins was a respected and popular member of the California state administration in Sacramento. According to Bernstein, Simpkins had a national reputation as a fierce opponent of pollution, especially pollution caused by car and truck exhaust. It sounds like Simpkins was a thorn in the side of some people in the transportation industry, but I can't believe it was enough of a thorn to cause his death. Frank asked a good question, Rocco. Was the killing race related? I admit we probably should investigate that angle thoroughly, but I find the race card far fetched. I'll go out on a limb and predict we won't find anything in Simpkins personal life that provoked his murder." Pete sat quietly for a few moments. "Unfortunately, that doesn't leave us much."

Rocco sighed. "This is really off the wall gentlemen, but do you suppose Simpkins' murder had something to do with the death of that five year old Rado boy a month or so ago? Riverside's intention to initiate a class action lawsuit against the Diesel Engine Corporation certainly was no secret. Maybe Simpkins represented a threat to someone."

Pete added, "You may be right, Rocco. The city's intentions were discussed openly up and down the valley for the past few months. Frank's even been out actively soliciting other communities along Interstate 64 and State Route 10 to join Riverside in the class action. He told me that Riverside had a better shot at securing class action certification if the city could get a few other communities to participate. That kind of effort could piss a few people off."

"Now that's an interesting theory." Rocco stood up and began to pace. He stopped and reached for his throat. "There's something about the Rado boy's death that sticks in my throat." Looking at Joe, he said, "If I can get Frank's approval, I want you and Rose to go down to New Haven and visit with Dr. Bernstein. We need to know more about the cause of the kid's death. Come to think of it, we don't know much about the Diesel Engine Corporation, either." He thought for a moment. "I'm gonna ask Frank to assign Rose to us for a few days. She could help us pull together background information on the company."

"Good idea, Rocco. After we meet with Dr. Bernstein, I'll make arrangements for Rose and me to drive over to Providence and talk with the bureaucrats at the Rhode Island State Capitol about D.E.C. We could stop in at that diner in North Attleboro while we're over there. I think North Attleboro is only a few miles out of the way."

Without the slightest hesitation, Frank Mancuso approved Chief Tarencelli's request to have Rose temporarily assigned to the Simpkins' murder investigation. When she was informed of the assignment, Rose was enthused. She saw the assignment as a means of avenging Dr. Simpkins' senseless murder. She agreed with Rocco that the first order of business ought to be a trip to New Haven to meet with Dr. Bernstein.

She called Dr. Bernstein and suggested they meet as soon as possible. "I'll have to rearrange my schedule, Rose, but helping find Julius' killer is more important than just about anything else I'm involved with right now. How about meeting at 10:00 tomorrow morning?"

The lobby directory showed that Dr. Bernstein shared an office suite with two physicians who specialized in patients with respiratory problems. Their suite was directly across from the elevator on the third floor of a large medical office building adjacent to New Haven Hospital. The receptionist announced the arrival of Rose and a Sergeant Joseph Godfrey and then led them down a hallway to Bernstein's office. Dr. Bernstein greeted them warmly. After Joe was appropriately introduced, he gave Bernstein a brief summation on what the police found at the crime scene and a status report on the investigation. Godfrey added, "We still haven't determined motive, Doctor. It may sound far fetched, but we're beginning to suspect it may have had something to do with the Rado boy's death. We need to get a better understanding of why the Rado family is filing a wrongful death complaint against D.E.C. and why the city's filing a class action against them."

"I'll do my best to explain, Sergeant. Let's start with the Rado boy's autopsy. The medical examiner found an abundance of tiny carbon particles in the boy's lungs. The particles were very small, about 2.5 microns in size, which is less than the thickness of a human hair. To put that into perspective, a human hair is 40 times larger. The particles were just too small to be stopped by his normal respiratory defenses. I believe chemicals in the particles caused the boy's chronic respiratory disease, and that, in turn, caused his heart to fail."

"The federal E.P.A. is starting to recognize that children are more vulnerable to the cancer-causing of chemicals in vehicle exhaust than adults. Children, age two and younger, are considered to have ten times the risk of adults, and children age two through fifteen are three times as vulnerable." Dr. Bernstein sat forward for emphasis. "None of us would knowingly mix up a batch of soot and nitric oxide and then spray the stuff on a group of children in a playground. But, that's exactly what those long haul diesel trucks are doing." He sat back. "I can't understand why the trucking industry is disputing the growing body of evidence that shows diesel exhaust is not only harmful, but it is, in fact, deadly."

Dr. Bernstein spun around in his chair, selected a document from his credenza, and turned back to face Rose and Joe. "A colleague of mine gave me a copy of a report he picked up while in Washington yesterday. It was prepared by an independent non-profit organization. Listen to this. 'New studies support the conclusion that exposure to particulate matter found in vehicular exhaust, especially the exhaust from diesel fueled vehicles, could shorten the life spans of children significantly. Roadway emissions, however, represent only one aspect of the problem. Children riding in school buses breathe two to five times more particulate matter than children exposed to roadway air. In-bus pollution comes from two major sources: first, ambient pollution builds up within the passenger compartment when buses drive through polluted areas like downtown Los Angeles; second, particulate matter will leak into the interior of the bus while the bus is operating. This is especially true in the case of older, higher polluting buses.'"

Joe Godfrey was stunned. He'd heard of the smog problem in Los Angeles, but thought that problem was strictly a southern California problem, certainly not a Riverside, Connecticut problem. "Doctor, am I hearing correctly? Are you saying that the people who manufacture diesel engines knowingly produce and sell products that can kill people, especially children?"

"I wouldn't put it quite so bluntly, Sergeant, but essentially that's what's happening." Sydney paused, and added, "Think about what Julius was attempting to do. My gut tells me that somebody, somewhere may have believed Julius represented a threat to their business."

Rose looked over at Joe Godfrey. She raised her eyebrows and then turned back to face Dr. Bernstein. "Are you suggesting that Dr. Simpkins death may have been related to his plan to monitor diesel truck exhaust?"

"I'm not suggesting anything yet, Rose. When the national media begin to understand the enormity of the diesel emissions problem, all hell could break loose. It wasn't a secret that Riverside retained one of the most respected vehicle emission authorities in the country and that the city was preparing to file a class action lawsuit against D.E.C. Think about it. The negative publicity could very well sink D.E.C."

Rose's mouth dropped open. Joe Godfrey stared at Sydney before exclaiming, "Well, I'll be a Texas longhorn, Dr. Bernstein. You may have just identified the motive for Dr. Simpkins murder."

"I won't argue that point, Sergeant. I have my suspicions." Bernstein took a deep breath. "Unfortunately there's more bad news. The Rado boy's lung tissue also revealed minute traces of asbestos. I haven't said this before, but I believe one or more of the manufacturers of diesel engines are using asbestos in their particulate traps. I'm not an attorney, but I'm pretty sure that's a violation of federal law."

35

Rocco's door was open, so Joe knocked on the door frame. "Got a minute, Rocco?"

"Sure, Joe, come on in and have a seat."

"I prepared a status report on the Simpkins investigation. I'd like you to look it over. Pete's already critiqued it." Joe handed Rocco a two-page document entitled, "Status Report—Julius Simpkins Murder Investigation." Rocco opened the bottom drawer of his desk, leaned back, propped his feet on top of the drawer, and commenced reading.

> Victim:
> Dr. Julius Simpkins, M.D. Clean air consultant from Sacramento, CA. Age 66. African-American. Under contract with the city of Riverside at the time of his death. Assassinated in front of the Performing Arts Center with one rifle shot to the back of the head fired from the fourth level of the Elm Street parking garage.
>
> Motive:
> Unknown at this time. Might be related to the city's plan to file a class action lawsuit against the Diesel Engine Corporation.

Rocco looked up and asked, "What's this about the Diesel Engine Corporation?"

"Dr. Bernstein thinks that Dr. Simpkins' death may be related to his being retained by Riverside. Maybe someone at D.E.C. didn't want Simpkins to uncover potentially damaging information about their engines, information that could be used against them in a Riverside civil action. Let's face it, Riverside's intention to file a class action against D.E.C. wasn't a secret.

Apparently, Frank has contacted at least four other cities in the valley and invited them to join the lawsuit. One or more people at D.E.C. may have panicked when they heard what Riverside was up to. It's conceivable that, if the Riverside action is successfully litigated, it could put D.E.C. out of business. At least, that's what Dr. Bernstein believes, and when you think about it, it makes sense. It wouldn't be the first time. People tend to flail out in all directions when their assets are threatened. Dr. Bernstein has an uncomfortable feeling about that company. D.E.C. is already up to its ears in trouble with the California Air Resources Board."

Rocco went back to reading the report.

> Evidence collected:
> One cigar butt. Brand - "Sinatra." Produced by the Johnson Cigar Company, Tampa, FL. Sent the cigar butt to the state forensics lab in Hartford. Recovered D.N.A. from the saliva and processed the results through the F.B.I. database. Only one hit—a retired F.B.I. agent. (I think there must be an error in the data base. We should run the D.N.A. findings through the F.B.I. file again.)

Rocco looked up again with a puzzled look on his face. "Please explain this bit about the D.N.A."

"We heard from the state lab in Hartford yesterday. They were able to recover D.N.A. from the cigar, but when they ran the findings through the F.B.I. database, they got only one match: a retired F.B.I. agent by the name of Robert Cicci. That doesn't sound right to me, Rocco. I'm not familiar with D.N.A. tests. Could the lab have made a mistake? If that's the case, we're back to square one."

Rocco lowered his feet and sat up straight. "D.N.A. findings are very accurate, Joe. I've been told that the folks at the Hartford lab are competent people. The F.B.I. database is a different story. The database is so new I can't express an opinion one way or the other. Congress established the database just last year. It's supposed to hold over one million genetic profiles, and it's open to law enforcement nationwide. I agree with your recommendation: let's run the results through the data base again." Rocco smiled. "We'd be laughed out of Connecticut if we charged an F.B.I. agent with Simpkins' murder." Rocco put his feet back on top of the file drawer and resumed reading.

One matchbook cover from Sam's Diner, North Attleboro, Massachusetts. Forensics unable to recover D.N.A., or clear, meaningful prints.

One Weber and Walther rifle. State lab confirmed that the rifle was the murder weapon. The bullet passed through Simpkins head and penetrated the Elm Street asphalt. The slug was dug out of the asphalt and was sent to the State lab along with the rifle. The lab was able to match the markings on the slug with the markings on the rifle barrel.

Witnesses:
One senior citizen. The man was sitting on a park bench across the street from the parking garage. Saw the killer fire the rifle from the roof, but because of the distance, wasn't able to describe him, except that he thought the man was Caucasian. The witness said that the man that fired the rifle was wearing a bright red shirt.

Suggested Plan:
• Compile a list of the tobacco shops that sell the Sinatra brand of Johnson cigars in the tri-state area, with emphasis on shops in and around North Attleboro.
• Visit tobacco shops in and around Pawtucket and North Attleboro. Interview shop employees and request lists of customers who purchase Sinatra cigars. Dom DeCarlo will be assigned this task.
• Meet with Rhode Island state officials to obtain information about D.E.C. Prepare a dossier on the company, incorporating the information that Desmond compiles while in California.
• Interview employees at Sam's Diner in North Attleboro to determine if any of their customers are cigar smokers.
• Contact police in Pawtucket, Providence, and North Attleboro. Inform them of our investigation and request their cooperation.
• Request a second, more thorough analysis of the saliva recovered from the cigar butt.
• Send someone to California to meet with the victim's widow and former associates to ascertain if the victim had any enemies.

Rocco finished reading, removed his feet from the file drawer, sat up, and placed the report on his desk. "If we have a positive D.N.A. identification, why do we need to do all of the rest of this, Joe?"

"The D.N.A. from the saliva proves only one thing, Rocco, that Cicci smoked the cigar. It doesn't prove that he was the one that threw the butt away. A good defense attorney could claim the cigar butt was left in someone's vehicle and was carried to Riverside in an ash tray and then discarded by someone other than Cicci. The D.A. will need corroborating evidence, Rocco."

Chief Tanencelli sat quietly for a few moments. "Okay. You're probably right. You're gonna need additional manpower to complete an investigation in a timely manner. You can have DeCarlo and Desmond full time for a while."

Rocco stood up and faced the window. "Human Resources told me last week that the city agreed to hire three college interns from the University of Connecticut. I requested that one of the interns be assigned to the Police Department, and they agreed. He's yours, Joe. The kid's name is Jack Clark. H.R. claims the kid's very intelligent. His counselor said the kid tackles assignments with ingenuity and enthusiasm. He's pre-law at UConn: he will enter law enforcement after he passes the bar. I suggest you use him to help track down the cigar lead. If you decide to send him out into the field on assignment, talk with me first. I'll have to check on our liability exposure."

"That's good news, Rocco. I can use a few more legs. When will he start?"

"He's taking his last final today. He's scheduled to report tomorrow morning." Rocco hesitated, then asked, "Are you sure you want to send DeCarlo off to Massachusetts and Rhode Island on his own? He's still wet behind the ears. Obtaining information about the cigar smokers will be critical to the investigation."

"I admit Dom is young and untested and has a weird sense of humor. But I have confidence in him. Dom will be a good investigator someday. I plan to visit a few tobacco shops with him before I send him out on his own. I'll have him call me every day and report on his progress."

Joe Godfrey was surprised when he met Jack Clark. At 6' 2", Godfrey towered over the diminutive Clark, who was only 5' 6" and skinny as a rail. Joe guessed he probably didn't weigh more than 140 pounds. Clark wore a sweat shirt with UConn across the front, faded Levi's, and deck shoes. Joe surmised that Clark was probably Irish to the core: narrow face, a large nose, fair complexion, and black bushy eyebrows framed by untamed black hair. He seemed to have a perpetual smile on his face.

Clark listened intently as Joe described the crime scene and the evidence collected thus far. "The only tangible evidence is the cigar butt, the cigar band, a match book cover, and the rifle. The cigar looks like our best bet. Call the producer and request the name of every retail outlet in Connecticut, Massachusetts, and Rhode Island. Tell whomever you talk with that you are an associate detective with the Riverside Police Department."

It didn't take long for Joe to recognize that Rocco's assessment of the young man was right on target. Clark didn't waste time: he went to the top of the list of company executives and called Johnson's president. The president wasn't in, but Clark informed the executive's secretary that he was involved in a murder investigation, convinced her that the list of retail outlets was needed immediately, and requested that she attach the list to an e-mail message and send it before the end of the day.

36

The next morning Joe Godfrey, Rose Nardello, Pete Desmond, Dom DeCarlo and young Jack Clark met in the in a small conference room adjacent to Chief Tarencelli's office to discuss investigative strategy and individual assignments. Joe distributed his two-page status report and waited while the team read through the document. "As you can see, people, we don't have much to go on. I was hoping we'd get more from the D.N.A. analysis of the cigar saliva. The F.B.I. database identified an F.B.I. agent as the person who smoked the cigar. There's got to be a mistake somewhere. I'll call the lab today and ask them to run their D.N.A. findings through the F.B.I. database a second time." Joe looked at Jack Clark. "Jack, tell us about your telephone conversation you had with the cigar company."

"Sure. I called the company headquarters in Tampa, and," Clark chuckled, "after a little haggling, persuaded them to attach a list of their retail outlets in the tri-state area to an email." He handed the list to Joe. "There are 41 outlets in Connecticut, 56 in Massachusetts and 27 in Rhode Island. Since the matchbook came from Sam's Diner in North Attleboro, I recommend we concentrate our tobacco shop visits to the shops in Pawtucket and North Attleboro." Jack handed Joe another list. "I listed three that I think we should call on first."

"Good work, Jack. Looks like we're gonna be busy for awhile. Rose and I will drive over to North Attleboro tomorrow morning and have breakfast at Sam's Diner. While we're in the area, I'll call on the two Pawtucket shops on the list." Handing the list to DeCarlo, Joe said, "You'll have to take care of the rest, Dom. Remember, we're only interested in customers who smoke the Sinatra brand. We need names and addresses. We may have to locate each and every customer and question them. I'll call the local police and let them know what we plan to do. If an owner or manager gives you a hard time, call me." Joe turned toward Rose. "You and I will split up while we're in Rhode Island, Rose. Rocco wants information about D.E.C. He wants you to visit the state capitol and the people at the city of Pawtucket to find out if there are any skeletons in the D.E.C.'s closet. Make some telephone calls and set up appointments for yourself.

"Pete, do you remember the name of that fellow in California who'd agreed to bring that special monitoring equipment to Connecticut? You know, Dr. Simpkins' friend?"

"I think it was Olson, Joe, but I'm not sure. I'll check with Frank."

"Make arrangements to fly out there to meet with him. You'll probably have to track him down through the California Environmental Protection Agency. I suspect he'll be able to tell us quite a bit about D.E.C. Rocco wants a detailed dossier on the company. While you're out there, meet with Mrs. Simpkins. Find out if the doctor had any enemies. Also, check out the race card. When you return, I want you to combine your notes about D.E.C. with the stuff Rose picks up in Rhode Island. Rose, since you have more experience with business information, you should prepare the write up."

Joe stood up and moved to the blackboard. He wrote in bold letters, "Possible Motive: Silencing a Business Threat." "I want you to give this motive serious consideration. It may open some doors in your mind that could be helpful to the investigation."

Later that day, Joe stopped at Pete's paneled cubicle. Rose was sitting in a side chair across from Pete. Joe jokingly asked Pete if he and Rose had solved the Simpkins' case yet. Pete laughed. "No, but we're close, Joe. Seriously, I was just telling Rose about the normal sequence of events during a murder investigation. Pull up a chair and join us."

Joe sat in the other side chair and laughed. "Maybe you should tell me after you finish telling Rose." Turning toward Rose, Joe asked, "Were you able to schedule appointments in Rhode Island?"

"Yes. The day after tomorrow I'm meeting with the woman who manages the Corporations Division at the State Capitol. After that, I'm taking the director of a group called Department of Business Regulation to lunch. I hope you'll be able to join us. After that, I'm meeting with Pawtucket Mayor Sylvia Estenes and her economic development director at 4:00 p.m. We should be able to find out if our friends at D.E.C. are in compliance with state statutes and if they've been involved with questionable marketing or manufacturing practices."

Joe said, "Just tell me where and when and I'll meet you for lunch. I'd like to have breakfast at that diner in North Attleboro. Being legitimate customers might give us a leg up with our questions. Let's leave early tomorrow, say 7:00 a.m."

Turning toward Pete, Joe asked, "Were you able to arrange your flight to Sacramento?"

"I leave Bradley on a 1:10 a.m. flight tomorrow. Charles Olson reserved a room for me at the Capitol Hotel. He and I will have breakfast together the following morning and then meet a few key C.A.R.B. people after breakfast. He said that he'd make sure everyone is briefed in advance about why I'm in California."

"Rose, do we know if Dr. Bernstein called Mrs. Simpkins?"

"Yes, he did. I talked with him this morning. Mrs. Simpkins agreed to meet with Pete whenever he's free." Rose tore off a page from a yellow tablet and handed it to Pete. "That's Mrs. Simpkins telephone number. Call her after you've completed your meetings at C.A.R.B. She suggested that you meet with Dr. Simpkins close friend, Oscar Jackson. His phone number's on the sheet, also."

Joe asked, "Any questions?" He stood up and said, "Okay. Rose, I'll meet you at the entrance to the parking garage at 7:00 a.m. You'll have to be the navigator. I don't know the route to North Attleboro."

"Not a problem, Joe. I could probably get us there blindfolded."

"You have a successful and safe trip, Pete. See you when you get back."

Joe was upbeat about spending the day with Rose Nardello: he hadn't enjoyed the companionship of an attractive woman for months. He had a broad smile on his face when Rose approached the passenger side of the unmarked patrol car. She was dressed in blue flats, a dark blue skirt, and a white short-sleeve blouse. *Even at 7:00 in the morning, this lady is beautiful,* he thought. Rose opened the rear door of the car and placed an overnight bag on the back seat. "Good morning, Rose." Joe's greeting was an accurate assessment of the weather. It truly was a good morning; the kind of autumn day that seemed to raise one's spirits. It was bright and clear with a cloudless blue sky. The shadows formed by the trees in front of City Center seemed to be more pronounced than usual.

As she slid into the passenger seat, Rose replied, "Good morning, Joe. You look handsome this morning. I haven't seen you dressed in a coat and tie before. I guess we both are trying to look our best for the citizens of Massachusetts and Rhode Island."

He laughed. "I just don't want people to think I'm from some hick town." As he guided the car out of the parking garage, he added, "I'm glad you're coming with me, Rose. I might get lost if I traveled into that hostile area by myself."

Rose laughed. "It's my pleasure, Sergeant Godfrey. I'm looking forward to watching a pro in action."

Joe turned and smiled. "I don't know about that. You may be the one that solves Dr. Simpkins' murder."

Rose fell silent. Joe's facetious comment, that she might be the one to solve the murder, triggered the memory of Dr. Simpkins lying face down on the sidewalk with half his head blown away.

Joe noticed the change and turned toward her. "Something wrong, Rose?"

She sighed. "Dr. Simpkins was a good man, Joe. Please pardon my language, but I want to do everything I can to help you catch the bastard who killed him."

Joe reached out, touched her hand. "We'll catch who ever did it, Rose, and you'll be a big help."

Both remained silent for a few minutes. Rose changed the subject by asking, "Where'd you live in Texas before you moved to Riverside?"

"I lived near the Mexican border, in a city about one third the size of Riverside called McAllen. I worked in a small county sheriff's department as the one and only homicide detective."

"How in the world did you end up in Riverside?"

"It's a long story. Suffice it to say, I came to Riverside by way of Norwich." Joe related how he'd befriended the Norwich, Connecticut, police chief during a murder investigation. "He's the one that told me about the opening in Riverside and recommended I apply for it." Joe laughed. "Chief Pierson must have said some glowing things when he recommended me. He probably gave Rocco an inflated account of my capabilities." Joe chuckled. "I got the feeling that Rocco was ready to hire me, sight unseen."

"I don't believe that for a minute, Joe Godfrey."

They rode in relative silence for rest of the trip, broken only by brief discussions of recent City Council decisions, and Frank Mancuso's attempts to enlist nearby cities to join Riverside's plan to file a class action lawsuit against D.E.C.

As they approached the Massachusetts state line, Rose asked, "Please don't answer if you think I'm getting too personal. You've been in Riverside for a couple of months. Are you happy here in Connecticut?"

Joe turned his head and looked at her for a few seconds. "I guess I'm happy. Leaving everything and everyone I knew has been difficult. I miss the open space for one thing. You can drive for miles and miles without encountering a single traffic light. And then there's adjusting to a new job. It hasn't been easy. I'm on pins and needles most of the time for fear of offending someone. My social life was limited before I moved, but now it's nonexistent." He thought for a moment, and added, "I guess I miss deep-sea fishing the most and one special fishing friend. I've been so busy preparing to take over for Pete I haven't had time to think about fishing." Joe stopped at a traffic light. He turned his head toward Rose again. "Fishing will come back into my life when I have more spare time. You can probably help me find a few spots where I can arrange deep sea trips."

Their brief eye contact supported Rose's earlier assessment: Joe Godfrey's eyes were quite captivating. They were a blue/gray, like Paul Newman's. "I'm sure I can, Joe. There are numerous fishing fleets that sail in and out of the small ports on Long Island Sound. I think we just entered city limits of North Attleboro. I guess we'd better pay attention to where we're headed. What's the name of the street we're looking for?"

"Norton Road. The number of the diner is 26558."

Rose didn't notice the sign for Sam's Diner until they'd driven past. The sign was partially obscured by a large tree. Rose rotated her head and looked out the rear window. "I think we just passed the diner, Joe." He made a U-turn at the next available intersection and pulled into Sam's parking lot.

The diner itself was set back from the road at the back end of a large parking lot. The building had been designed to simulate an old railroad dinning car: a metal shell with rounded corners and circular windows. The interior was vintage '50s: plastic counter tops and Naugahyde coverings on the booths and stools. Two large fans hung from the ceiling at each end of the diner to circulate the air.

Rose slid into the first booth to the right of the entrance. Joe sat on the opposing bench. "Are you as hungry as I am, Joe?"

"For the past half hour, my thoughts have been focused on a heaping plate of scrambled eggs."

A middle-aged waitress appeared with menus. She waited while Rose and Joe examined the selections and left with two orders of Denver omelets, toast, and coffee. While they waited, Rose and Joe scanned the interior of the diner. Joe's eyes gravitated to the smoking section. It was small, only two tables, and partially walled off at one end of the diner. Except for a young couple drinking coffee and smoking, that end of the diner was empty. Joe thought, *If this were a Texas diner, that smoking section would be filled.*

Rose asked, "Did you notice the smoking section at the end of the diner?"

"Yes. It's small by Texas standards. I'll ask waitress about cigar smokers when she returns."

Noticing the condition of the carpeted floor, the dessert displays, and the equipment behind the counter, Rose commented, "I'd say this place is well-managed. My mother would say, 'Everything appears to be in its place, and there appears to be a place for everything.' There's a dish filled with matchbooks next to the cash register. I'll grab one." Returning to the booth, she handed it to Joe. "No surprises. Its looks just like the one you found at the parking garage."

When the waitress delivered their order, Joe asked, "Do you have a moment to settle a friendly argument my friend and I are having?"

The waitress looked around to see if any customers had slipped into the empty booths while she was in the kitchen. "Maybe. What's the question?"

Rose said, "My friend doesn't believe there are any cigar smokers left in this state. What do you think?"

The waitress looked at Rose. "I've seen a few." She thought for a moment, and then added, "We've got a couple of regulars that smoke cigars." She chuckled, "I'll bet their wives make those dudes smoke them ugly things out back in a barn somewhere."

Joe asked, "How frequently do the cigar smokers come into the diner?"

"One old timer comes in every mornin'. The other guy, he comes in when he ain't traveling. I guess he's some kind of a businessman. All I know about that boy is that he's good looking and tips well."

Joe asked, "Has he been around lately?"

The waitress was slightly taken aback by Joe's question. "Why you interested in our customers, mister? Are you a cop?"

"Yes." Joe flipped open a wallet size, leather pouch to display his police shield.

"Damn! I shouldn't a said anything." She began to walk away.

Rose rushed after her and whispered, "Wait. Please wait. A friend of mine was murdered recently."

The waitress stopped and looked at Rose.

"My friend was a distinguished scientist. We're just trying to track down a few leads. We think the murderer was a cigar smoker and that he may have frequented this diner. Please help us."

She studied Rose for a moment. "I can't talk here, lady. I get off work at 2:00. If you want to talk, meet me out front at 2:00 and we'll go someplace else." She whirled around and walked away.

"What do you think, Joe?"

"It's a long shot, Rose, but it's worth pursuing. We'll come back here at 2:00." Joe smiled and added, "You did well, Rose."

"Miss...? We didn't get your name."

"Agnes. What's yours?"

"My name is Joe, and this is Rose." Agnes reached out to shake Rose's hand first before accepting Joe's. Joe asked, "Where can we go to have a cup of coffee?"

"Let's go to Jessie's, down at the corner. We've got to talk quietly, though. I don't want anybody hearing me talking to you and tell my manager."

When they were seated Joe resumed his questioning. "Tell us about that young cigar smoking regular you mentioned this morning. The one you think might be a businessman."

"I don't know much about that man, except that he's a good customer and that he don't live in North Attleboro. He lives somewhere out in the country. He only comes in for breakfast or lunch once in a while, when he's in town." Agnes looked at Rose and giggled. "He's sure a good looker." Joe couldn't help but smile. He glanced at Rose, who was also smiling.

"Does he meet anyone in the diner or does he eat alone?"

Agnes thought about that question for a moment. "Most of the time he talks with Rick, or he eats alone. Rick might know something about him. Rick, he's our manager."

Joe asked, "When did you last see this man?"

"Let's see. Maybe two days ago. I heard him tell Rick that he just returned from a business trip."

Joe pulled a small appointment book out of his pocket. He pointed to a date a week before Dr. Simpkins murder, and asked, "Did he come in for breakfast or lunch around this date?"

Agnes looked at the date and then into Joe's eyes. "I don't know about that. I don't get involved with our customer's activities."

"Okay, we understand. Can you at least describe this man?"

Agnes sat motionless for a moment. She looked out of the window as she thought about that question. "He looks like an Italian: dark hair, dark skin. He looks like he needs a shave all the time. You know, like an Italian."

Rose asked, "How big a man is he?"

Waving her hand over her head, she said, "He's way over my head. The guy's a well built dude." Reaching for her arm, she said, "His arms big as my legs."

Rose asked, "How old a man would you say he is?"

"Hum, maybe early forties."

"Do you recall hearing a name while he talked with Rick?"

"No." Agnes's eyebrows suddenly went up. "Hey, that ain't right. I remember Rick called him Phonz, You know, like that fellow in that old TV show."

"That's good, Agnes. Did Rick use a last name?"

"No. I never heard a last name."

Rose's next question brought a smile to Joe's face. "What sort of clothes does this man wear?"

"He's a good dresser. When its cold outside, he wears a turtle neck and a sport jacket," Agnes chuckled, "and them girly shoes. You know, loafers with little bows. When it's hot, he wears a sports shirt and sometimes a Red Sox baseball cap."

Joe asked, "If we need more information about your cigar smoking customer, would you be willing to help us?"

"How else can I help? I don't want any trouble."

"I'd like to have one of my men wait in an unmarked patrol car in the parking lot until your customer returns and then follow him."

"That doesn't sound like a good idea. He might not be back for days. Besides, Rick won't put up with you parking a police car in the lot all day."

"Okay. I understand. We can park on the street." Joe sat back and thought for a moment. "Since we don't know what your customer looks like, we'll need you to signal us when he arrives."

Agnes leaned forward. "How I do that without getting my rear end shot off?"

Joe turned and pointed to an "Open" sign in the window. "Do you use an open sign like that?"

"Yep. Just like that. Why?"

"Maybe you could turn your sign upside down when he comes into Sam's. That could be our signal. When he leaves, you could turn it back."

Agnes studied Joe's eyes, and then looked at Rose. "I'm not gonna get fired, mister. I need the job. You can check with Rick. If it's okay with him, I'll do it."

"Good. We'll talk again in the morning, after I meet with Rick. In the meantime, take my business card. Call me on my cell phone if anything important happens between now and then."

Agnes took the card and nodded. Joe asked, "Do you think Rick is at still the diner now?"

"He might be."

Joe looked at Rose. "I think we should go back to the diner and see if we can talk with Rick before he leaves for the day." Joe reached out to shake Agnes's hand. "Thanks, Agnes. You've been a big help."

The cashier at Sam's told Joe and Rose that Rick left at 2:00 and wouldn't return until tomorrow morning at 5:00.

"What's your opinion, Rose? Do you think we should assign someone to stake out the diner and wait for our friend to show up? It could be a false alarm and a big waste of time."

"I think you should. How else can you find out if this particular cigar-smoking customer is or isn't the person you're looking for?"

"Okay. I'll come back in the morning and talk with Rick."

They discussed the logistics of staying in the area until the next day. It was agreed that Rose would stay with her parents in Pawtucket, while Joe would find a motel close to the diner. Joe decided that he'd better stop at the North Attleboro police station to brief the police chief before he dropped Rose off at her parent's home in Pawtucket. "We'll need his approval and cooperation if the surveillance plan has any chance of succeeding. Besides, he may recognize the sketchy description of our mysterious cigar-smoking friend. I'd better call the Pawtucket and Providence police chiefs as well and alert them that we'll be visiting tobacco shops in the area."

The North Attleboro Police Department occupied the east-end of a new, two level brick Public Safety Building. The main North Attleboro Fire Department was at the other end. Two large doors to the firehouse were open when Joe turned into the parking lot revealing bright red fire vehicles and assorted fire equipment. Joe opened the glass door that led into the lobby of the Police Station to allow Rose to enter first. He removed his badge from an inside jacket pocket as they approached a uniformed female receptionist stationed behind a waste high, wood counter approximately six feet wide. Two large floor-to-ceiling glass walls on each side of the counter separated the lobby area from administration and operations. When receptionist saw Joe advance toward her, she stood up and slid open a glass window. "May I help you, sir?"

Joe displayed his badge, introduced Rose and himself, and asked to see the police chief. After making the appropriate phone call, the receptionist said, "Chief Buckley will be with you in a few minutes. Please have a seat. May I get you something, a cup of coffee or a soft drink?" Both Joe and Rose declined the offer.

Joe was mesmerized by the activity on the other side of the glass: male and female uniformed employees were scurrying about noiselessly like fish in a tank. A few plainclothes detectives sat at desks inside paneled enclosures talking on telephones, reading documents, or working at computers. Joe turned and asked, "Do we look as disorganized as that, Rose?"

"I hope not, Joe. It looks like a zoo in there."

Joe asked the receptionist which divisions were on the other side of the glass. "Over to the left is the administrative offices and investigative divisions. Over to the right is our 911 dispatch section. Booking, holding cells, and interrogation rooms are on the upper level." She smiled and added, "911 always looks that chaotic."

Rose and Joe were led into Chief Buckley's office and were greeted warmly. Joe commented, "It looks like you have a busy department, Chief."

Buckley laughed. "Our community is growing rapidly, Sergeant. Sometimes I feel like a one-armed paper hanger. What can I do for you?"

Joe summarized the status of the murder investigation and the objective of the surveillance at the diner. "I only have enough manpower to assign one man to a shift: four hours on and four hours off for twelve hours. We need help with the remaining four hours that the diner is open. Could you give us some help during the early morning hours or at night?"

"Unfortunately, I can't provide much support. Like most cities in this state, we've got budgetary problems. But, I definitely will place an unmarked across the street from diner from the time it opens at 6:00 a.m. I can leave it there until 10:00. After that, I can't make any promises."

"That would be very helpful, Chief."

37

Joe's watch read 4:35 p.m. when he turned into the driveway of the Nardello home. Rose led the way up the walkway to the front door. She pointed to a beautifully manicured collection of rose bushes off to their right. "See those roses, Joe? Dad planted those the day I was born. The sentimental galoot said that he thinks of me whenever he waters them."

Rose opened the door and called, "Mom, I'm home."

Teresa rushed from the kitchen and embraced her daughter. "Your telephone call was a pleasant surprise, honey. We had no idea you were in town."

"It was a last minute thing, Mom." Rose turned and touched Joe's elbow. "Meet Detective Sergeant Joe Godfrey of the Riverside Police Department."

"Welcome to our home, Sergeant."

Rose explained that she was helping the Riverside Police with the Simpkins' murder investigation. "Since I knew Dr. Simpkins better than anyone else at City Hall, Frank asked me to work with Sergeant Godfrey for a few days and help prepare a dossier on Dad's neighbor, the Diesel Engine Corporation. I have an appointment at the state Capitol tomorrow morning."

Teresa's eyes widened. "Why D.E.C., Rose?"

Rose glanced at Joe. He nodded. Rose said, "Remember me telling you a few months ago that Ethyl Radio's boy developed emphysema and died? The physicians at New Haven Hospital believe that the emphysema was caused by the inhalation of harmful chemicals from the exhaust of diesel trucks. When Frank learned that most of the diesel trucks registered in Connecticut are powered by D.E.C. engines, he recommended that the City Council file a class action against D.E.C. on behalf of city's children. He also encouraged the Rado family to file a wrongful death claim against D.E.C.

"We need to learn more about the company. Are they complying with Rhode Island and Connecticut vehicle emission regulations? Are they a corporation in good standing? Have they broken any laws? Tomorrow, I have an appointment with the Rhode Island corporations commissioner. The information I pull together may have a bearing on whether or not we proceed with the class action lawsuit."

Teresa frowned and turned toward Joe. "Why is the police department interested in D.E.C., Sergeant?"

"At this point in time, we aren't, Mrs. Nardello. I'm just tagging along. That's Rose's assignment." Smiling, he added, "I wouldn't know what questions to ask the bureaucrats at the state Capitol."

Joe asked if he could look at a phone directory. Teresa retrieved two directories, one for metropolitan Providence and another for Pawtucket. "Please make yourself comfortable at the dinning room table, Sergeant. Would you like a pad and pencil?"

"Yes, please."

While Joe was comparing Clark's list of tobacco shops in and around Pawtucket and North Attleboro with the listings in the yellow pages, Teresa and Rose moved into the kitchen.

"It's good to be home, Mom. How's Dad? Is he still down in the dumps?"

"Something is bothering him, Rose, but he refuses to talk about it. He started to tell me the day Dr. Simpkins was murdered but changed his mind. I have a feeling it has something to do with the business. I can't help him unless he's willing to share."

"When he gets home, I'll suggest that we sit out on the porch. He can smoke his pipe. That usually relaxes him. Maybe he'll open up."

Joe called out, "Rose. I've found what I need. I'll be leaving now."

Teresa asked, "Can you stay for dinner, Sergeant?"

"Thank you, no, Mrs. Nardello. I've got a lot of work to do before Rose and I return to Riverside." Turning toward Rose, he said, "I'm going back to the diner first thing tomorrow morning and try to talk with Rick. Then if I have time, I'll visit the other Pawtucket tobacco shop. I'll come by around 10:00 a.m."

After Joe left, Rose asked her mother, "When do you expect Dad?"

"He won't come home until after eight. He has a Rotary Club meeting tonight. He'll go directly from work."

"I think I'll call Rita. I haven't talked with her for ages. I'd like to get an update on the kids."

Joe found Gibby's Tobacco Shop nestled between a hardware store and an appliance store in the older section of downtown Pawtucket. The buildings were early 20th century tenements with retail on the ground floor and apartments on the second and third floors. All three ground floor stores—tobacco, hardware, and appliance stores—featured large front windows with huge signs above the windows. A doorway separated the tobacco shop from the hardware store. Joe surmised that the door led to a stairway to the upper floors.

Joe parked across the street from the tobacco shop. He watched and waited until all of the customers had departed before he entered. A woman behind a counter greeted him with an enthusiastic "Good afternoon. May I help you?"

Joe grinned broadly: he didn't want the clerk to feel uncomfortable or threatened. He moved toward the counter and reached out to shake the woman's hand. "Good afternoon. I'm Sergeant Joe Godfrey from the Riverside, Connecticut, police department." As he said this, he displayed his detective's badge. "May I speak with the owner or the manager?"

The woman was momentarily startled by the sight of the badge, but quickly recovered her composure. "I'm Mrs. Gibarelli. My husband is off this afternoon. How can I help you, Sergeant?"

"Our research shows that you are one of the tobacco shops in Pawtucket that sell Johnson cigars. Is that correct, Mrs. Gibarelli?"

"That's right. We've been a Johnson retailer for over 30 years."

Joe explained that he was involved in a murder investigation and why Johnson cigars might be important. "Do any of your customers smoke the Sinatra brand, Mrs. Gibarelli?

"No, we haven't sold a Sinatra cigar in a long time, Sergeant."

Joe tried not to show his disappointment. He told himself that it was probably unrealistic to have expected to hit pay dirt on the first try. "Even though you don't have any Sinatra customers, do you have a list of your Johnson customers? The information will be considered confidential, Mrs. Gibarelli."

"We have a list. We mail a newsletter to our customers every two months. Before I give it to you, I'd want to check with my husband. Do the Pawtucket Police know of your visit, Sergeant?"

"Yes, I cleared my visit with your police chief. He is fully aware of our investigation. He agreed to help, if we need it."

Smiling, Mrs. Gibarelli said, "I don't see a problem, Sergeant, as long as you can convince me that you won't share the information with a competitor." Joe returned the smile and held up his hand. "Scout's honor, Mrs. Gibarelli. I won't share the customer list with anyone."

"It'll take me awhile to compile the list. I can mail it to you by the end of the week. Do you have a business card?"

After leaving Gibby's, Joe located a pay phone in the lobby of the Holiday Inn just off Pawtucket Road and called Riverside. He gave Rocco a brief update on his conversation with the waitress at Sam's Diner and then requested permission to use young Clark in a stake out of the North Attleboro diner. Rocco said he'd check with Human Resources. When they'd finished talking Joe asked Rocco to have his secretary switch the call to Dom DeCarlo's extension.

"Dom, have you got your tobacco shop list handy?"

"Yeah, I got it right here."

"Check off the Pawtucket store on River Road. It's called Gibby's. I talked with the owner's wife this afternoon. I struck out. She said that she doesn't have even one Sinatra customer. I should have enough time to check out the other Pawtucket store tomorrow before I head back to Riverside. Tell Clark that the three of us will have to drive back over here on Monday. I want you and Clark to stake out Sam's diner while I hit a few more tobacco shops. Tell him to pack a bag. He'll be over here for a few days. I'll explain when I get back."

Dom chuckled. "Wait until you hear this one, Joe. Clark called the Johnson Cigar Company again and found out they maintain a record of which Johnson brands are sold at each of the retail outlets. They emailed the new information this morning. It should save us a lot of time. If you'd had the information yesterday, you wouldn't have called on that River Road store. They haven't placed an order for a single box of Sinatra's all year. That young Clark is a smart son-of-a-gun, Joe."

"That's outstanding. How many of the shops in the Pawtucket/Providence area ordered Sinatra's this year?"

Dom ran his finger down the list. "Let's see. It looks like only six."

"What about the other Pawtucket store, Dom? Have they ordered any Sinatra's?"

"Yeah, they did. The other five stores are in Providence and Cranston."

"Tell Jack I'll buy him a beer when I get back."

38

"Rita, it's Rose."

Rita exploded with delight. "Rose! What a pleasant surprise. Are you in Pawtucket?"

"I'm over at my parent's house. I'm staying the night. May I come over and visit?"

"You bet. I'll make a pot of coffee. Jon and Elizabeth are both home. They'd love to see you."

"I'll be there in about 20 minutes. I can only stay for an hour. Dad's at a Rotary Club meeting until 8:00. I want to talk with him when he gets home."

Rose looked forward to reconnecting with Rita's children: she hadn't seen either for over a year. She last saw Jon and Elizabeth at the latter's graduation from high school. Now both Fernandez children were attending a community college in Providence. Jon had his mother's coloring: dark skin, black hair that reached to his shirt collar, and dark brown eyes. His shoulders were broad and his arms and legs were muscular. He was tall like his biological father, over six feet. Elizabeth on the other hand was short, like her mother, had fair skin, blue eyes, and light brown hair that cascaded over her shoulders.

Rounds of hugs and kisses ensued when Rose arrived. She, Rita, and the children moved into the living room and reminisced. After ten to fifteen minutes of belly laughs over things that had happened while Rita and the children were homeless, Jon sensed that Rose wanted to have a confidential talk with his mother. He suggested that he and his sister adjourn to the sitting room to watch a movie.

When they were alone, Rose said, "Dad told me about your promotion, Rita. Congratulations! I'm proud of you."

Rita smiled and said, "I'm proud of me, too. I want to be the best controller your father's ever had. I'm taking a cost accounting course at the same community college the kids are attending. It's only one night a week, but it's still taxing. I was never a good student to begin with."

Rose looked down at her coffee mug. Her knuckles began to turn white as she squeezed the mug tightly with both hands. After a moment of silence, she raised her head slowly. Rita could see that the sparkle that had been in her friend's eyes just a few moments ago was now replaced by a look of concern.

"Mom's worried about Dad, Rita. Apparently, he's been edgy and stressed lately, but he won't talk about it. Has anything happened at work that would distress him?"

"I've noticed a change, too, Rose. He's been very quiet lately. Even keeps his office door closed, which is very unusual. Agnes told me that he hasn't visited with the men on the docks for over two weeks. It might be that blowout he had with Mr. Osborne."

Rose frowned. "Isn't Osborne the president of D.E.C.?"

"That's the man."

"What happened, Rita?"

"I was meeting with your father in his office. We were going over the quarterly results when Osborne burst into the office without knocking. He slammed the door shut and yelled at your father. It frightened me, Rose. I nearly peed my pants. I don't know what that man's problem was, but it sounded like he was upset about a man that your father had sent to talk with him. I don't know any more than that. Your father asked me to leave and to shut the door on my way out. I stood next to Agnes's desk for a few moments, not knowing what else to do. We both heard Osborne threaten to cancel the testing contract the firm has with D.E.C. That might be the reason your father is stressed. That contract is critical to the company's profitability."

Mario came home just after 8:00 p.m. When he saw Rose, he dropped his briefcase and rushed across the living room to greet her. They flung their arms around each other and embraced. Rose may have been overly sensitive, but she thought her father's hug was stronger and longer than usual. When she was able to back away, she looked into his bloodshot eyes. "Are you okay, Dad?"

With a catch in his voice he said, "I'm okay." He looked away, avoiding her eyes. He asked, "What brings you to our all-American city?"

Rose sat down alongside her father on the living room couch. "It's beginning to look like your neighbor, Winston Osborne, may have a few problems, Dad. A New Haven medical examiner found tiny carbon particles in the Rado boy's lungs during an autopsy. Based on the M.E.'s finding, Dr. Bernstein believes that the particles came from the exhaust of D.E.C. engines. Our City Council agrees with Dr. Bernstein and directed a large New York law firm to prepare a class action against D.E.C. on behalf of the children of Riverside. The city needed facts and data to support the action, however, so we retained Dr. Simpkins. We think Dr Simpkins was murdered a few weeks ago to stall the law suit.

"I'm over here compiling background information on D.E.C. We're interested in D.E.C.'s record of compliance with environmental regulations here in Rhode Island. I have an appointment at the state Capitol tomorrow morning."

Mario locked his hands together so tightly they turned white. "Are you saying that the City Council thinks that D.E.C. had something to do with Dr. Simpkins' murder?"

When Teresa heard the exchange between her daughter and husband, she slowly moved from the kitchen. She stood in the doorway to be closer to the conversation.

"I can't go into the details now, Dad, but I can tell you this much. Chief Tarencelli believes there might be a link. Since I knew Dr. Simpkins better than anyone else at City Hall, he asked me to help with the investigation. I've been assigned to the Police Department for a few weeks."

The blood drained from Mario's face. His jaw dropped, and his eyes practically popped out of his head. Slowly, he lowered his head into his hands. Concerned, Rose slid forward. "Dad, what's the matter?" Mario didn't respond. He just sat there holding his head. Rose looked at her mother, and then turned back to her father. "Please talk to me, Dad. Everyone is concerned. Did something happen at work? Did you have a run in with Mr. Osborne? Is that why you're down?"

Mario looked at his wife pleadingly. Teresa moved from the doorway into the living room and stood in front of her husband. "You've got to tell her what's bothering you, Mario."

Mario grabbed the arms of his chair, flung himself up and in a heated voice said, "I'll tell her, but not now. I need time to think."

The following morning, Rose sat quietly with her parents in the living room. Mario leaned forward and rested his hands on his knees. "I did something very stupid, Rose. Winston Osborne asked me to help him find an enforcer a few weeks ago. He said that he needed someone who'd help him convince a man to stop interfering in his engine business. Unless I agreed to help, he threatened to cancel the testing contract we've had with D.E.C. for years. The company's income depends on that contract, Rose. Without it, the business wouldn't have shown a profit last year. I was between a rock and a hard place."

"Why did Osborne want an enforcer, Dad?"

Mario raised his sad eyes and looked at his daughter. "I can't answer that, Rose, because I don't know. He didn't tell me and I didn't ask. I could speculate, I suppose, but that wouldn't do any good. He didn't give me any names, or what the convincing would entail. I'm sorry to say I didn't ask." Rose stared at her father, unable to comprehend the significance of what she was hearing.

Mario leaned back in the chair and recounted an abbreviated version of what happened when he met with Winston Osborne. When he'd finished, he stood up and began to pace. "I have to give Osborne credit. He persisted. He promised to extend the contract for another two years and increase the fee by 50 percent if I'd help." Mario stopped pacing and looked down at his wife. He said sheepishly, "I contacted your brother."

Teresa cried, "You promised you'd never get involved with Mark." Suddenly, her eyes opened wide. "Did the so-called enforcer have anything to do with what happened in Riverside?"

"I wish I could say no, but I can't." Mario sat down and put his face in his hands. Rose was stunned. She didn't know what to say.

Teresa asked, "What do you intend to do about this, Mario?"

"I don't know." He leaned forward, ran his fingers through his hair and closed his eyes. "Osborne said that all he wanted to do was convince someone stay out of D.E.C.'s business." Mario shouted, "Damn!"

He stood up, put both hands on his forehead and began to pace again. "If there is a connection, I could be charged as an accessory to murder. What can I do, Rose? I can't talk with the police."

Rose sat quietly for a few moments as she thought through the situation. Finally, she looked up at her father. "The incident in Riverside may have nothing to do with what you and Osborne talked about, Dad. On the other hand, I may have a serious conflict of interest on my hands. If I tell Sergeant Godfrey about what you did for Osborne, he'll be forced to ask you and Mr. Osborne a lot of embarrassing questions. If he uncovers evidence that shows there is a direct link between the death of Dr. Simpkins and D.E.C., you may be right. It's conceivable you could be charged as an accessory. I think we'd better seek legal council. Who do we know?"

Teresa responded. "If your father hadn't contacted Uncle Mark, he'd be my obvious choice"

"I think we should talk with him anyway, Mom. He's got as much to loose as Dad, maybe more. I expect that he'll go out of his way to help."

Mario shook his head. "Let's think this through carefully before we talk to your brother, Teresa. I'll bet Mark doesn't know any more about what happened in Riverside than I do. And it wouldn't surprise me if Mark has never heard of Dr. Simpkins. No, I don't think Mark can help." He leaned back in his chair. "I don't think we should talk with anyone."

Rose looked at Teresa, and then turned toward her father. "Put your feet in my shoes, Dad. Your information may be material to a murder investigation. It's plausible that someone at D.E.C. may have contracted for Dr. Simpkins' murder. I can't just ignore that. Dr. Simpkins was a good man. If that horrible Osborne person was responsible for his death, he'll have to pay and pay dearly. Maybe you should write an anonymous letter or make an anonymous phone call."

"I understand how you feel, Rose. But I have to think about the future of this family." In the most authoritative voice he could muster, Mario announced, "I don't want any of us to say anything to anyone about this matter."

He stood up and walked out of the room, leaving a startled daughter and wife with their mouths open. Tears began to form in Rose's eyes. Teresa grasped both of her hands, but couldn't say anything: she was to dumbfounded.

Mario left for work early the next morning to avoid a confrontation. Mother and daughter chatted during breakfast about the Fernandez children and about Rita's decision to take an accounting course at the community college, but shunned any mention of the disagreement that they'd had with Mario the previous evening. After clearing the table and loading the dishes in the dishwasher, Rose said, "I guess I'd better shower and get ready. I expect Joe will pick me up around ten." She hugged her mother, and added, "We'll work it out, Mom. Don't worry."

39

It turned out to be a whirlwind day for Rose and Joe. Beginning with an appointment at the state capital at 10:00 a.m., they met continuously with state and city bureaucrats until mid-afternoon. Rose was able to defer thoughts of the previous night's confrontation with her father and concentrate on asking meaningful questions during the meetings, listening to the answers, and taking copious notes. The effort had been exhausting, however. Joe suggested they take the Interstate back to Riverside rather than take the rural route they'd traveled the previous day on their way to North Attleboro. Rose readily agreed: she felt that a change of scenery might lift her spirits.

Rose was unusually quiet and glum during the trip. Joe didn't ask any questions, but he suspected that something unpleasant had occurred after he'd left the Nardello home the previous afternoon. As they crossed the State line from Massachusetts into Connecticut, Rose said, "I'm sorry, Joe. I haven't been very good company. My mind has been fixed on something my father said last night. Tell me about your visits to the tobacco shops. Any luck?"

"I guess I'd have to say partially. Only one of the two shops I visited carried the Sinatra brand, but they hadn't sold many this past year. I did get a list of their customers. I doubt the list will do us any good, however." Joe took his eyes off the road for a moment and looked toward Rose. "What was your take on the meetings today?"

"As far as the state of Rhode Island is concerned, D.E.C. appears to be a good corporate citizen. But, I have to tell you, I was shocked when that fellow at the secretary of state's office told us the size of the fine imposed on D.E.C. by the State of California. Two million! Wow! I had no idea the fine was that big. I'm sure Pete will have something to say about that when he returns. Then there was the revelation that D.E.C. was caught dumping waste oil into the Pawtucket sewer system. That's unconscionable! If a company thinks it can violate a common sense regulation like that, they're capable of anything. There was one other thing that caught my attention. Osborne and his sister own most of the stock in D.E.C., but apparently she isn't involved with the business, certainly not the day to day operations of the company. That could mean that her brother does what he wants. He may be a loose canon."

"I agree. At some point you may have to have a talk with the sister."

"That should be interesting. I'll bet they're estranged."

"Pete's due back tomorrow. It's important that the two of you go over everything that you've learned about D.E.C., write it up, and send to the District Attorney. My intuition is telling me that D.E.C. is hiding something. Concentrate on D.E.C.'s record of compliance with environmental regulations. Look for red flags."

Joe turned his head and asked, "Is your cell phone handy, Rose?"

"Yes, it's in my purse."

"Call the department for me please, and try to track down DeCarlo. I need an update on the F.B.I. database search for a D.N.A. match. If he hasn't heard from anyone yet, tell him to drop everything and call Hartford." After Rose completed the call to DeCarlo, Joe asked, "Would you mind if we stopped in Windsor Locks on our way? I'd like you to meet my cousin Ginny Newburg."

Although unenthusiastic about the idea of delaying her arrival in Riverside, Rose said that would be fine. "I don't have any plans for this evening."

"I know you're tired. I promise that I won't keep you out late." Joe recited the phone number and Rose initiated the call. "When the receptionist comes on the line, hand me the phone and I'll talk with her."

The unexpected telephone call from her cousin energized Ginny. "Will you have time to have dinner with me?" Joe checked with Rose and she agreed. Ginny suggested they meet at the Blue Hills Inn, just off the Interstate in the community of Blue Hills. "Where are you now, Joe?"

"We just crossed the state line. The last sign I saw said Union."

"Hold on a minute while I look at a Connecticut map." Ginny opened a desk drawer, retrieved the map and quickly located the correct exit number. "Let's see, Blue Hills is near the intersection of I-291 and 91. Go south on 91 and get off at Exit 66, and then look for their sign. I'll leave now. I think you could get to the Blue Hills Inn by 5:30. Call me on my cell phone when you get to I-291." Ginny buzzed her secretary and instructed her to cancel a meeting that was scheduled for 4:00 p.m.

Joe could feel his attraction toward Rose Nardello was growing. He was of the opinion that Rose Nardello was an extraordinary woman: sensitive, intelligent, and beautiful. Joe had trouble understanding why she was still single, so he thought it would be a good idea to get another opinion. Ginny Newburg was Joe's only relative within 1,000 miles of Riverside. He wanted Ginny to be the one that sized her up.

Rose spotted the Blue Hills Inn sign immediately after exiting the Interstate. As they pulled into the parking lot, Rose saw an attractive woman standing at the front entrance, waving. "That lady waving must be your cousin, Joe."

"That's her." Ginny noticed the pride and excitement in Joe's eyes when he introduced Rose, "Ginny, I want you to meet the best looking lady in Riverside, Rose Nardello. And Rose, say hello to my cousin and best friend, Ginny Newburg."

The chemistry between Rose and Ginny was evident from the beginning. Joe didn't have to say very much during dinner: the two ladies carried on a continuous conversation without involving him. Except for answering an occasional question, Joe felt like a fixture hanging on the wall. But he didn't mind. That was exactly what he'd hoped would happen.

The digital clock on the dashboard read 7:45 p.m. when Joe and Rose exited I-64, drove past the Green, and entered the City Center parking garage. Joe held onto Rose's hand while he said, "Thanks for coming with me, Rose. It was a productive trip. But most of all, I enjoyed being with you. Maybe we could arrange to have dinner together. Are you free Saturday night?"

Rose was both startled and pleased. A broad smile creased her face. "I'd be delighted to have dinner with you, Joe Godfrey. If I'm not free, I'll change plans."

"Great! Do you have a preference? Should we have dinner in the country, or would you like to have dinner in the city?"

"Let's have dinner in the country. We have a marvelous restaurant in Westwood. It's right on the River. I'll make a 7:30 reservation for a window table."

"That sounds good to me. I'll need a map to get to your home."

"I'll draw one and give it to you tomorrow. Well, I guess I'd better get started. I have another half hour drive ahead of me."

40

Riverside Police Chief Tarencelli sent out an interoffice memo to all city employees suggesting that one or more employees may have witnessed something suspicious or out of the ordinary during Dr. Simpkins' recent visit to Riverside. The memo stated in part, "You may think what you observed or heard was insignificant and unrelated to the murder. Please don't try to interpret the importance of that information. Let us be the judge. What you observed or heard may be crucial."

Marie Lombardo, Frank Mancuso's secretary, reread Chief Tarencelli's memo a third time. She walked over and stood by the open door to her boss's office with the memo in her hand. "Mr. Mancuso, do you have moment?"

"Please come in, Marie. You look perplexed about something."

"I guess I am, sir. Did you read Chief Tarencelli's memo about the Simpkins investigation?"

"Yes. What about it?"

"It may not be important, sir, but I thought I'd better tell you anyway." Marie described the unusual phone call she'd received just days before Dr. Simpkins murder. "The man introduced himself as an old friend of the doctor's and asked if I knew where Dr. Simpkins was staying while in Riverside. I told him I didn't know but guessed that it might be the Riverside Inn. The more I think about that phone call, the more uncomfortable I feel. It seems implausible to me that Dr. Simpkins would not tell a close friend that he'd been retained by the city and where he'd be staying. Another thing concerns me. If Simpkins didn't tell this so-called close friend, who did? Only insiders knew about your decision to retain Dr. Simpkins."

Frank placed the document he'd been reading on his desk and leaned back in his chair. "Those are damn good questions, Marie, but I don't have the answers. Maybe Chief Tarencelli can provide some insight. Let's go talk with him."

Frank led the way across the breezeway connecting City Administration from the Police and Fire departments, and went directly to the office of Rocco Tarencelli. Although the Chief's office door was open, Frank elected to stop at his secretary's desk and ask if the Chief was free, instead of walking in unannounced.

When informed that Frank Mancuso wanted to see him, Rocco hustled out to greet him. "This is a pleasant surprise, Frank." Chuckling, he added, "I see that you brought the boss with you. Hello Marie. Come on in and have a seat. Cup of coffee or a soft drink?" Both declined the offer. "What brings you to our humble digs?"

Frank watched Rocco's facial expression carefully while Marie retold the story of the unusual phone call that she'd received just before Dr. Simpkins was shot. He could see that the story was having a significant impact.

"Is there anything else you'd like to tell me, Marie?"

"No, sir."

"Marie, you were wise to tell Frank about that call." Rocco stood, signaling that the meeting was over. "Well I guess that's it. Thanks for coming over to tell me about the phone call." Rocco reached out to shake Marie's hand, but pulled it back and asked another question, "Doesn't every incoming call go through the receptionist in the lobby?"

"Yes, sir. Betty screens each call." She smiled. "If the caller acts strange, or begins to rant and rave about something, Betty will say the city employee is not in. She'll try to get the person's name, and say the employee will call back."

"What would happen if the potential flake came through the door and asked to see one of our employees?"

"She'd essentially do the same thing, I guess. She'd size up the visitor to determine if she or he had legitimate business with the city."

Rocco thought that over and said, "If you hear or think of anything else that seems out of the ordinary regarding Dr. Simpkins' visit, please come back and see me."

After Marie and Frank left, Rocco sat at his desk and contemplated what the secretary had said. His body was quiet, but his mind was churning. Marie was correct. If the caller had been an old friend, it's logical to assume that Simpkins would have contacted him before he arrived in Riverside and would have told him where he was staying. It just didn't make sense. Maybe Dr.

Simpkins said something to Rose Nardello about having a friend in Riverside.

"Morning, Rose, it's Rocco Tarencelli. Do you have a moment to answer a question?"

"Certainly, Rocco, what's your question?"

"Did Dr. Simpkins ever mention having a friend living in or near Riverside?"

"Only Dr. Bernstein, Rocco. They seemed to know each other quite well, at least professionally. He never mentioned anyone else."

"Thanks, Rose."

Within minutes, Rocco was on the phone calling Frank Mancuso. He told Frank about his conversation with Rose. "There's something very strange about the phone call Marie received. Think about it, Frank, the caller knew enough about our city administration to ask for you. That leads me to believe that he could have been nosing around City Hall before he made that call. Maybe someone will remember seeing a stranger in our midst. It might be helpful if we schedule a general meeting with all city employees. What do you think?"

"That's a good idea, Rocco. I'll send out a memo right away. How about first thing Friday morning in the Council Chambers?"

"That works for me, Frank."

Walking out of Council Chambers with Joe Godfrey, Rocco commented, "I don't think that little get together did much good, Joe. I was hoping someone would remember seeing something unusual or maybe a stranger in the building. I guess I expected too much."

Rocco heard a soft voice behind him ask, "May I speak with you, sir?"

Both Joe and Rocco turned around and looked into the eyes of an attractive young lady. "Certainly, Miss." Rocco pointed to a bench in the hallway. "Please sit Miss…"

"Johnson, Betty Johnson, Chief. I'm the receptionist for the administrative departments."

"I'm glad to meet you, Betty." Placing his hand on Joe Godfrey's shoulder, Rocco added, "This is Sergeant Godfrey." Sitting down on the bench next to Betty, Rocco asked, "Do you have some information for us?"

"As you said during the meeting, I'll let you be the judge." Betty described her encounter with a well-dressed businessman at the reception desk just prior to Dr. Simpkins death. "He asked to see Dr. Simpkins. Well, I didn't know who Dr. Simpkins was at the time, so I called the city manager's secretary. She told me that Dr. Simpkins was a consultant from California and wasn't expected to arrive until the following day. I remember thinking, *That's strange. He doesn't seem to be disappointed.* Then he asked me if city visitors stayed in a certain hotel. I told him that I didn't know anything about that either. He didn't say another word; just turned and walked out. Dr. Simpkins was killed only a few days later."

"Can you describe this man, Betty?" While Betty did her best to recall what the visitor looked like, Joe Godfrey took notes. "That was a thorough description, Betty. I'd like you to meet with an illustrator. Maybe we can come close to creating a picture of the man."

41

Rose tossed and turned most of the night. The unpleasant scene with her father earlier in the week kept running through her mind. She sat up and looked at the bedside clock: 5:35 a.m. *I guess a good night's sleep isn't in the cards tonight. That's okay. It's Saturday. I can nap later. I'll get up, make a pot of coffee, and read the newspaper.* Rose shuffled into the bathroom and splashed water on her face. She looked at her refection in the window and thought. *If Joe Godfrey is right and the D.N.A. recovered from the cigar butt is enough to identify Dr. Simpkins' killer, Dad's compact with Osborne might never become an issue. On the other hand, if the D.A. needs corroborating evidence, Dad's testimony could be crucial.* Rose leaned on the sink with both hands and mumbled, "Damn! Make a decision, you dope."

She retrieved the morning newspaper, poured a cup of coffee, and sat down on her favorite chair in the living room. She attempted to read the front page, but found that she couldn't concentrate. Doing nothing about a problem was an abhorrent thought to Rose: it just wasn't in her nature. She placed the newspaper on her lap. *I've got to stop procrastinating. I don't have a choice. I've got to drive over to Providence tomorrow morning and confront Uncle Mark. Stop thinking about the investigation, and start thinking about pleasant things, like your dinner date with Joe Godfrey tonight.* Rose stood up and walked into the kitchen to refill her coffee mug.

Joe rang the doorbell under the small hand printed sign that read "Rose Nardello." A few seconds later, he heard the front door click open. As Joe entered the lobby at the bottom of a staircase, he heard Rose call out, "Come on up, Joe."

Rose was standing in the doorway when Joe reached the top of the stairs. His mouth fell open. She was stunning! Rose had chosen a black, long-sleeve silk dress accentuated by a simple string of pearls. Her black hair framed her well-proportioned and beautiful face. After a momentary pause, Joe said, "You look lovely, Rose."

"Why thank you, Joe Godfrey." Rose reached out and touched his arm lightly. "You're pretty handsome yourself."

Joe hadn't had time to add a Northeastern touch to his wardrobe since he moved from Texas. He wore a western-cut tan jacket, white shirt and string tie, a pair of tight fitting brown slacks, and brown boots that he'd obviously spent time polishing.

"Those stairs should keep you slim, Rose."

"I don't mind the climb, except when I'm carrying groceries. I usually have to make two trips. We have time for a glass of wine or a cocktail. Do you have preference?"

"Yes, I'd like a glass of white wine."

From the day he met Rose in Frank Mancuso's office, Joe thought Rose was an especially attractive lady. Now, as he watched her open a bottle of wine in the kitchen, he realized that his feelings were changing: she no longer was just a fellow employee. He'd become physically attracted to the woman: he wanted desperately to hold her in his arms and kiss her. He looked away and he noticed the view through a large bay window on the opposite side of the living room. He walked across the room and looked out. The view was so beautiful he felt a shortness of breath. *No wonder Rose is willing to drive over 20 miles each way to get to work,* he thought.

Joe turned back and looked into the kitchen again. It was small but bright and cheery: everything was white. A small dinning area separated the kitchen from the living room. The walls of the dinning area were painted in a mocha color to compliment the oiled walnut dinning table and chairs. Looking to his right, Joe could see into Rose's neatly decorated bedroom.

"Want crackers and cheese with your wine, Joe?"

"Yes, please."

Rose's description of Lift the Latch Inn had been thorough. As soon as Joe walked through the door, he felt like he'd been to the restaurant before. A hostess led them to a window table, offered menus, and departed. The view of the river rapids and old water wheel held their attention for awhile. It was a wonderful view, something Joe had never experienced before. As darkness fell, the river became less important as they began to get to know each other. As they discussed their personal feelings about people and things, their eyes rarely wavered from each other: Joe feasted on the lovely woman sitting across from him; Rose, in turn, felt her heart pound. Before dessert was served, they were holding hands.

42

The traffic on Hope Street seemed abnormally heavy for noon on a Sunday. *There must be lots of churches in the neighborhood*, Rose thought. She turned onto Cypress Street and couldn't help but notice that fallen tree leaves were everywhere, especially in the street gutters. She smiled at the familiar crunching sound when she pulled up to the curb in front of the Aquavia's home.

Rose knew every inch of her Uncle Mark's home: when she was a child, the Nardellos had been frequent visitors. The home was a red brick, two-story structure set back from the street, slightly elevated above the street level. As Rose began the short walk toward the columnar porch, she smiled as she recalled the occasions when she and her two cousins, Howard and Elizabeth, would jump into piles of leaves on the front lawn. Rose didn't have to announce her arrival: her uncle Mark had been looking out of the bay window in the living room when she pulled up to the curb.

Mark and his wife Loren were standing in the doorway when she reached the entrance. Enthusiastic hugs ensued. Loren said, "Age has been good to you, Rose. You're more beautiful now then when I saw you last."

"Stop with those compliments, Aunt Loren. My head is already too big."

Mark gently took Rose's arm and led her into the house. "Loren's correct, Rose. You look marvelous. Have you lost weight?"

"Thank you, Uncle Mark. Yes, I've lost about ten pounds since Labor Day. I joined a gym."

"How frequently do you work out?"

"Three times a week after work. The gym is on my way home, so I can't make excuses."

"I remembered that you like Italian food, so I made a 12:30 p.m. reservation for us at Emily's. It's a new restaurant in East Providence. Is that okay?"

"That's fine, Uncle Mark." Turning to Loren, Rose said, "I hope you don't mind me taking your husband away for a few hours on a Sunday, Aunt Loren."

Loren smiled. "Not a problem, young lady. We'll have time to visit when you return."

While Mark was introducing himself to the restaurant hostess, Rose surveyed the interior of Emily's Restaurant. The building had been the East Providence branch of the Rhode Island National Bank until the bank moved into a larger building to accommodate an expanding base of customers. Emily Proctor bought the old bank building and transformed it into a restaurant. She retained a financial theme, however: murals of different types of financial transactions were painted on the walls, and cloth statuettes of bank clerks and bank related signs were strategically positioned throughout. By employing her imaginative flare, Emily transformed the old bank built-ins into key restaurant features: the old vault was reconfigured into a private dining area for families, for small groups of friends, or small business meetings; the stand-up teller stations became the restaurant bar; and the drive-through station became a pick-up location for take out orders.

Mark asked, "Do you like it, Rose?"

"What a marvelous idea. It's wonderful." Pointing to the old vault, Rose said, "Having lunch in the vault must be a hoot."

"You're right. It's fun. To make eating in the vault even more entertaining, Emily developed a game that involves the old safe deposit boxes. Customers can win free meals if they can guess the location of 'secret' documents in one of the boxes. Emily presents a series of clues with each menu. It's a lot of fun, especially for a family."

Rose ordered a Cobb salad, chopped and mixed the way she liked it. Mark ordered a chicken salad and two glasses of chardonnay. For over an hour they nibbled on the salads, sipped wine, and recalled many happy times that the two families shared holidays together.

"Well, young lady, I think we've had enough of this mindless chatter. You didn't drive all the way over here just to have lunch with me. What's on your mind?"

Rose leaned forward and placed her elbows on the table. "I need to talk with you about Dad. He's depressed about something. The day before yesterday I drove over to Pawtucket with a Riverside homicide detective to meet with a few state officials. While I was in town, I visited with a friend of mine who also happens to be one of Dad's key employees. She told me she thought that Dad was upset about a run-in he'd had with Winston Osborne, the C.E.O. of the Diesel Engine Corporation. I dismissed the idea initially. But it turns out that Rita was partially right."

Rose leaned back in her chair. "Apparently, Osborne blackmailed Dad into helping him. He threatened to cancel a very important contract between Nardello Trucking and D.E.C. that has existed for years unless Dad helped him find a thug to put the fear of God into a competitor. I'm beginning to think that Osborne wanted to do more than frighten someone, Uncle Mark."

Mark's facial expression changed. His smile turned into a frown and his eyes seemed to take on a menacing look.

Rose sighed. "Dad told me about the meeting that you and he had recently. He said that he asked you to help him satisfy Osborne's request. I need to know what you talked about and who you contacted." When Rose realized that she'd touched a nerve, an overwhelming sadness enveloped her, and a frightening thought crossed her mind. *Could her father and uncle have had something to do with Dr. Simpkins' death?* She shivered and looked away, and then reached for her briefcase. She retrieved a sheaf of documents held together by a large paper clip.

"I want to read something, Uncle Mark, and then I'd like you to comment. 'It is a Federal crime or offense for anyone to conspire or agree with someone else to do something which, if actually carried out, would amount to another Federal crime of offense.'" She stopped reading and reinserted the papers into her briefcase.

Mark stared at Rose for a few moments, and then forced a laugh. "I know what conspiracy is, Rose. Why did you read that definition?"

"A five-year old boy died recently because he involuntarily inhaled chemical poisons emitted from diesel engines manufactured by the Diesel Engine Corporation. The city of Riverside retained Dr. Julius Simpkins, a nationally recognized authority on vehicle emissions, to help the city prepare a class action lawsuit against D.E.C. and help the family of the boy prepare a wrongful death claim against D.E.C. That consultant was killed a few weeks ago. All indications point to premeditated murder."

Mark was able to force his body to relax. "I'm sorry to hear that, but you haven't answered my question. Why did you read the conspiracy definition?"

"Because I'm concerned about what you and Dad may have discussed and who you contacted."

"I'll say this as lovingly as I can, Rose. Please don't take offense, but it's none of your damn business what your father and I talked about, or who I contacted as a result."

Her jaw dropped, but she was able to recover her composure within seconds. She became defiant and leaned forward. "That's where you are dead wrong, Uncle Mark. As an administrative officer of the city of Riverside, it is my duty to try to find out why Dr. Simpkins was murdered and who murdered him."

Mark was visibly angry, but his anger was muted by discomfort. Could the murder of Dr. Simpkins have had anything to do with his telephone call to Paul DeCurcio?

"Listen, and listen carefully, young lady. Until I saw a story in the Providence Journal about Dr. Simpkins death, I'd never heard of the man. So why are you talking with me about him?"

"I'll ask you again, Uncle Mark. Who did you contact after you talked with Dad?"

Mark slapped the table with his open palm and said, "I think you've forgotten who you're talking to. You're way out of line! The lunch is over." Mark stood up, plucked the bill off the table, turned, and began to walk toward the cashier. He stopped abruptly, spun around, and returned to the table. He leaned over and within inches of Rose's face, whispered, "Back off, Rose. I advise you not to dig any deeper. Your family's health could be at risk." Mark straightened, turned and walked to the cashier's station.

They returned to the Aquavia home without saying a word to each other. Rose kept the engine running while Mark got out. As Mark was about to slam the door, she said, "I'm sorry I upset you, Uncle Mark."

Mark leaned into the car and said, "Heed my advice young lady. Don't push your luck."

Mark had an uncomfortable feeling that his niece may have stumbled onto something that could be very embarrassing, and might even be a serious threat to his law practice. But, before he could defend himself, he had to learn the nature of the threat. He placed a call to Paul DeCurcio.

"Why, hello, Mark. This is a pleasant surprise. How's that lovely wife of yours?"

"Hold the goodwill crap, Paul. You may not think it's so pleasant after I tell you why I'm calling. I just had lunch with my niece, Rose Nardello, Mario's daughter. She's a senior administrator with the city of Riverside,

Connecticut." Mark breathed deeply. "What do you know about a Dr. Julius Simpkins, Paul?"

"Doctor who?"

"Dr. Julius Simpkins. He was a consultant retained by the city of Riverside to help them prepare lawsuits against the Diesel Engine Corporation."

"I never heard of the guy. You used the word 'was.' Is that a significant part of this conversation, Mark?"

"My niece told me that Simpkins was murdered a few weeks ago. The Riverside police are beginning to suspect that someone at D.E.C. may have had something to do with his demise. I think you and I had better have a talk."

"Wait a damn minute. Why are you telling *me* this?"

"Because I asked you to do me a favor awhile ago, remember? Mario said a business friend of his needed to put the fear of God into a competitor. You agreed to call someone and arrange for him to meet with that someone. Since I didn't hear from you, I assumed that you were able to take care of Mario's request. I'm beginning to have a bad feeling about this, Paul. That damn phone call may come back and bite us. What I need to know is whom did you talk with and should I be worried?"

The silence on the other end of the line was deafening. It was a clear indication that the answer to his question would not be pleasant. Mark began to perspire. "Paul, are you still there?"

DeCurcio whispered, "I called Tony Summa."

"Shit!" Mark pounded his desk. He correctly surmised that if Summa were involved, the unfortunate target would have undoubtedly experienced physical harm: violence was just part of Tony Summa's nature. To make matters worse, Summa wouldn't have cared whether or not the violence was a crime. The man had no conscience. "When can we meet, Paul?"

"Let's meet in my office in 30 minutes."

43

Following the contentious meeting with her uncle, unpleasant images dominated Rose's thoughts during the drive back to Riverside. She was so distressed she was on the verge of hyperventilating. The confrontation with her uncle had reinforced her suspicion that Mark Aquavia and her father were involved in something onerous, something that could possibly destroy careers and family reputations. She visualized her father being arrested, handcuffed and locked up in a prison cell, and the family's good name being pillaged in the press.

Rose pulled off the road, parked on the shoulder, and began to pace back and forth next to the vehicle. When she finally regained control of her emotions, she stopped pacing, closed her eyes, and leaned her arms against the roof of the car. Rose could only speculate about what had happened between her father and her uncle, and she knew from experience that speculation without facts was a dangerous road to travel. To make matters worse, she hadn't the slightest idea of how to go about uncovering the facts. Rose concluded that she had only one option: go back to Pawtucket and extract the facts from her father. She climbed into the car, made a U-turn, and drove east.

Mario was raking leaves in the front yard when Rose parked at the curb. When Rose stepped out of the car, he stopped and leaned on the rake. "What brings you back so soon, honey? Did you forget something?"

"No. It was a spur of the moment decision to come back. I was uncomfortable with our last conversation, Dad. I think you and I need to talk some more."

"Oh. That could be a problem if you mean you want to talk about Winston Osborne."

"Don't prejudge my questions even before you hear them, Dad. Give me a little slack. Should we talk inside, or would you rather sit on the porch?"

"On the porch. You go in and say hello to your mother while I put my tools away. Ask her to make a pitcher of iced tea."

The Nardellos used their screened-in porch extensively: spring, summer, and fall. It was a long and narrow, bright space that ran across the entire width of the house. The space was bright because it was predominately white: the inner wall and trim were white, and most of the furnishings were white whicker. A two-seat swing, covered with a bright red and blue fabric, dominated one end, and a large plant rack filled with a variety of colorful flower pots occupied most of the space at the other end of the porch.

Rose was already seated when Mario climbed the front stairs, pushed open the screen door and sat down next to his daughter. She didn't hesitate. "Here's my dilemma, Dad. Although I'm not a police officer, I am temporarily assigned to the department." Rose leaned forward. "Because of that responsibility, I can't just ignore what you told me about Osborne." Rose leaned back and folded her arms across her chest. "I drove over from Riverside this morning and had lunch with Uncle Mark. I asked him about the meeting you and he had a few weeks back."

Mario leaned back. His eyes glazed over and his face turned red with anger. He didn't make a sound for a few moments. He stood up and nervously walked to the end of the porch. He turned around and said, "I asked you not to do that, Rose. What did Mark say?"

"Essentially nothing. He just got angry and walked out of the restaurant."

"I'll bet Mark called Paul DeCurcio the moment you left."

"Who's Paul DeCucio?"

"He's the treasurer of the local Teamsters union. I may have a serious problem, Rose."

"Did you meet with this man DeCucio, too?"

"Yes."

"Who else did you meet with, Dad?"

Mario hung his head and mumbled, "Tony Summa."

"The crime boss here in Providence? My God! We can't waste time by playing footsy with each other. You're going to have to be honest with me. Did you meet with anyone else after you talked with Summa?"

"No, but Summa arranged for someone to talk with Osborne. The contact approached Osborne on a busy street down in Newport. That's why Osborne was so upset when he barged into my office and frightened Rita. I don't know any more than that, Rose."

While Rose was wrestling with the question of whether or not she should tell Joe Godfrey about her father's agreement to help Winston Osborne, Mark Aquavia, and Paul DeCurcio were grappling with their own problems. Within 30 minutes of Mark's telephone call, the two men were meeting at DeCurcio's office at union headquarters. They began their discussion by reviewing what they knew about Mario Nardello's initial request for help. Mark said, "I know Mario. He wouldn't threaten or hurt anyone unless he was really provoked or threatened. Hurting another person for no good reason would be totally out of character. My read on the situation is that Mario was somehow coerced into contacting me. He wasn't the one that wanted an enforcer. He was just a messenger, Paul. But that leaves us with the question, if it wasn't Mario who wanted the enforcer, who the hell was it?" Neither man could recall if Mario had spoken of a specific person during their meetings with him. Mario mentioned only that he was trying to help a business friend. They decided that they'd also have to confront Mario and "persuade" him to talk.

Paul admitted that he hadn't given his decision to call Tony Summa very much thought. In hindsight, it was probably a mistake. He said that he'd automatically thought of Summa because the man had a reputation of being an efficient enforcer and would do anything for a buck. Summa was ruthless but also unpredictable: it was rumored that Summa had already killed three people.

Although it was a repugnant thought, both men agreed that the first order of business was to approach Summa to find out if there was a connection between Mario Nardello's effort to find an enforcer and the subsequent assassination of Dr. Julius Simpkins in Riverside. If there were a connection, they'd have to convince Summa to eliminate that connection immediately. Mark was beginning to understand why his niece had read aloud the definition of a conspiracy while they were having lunch. Mark smiled to himself. *That Rose is a smart young woman. I'd better have another talk with her.*

Mark Aquavia and Paul DeCurcio were escorted by one of Tony Summa's bodyguards along an elaborately decorated hallway and into a book filled office. It was the first time that either man had visited Summa's home. Mark, an amateur art collector himself, was surprised by the quality of the art work hanging on the walls of the hallway. Summa's choice of paintings showed his deep interest and affinity for the sea and his loyalty to local artists. Mark knew some of the artists personally and was fully aware of their talent. If he hadn't been preoccupied with a potentially devastating problem, he would have stopped and studied the works more carefully.

Tony Summa was seated in recliner watching the daily stock market report on his big screen television when they entered. He paid no attention to the visitors. Mark thought, *This guy's got to be one big contradiction.* Paul walked over and stood in front of the TV blocking Summa's view of the screen. "What the hell are you trying to do, DeCurcio, piss me off? If you are, you're doing a pretty good job." Summa gave Paul his usual steely-eyed stare, but Paul didn't back off.

"We have a problem, Tony. Mario Nardello told his daughter that he met with you and asked for your help. He asked you to find someone to do a little 'persuading" for a price."

"So what if he did? Who gives a shit? It's a free country and his daughter ain't the fuzz."

Summa kept watching the television while Mark and Paul looked at each other. DeCurcio nodded. Mark cleared his throat and said, "Not exactly, Tony."

Summa bolted upright in his chair and turned toward Mark. "What the hell do you mean, not exactly."

"A few weeks ago, a Dr. Simpkins was whacked on a Riverside, Connecticut, street, in broad daylight. Dr. Simpkins was working for the city, helping prepare a couple of lawsuits against a Pawtucket company, the Diesel Engine Corporation. Paul and I put two and two together, Tony, and we think it was your man who wasted Dr. Simpkins. My niece works for the city of Riverside. She's one of the managers over there. She's helping the Riverside Police find the person who whacked the doctor."

Summa tried to stare down Mark. "I never heard of a Doctor what's-his-name. What you're saying is strictly bullshit."

Paul moved forward and said, "We don't think so, Tony." Summa turned his stare on Paul, but Paul didn't flinch. "You'd make a lousy actor, Tony. Who did it?"

Summa's facial expression slowly changed from defiance to a sinister smile. "The guy who did it is an ex-F.B.I. agent. He was paid good money to do the job." He leaned back and added, "I guess I'd better do a little house cleaning."

Paul said, "We agree: the sooner, the better, Tony. In the meantime, what are we gonna do about Mark's niece? We can't let her talk with the police."

"I'll send someone to have a talk with her. I'll make sure she understands what's at stake. When I finish with her, it'll be crystal clear that if she talks to anyone about my conversation with her father, he's history." Summa turned back to the TV.

Mark barked, "What does that mean, 'when I finish with her'?"

"I intend to scare the living shit out of her, that's what I mean. Maybe I'll give her the name of the guy who paid for the kill, but no more. Now get the fuck out of my house. I don't want to hear any more about Riverside, doctors, Mario Nardello, or nieces."

44

Dom DeCarlo didn't bring good news to the meeting with Joe Godfrey. A second search of F.B.I.'s computerized D.N.A. file produced the same result as the first: it identified an F.B.I. agent, Robert Alphonse Cicci, as the person who smoked the cigar. Although Joe continued to believe the search had to be faulty, he agreed with Rocco that they couldn't ignore the finding any longer: they had to investigate this Cicci person. Rocco suggested that Joe challenge the persuasive skills of young Jack Clark to obtain a copy of Cicci's personnel file from F.B.I. headquarters in Washington. If that didn't work, Rocco said that he might have to employ his considerable political influence with the U.S. congressman from Western Connecticut to obtain the file.

It took Clark six phone calls, but the young man was able to cajole, and finally persuade, the supervisor of records at F.B.I. headquarters in Washington to fax him a copy of Cicci's personnel file. Joe found that the file was replete with contradictions: commendations for bravery interspersed with reprimands for brutality that Cicci exhibited during arrests. He surmised that the latter problem may have served as the basis for the man's numerous transfers. He reread the file a second time. The image of an F.B.I. agent with a sadistic streak began to hatch in Joe's mind, and he began to write notes in the margins.

Three items in particular stood out and provoked his curiosity. Point one: while stationed in Chicago, Cicci had been a member of the F.B.I.'s elite sniper team. Point two: Cicci was transferred to the Boston Field Office only one year before he retired. Point three: Cicci retired early for no explained reason. Joe wondered. Had he been offered a more lucrative job with a private security firm? Godfrey had to find out. He initiated a call to the chief of the Boston Field Office.

Godfrey's conversation with Elliot Dirksen, manager of the F.B.I.'s Boston Field Office, proved to be considerably more productive then he'd hoped. Dirksen was more than forthcoming with his remarks. He seemed genuinely proud that he and Robert Cicci detested each other and that he forced Cicci into retirement. In spite of his obvious dislike for the man, Dirksen reluctantly admitted that, on balance, Cicci was a good agent. Dirksen also confirmed that Cicci was an avid cigar smoker.

"Do you know what Cicci has been doing for a living since he left the F.B.I., Mr. Dirksen?"

"The resident agent in Providence told me just the other day that Cicci was working as a body guard and general handy man for a Rhode Island mobster by the name of Tony Summa." Dirksen summarized what he knew about Tony Summa. "Summa's crime family limits its activities to Rhode Island, but concentrates on the Providence/Pawtucket area. I can't imagine why you'd find one of Cicci's cigars in Riverside."

"What can you tell me about his expertise with a rifle? The file shows that he was a marksman."

"Cicci was one of the best. He was especially effective during hostage situations." Dirksen sighed, "Cicci has killed two people that I'm aware of, Sergeant, but only in the line of duty. He killed to protect other agents."

"Something else caught my attention when I read through his file, Mr. Dirksen. While he was assigned to the Chicago field office, he infiltrated a narcotics organization. His undercover work resulted in the breakup of the largest drug distributor in Chicago. The file says he received a commendation. What can you tell me about that?"

"I didn't use him on undercover assignments, so my answer is strictly second hand. He had a reputation as one of the best disguise artists in the Bureau. In my opinion, Robert Cicci is a frustrated actor."

"Thank you, Mr. Dirksen. I'll keep in touch."

Rose knocked on the open door to City Manager Frank Mancuso's office. "Got a minute, Frank?"

"Come on in and have a seat, Rose. Did you have a productive trip to Rhode Island last week?"

"We did. Remember the match book cover from a North Attleboro diner that the police found on the top level of the parking garage?" Frank nodded. "Joe and I had breakfast at that diner on Tuesday. One of the waitresses told us that one of her cigar-smoking customers announced about a month ago that he was going on a business trip. She didn't recall seeing the guy during the time Dr. Simpkins was visiting Riverside. It's a real long shot, Frank. But, think about it. How many customers of a North Attleboro diner are apt to leave a match book cover in a parking garage in Riverside? Joe thought that was too much of a coincidence to ignore. He's arranged for two of his guys to watch the place for a few days and see what happens."

Rose leaned forward and placed a document on Frank's desk. "I completed the D.E.C. report. That company is a puzzle, Frank. They continue to thumb their noses at most state and federal regulations promulgated to control harmful emissions. They've even violated local ordinances. There's a copy of a letter from the Pawtucket city attorney accusing D.E.C. of dumping chemicals into the local sewer system. Although on paper D.E.C. has the appearance of being a valued employer in Rhode Island and a good corporate citizen, I think otherwise."

"Good work. I'll read it while I eat lunch. Then I'll fax a copy to Jason Roberts in New York."

Joe Godfrey's watch read 10:30 when he, Dom DeCarlo, and young Jack Clark pulled up to the curb in front in front of Sam's Diner in two unmarked police cars. The two vehicles had caravanned from Riverside with Joe and young Jack Clark in one car, and Dom in the other. Joe planned to leave one vehicle in North Attleboro with Clark and DeCarlo. He intended to use the second car to visit a few more tobacco shops in the Providence area.

Dressed in casual attire—loafers, sport shirt and slacks—Joe entered Sam's Diner and was greeted by the waitress, Agnes. "Well, if it ain't the policeman from Connecticut. How you been?"

"Good morning, Agnes. I'm glad you remember me. Have you seen our cigar smoking friend since we were here last week?"

"No, he hasn't come in during my shift."

"Is Rick here?"

"He's in the kitchen. I'll get him. "

Rick exited the kitchen and walked toward Joe wiping his hands on an apron. "Good morning, Sergeant"

"Good morning, Rick. We're ready to start our surveillance this morning. The North Attleboro police will cover the first shift tomorrow morning. Two men will alternate shifts: four hours on and four hours off. That should cover the entire time the diner is open. Were you able to explain our plan to the waitress who relieves Agnes?"

"Yeah, I talked with her day before yesterday. Like I told you last week, Sergeant, if there's the slightest hint of trouble, I'll have to cut off our cooperation immediately."

"I understand, Rick. We'll try to be invisible."

Just after noon on the second day of the surveillance, Robert "Phonz" Cicci pushed open the front door, walked to the smoking section, and sat down at a table. Young Jack Clark was sleepy. He was finishing the fourth hour of his shift. He turned the key in the ignition and tuned the car radio to National Public Radio station to listen to the news. He raised his arms above his head to stretch, yawned, and glanced for the umpteenth time at the sign in the window of the diner. His arms dropped immediately, and he mumbled, "Shit!" The sign had been turned upside down. Clark pulled out his cell phone and called Dom DeCarlo, who was asleep in a motel room three blocks away.

"You stay put, Jack. I'll walk. If he leaves before I get there, get a picture of the guy so we can make a positive I.D. Get his license plate number, too. How many cars are in the lot right now?"

"Six."

"Write down the plate numbers of all six. While you're at it, describe each car: color, make and model. I'll be there as quick as I can."

Clark kept shifting his eyes back and forth from watching the front door of the diner to checking to see if the sign had been turned. At approximately 1:15 p.m., Clark thought he recognized the man that was descending the front stairs of the diner. He quickly checked the photo from the F.B.I. file, but he still wasn't sure it was Cicci. Just then, the sign was turned to the upright position. *Son of a bitch! That's gotta be him.* Clark looked around to see if he could see DeCarlo. No such luck. *Damn it! Come on, Dom. Hurry up. I don't want to do this alone.* Cicci walked over to the only BMW in the lot and unlocked the door. But, instead of sliding into the driver's seat, he leaned his back against the driver's side door, pulled a cell phone out of a small pouch on his belt, and made a call.

DeCarlo arrived just in time to see Cicci clip the phone back on his belt and slide into the driver's seat. DeCarlo quietly opened the driver's side door of the unmarked and slid in. He and Clark watched as Cicci left the parking lot heading east. Clark was already on the phone talking to Joe Godfrey when DeCarlo pulled away from the curb and began to tail the target.

Cicci drove less than ten blocks before his F.B.I. experience kicked in: he recognized that he was being followed. *Amateurs,* he thought. He executed a quick right turn, a left turn, another two quick rights, and pulled into an alley behind a gas station and parked. He waited. The car that had been following him was no longer in sight. Cicci smiled. He was proud of himself: he could still elude a tail with a few simple moves. He remained parked in the alley for several minutes, contemplating the significance of the tail. He concluded that it had to be a rookie North Attleboro policeman who was pursuing him, probably for some minor traffic violation that he didn't even know he'd committed.

Dom shouted, "Shit! I lost him, Jack. I don't know how I screwed up. He must have realized that he was being followed and took evasive action. Joe isn't gonna to be happy about this. Thank goodness you got a picture of the guy and a license plate number. Call headquarters and have someone track down the owner of that BMW."

Joe Godfrey leaned over the counter and watched as Angela Capaldo, wife of the owner of Mike's Tobacco Shop, described the six customers who frequently purchased Sinatra cigars. He was about to ask a question, when his cell phone rang. He straightened and said, "Please excuse me, Mrs. Capaldo. I should answer this call." He unclipped the phone from his belt and said, "Joe Godfrey." He didn't say a word during Jack Clark's account of the botched tail, but Mrs. Capaldo noticed that his facial expression changed dramatically from a broad smile to a frown. "Thanks for calling, Jack. I can't talk right now. Meet me at Sam's Diner in an hour."

"Something wrong, Sergeant?"

"No, nothing that can't be repaired, Mrs. Capaldo. Thanks for asking. Where were we?" Joe returned his phone to his belt and leaned forward. "Tell me more about these six men, Mrs. Capaldo."

"Normally, my husband waits on our customers, but I'll tell you what I know. I believe that four of the men are retired and live in that senior's complex down the street. A fifth is a banker and works for Pawtucket Savings Bank. I don't know much about the sixth man except the name, Robert Cicci. He's a heavy cigar smoker. He comes in, maybe once every three to four weeks and buys a full box of Sinatras. Mike told me he lives in a small town west of here."

"Can you describe this one, Mrs. Capaldo?" pointing to Robert Cicci's name.

"Oh, that man. He's the handsome one. He may have been an athlete when he was younger: slim waist and broad shoulders. Has the look of someone whose parents or grandparents came from the Mediterranean: dark skin, black hair, and," she giggled, "that ever-present five o'clock shadow. He looks like he needs a shave every time I see him."

As Joe was writing down Cicci's address in Quaddick, Connecticut, he asked, "How is it that you have this man's address?"

"We mail a flyer to our customers every month notifying them of special offers and sales."

Joe placed the notebook in his pocket and prepared to leave. "Thanks, Mrs. Capaldo. You've been a big help. Here's my card. If you think of anything else, please call me."

DeCarlo and Clark were sitting in their unmarked police car across the street from Sam's Diner when Joe pulled up and parked behind them. He climbed into the back seat of their car and announced, "Don't worry about the botched tail. I was able to get the home address of our cigar-smoking friend. The wife of the owner of Mike's Tobacco Shop in East Providence gave it to me." Two very relieved detectives listened as Joe explained how he'd obtained Cicci's address. "The pieces are beginning to fall into place, gentlemen. I may be overly optimistic, but I think Dr. Simpkins' killer is a retired F.B.I. agent that goes by the name of Robert Cicci."

Dom turned around and said, "Joe, I don't mean to be disrespectful, but aren't you jumping the gun? I find it hard to believe that an F.B.I. agent would turn so quickly."

Joe patiently summarized the evidence collected thus far, and then like frosting on a cake, recounted his conversation with the chief of the F.B.I.'s Boston field office. "Dirksen told me Cicci was a sharpshooter and a master of disguises. He was also a hot head. He and Dirksen hated each other. Cicci may have flipped because he was angry about being pushed out of the Bureau. I may be off base, Dom, but my gut is telling me that Cicci is the guy. I'm going to call Rocco and suggest we meet the D.A. I can't see any reason for us to stay over here in North Attleboro any longer. You can go ahead and head back. I'm going into the diner and thank everyone before I take off."

45

Following a few introductory remarks, Police Chief Tarencelli turned toward Joe Godfrey. "Sergeant Godfrey will present the evidence collected so far."

Joe leaned forward. "Ms. Anderson…"

"Please, call me Caroline, Sergeant. I'll call you Joe. No need to be formal. We're just reviewing the evidence to see if it's strong enough to take to the Grand Jury."

Smiling, Joe said, "I appreciate that, Caroline." The Riverside district attorney returned the smile. For the next half hour, Joe Godfrey systematically presented evidence to support his opinion that Robert Cicci, a former F.B.I. agent, was Dr. Simpkins' killer. He reviewed what the police had found at the Elm Street Parking Garage: a matchbook cover from Sam's Diner in North Attleboro, Massachusetts; a cigar band from a Sinatra brand cigar produced by the Johnson Cigar Company; and a cigar butt. He read the report from the State Laboratory in Hartford about their D.N.A. analysis of the saliva from the partially smoked cigar, and summarized the content of Cicci's personnel file obtained from F.B.I. headquarters in Washington. At the conclusion of his remarks, he slid an 8" x 10" of Cicci across the conference table.

"Yesterday, Detective Desmond showed this photo to a young woman who covers the check-in desk at the Holiday Inn, the one at Exit 64, just off Route 10. The young woman recognized the man in the photograph immediately. Robert Cicci had asked her to put a rather bulky envelope in the hotel safe for a few days. She remembered because she thought maybe the envelope contained a large amount of cash." Joe chuckled. "I'm sure a request like that doesn't happen very often at a Holiday Inn."

DIESEL DEATH

District Attorney Anderson closed her notepad and said, "I think I've heard enough, Rocco. Sergeant Godfrey has been thorough and convincing. Thank you, Sergeant. I'll call the Grand Jury into session within a few days and ask for an indictment. You said this Cicci lives in the village of Quaddick in eastern Connecticut. That's a rural area, as I recall. If I'm not mistaken, the only law enforcement presence in that part of the state is the State Police. I suggest you contact them right away. Undoubtedly, they will have to accompany you when try to arrest our friend Mr. Cicci."

Tony Summa telephoned Cicci at his unlisted number and left a message. "Phonz, it's Tony. Call me. I've got another assignment." Cicci returned the call the following morning and arranged to meet at 9:00 p.m. at Summa's 44-four foot yacht docked at a marina in North Kingston. Phonz knew the area well: Summa had hosted a Labor Day celebration on the yacht for members of his so-called "family." Cicci smiled when he recalled the raucous affair. Tony hired a group of sparsely clad dancing girls to circulate on the decks, showed porno films in the salon, provided drugs, and served every alcoholic beverage imaginable.

Phonz couldn't recall the last time he'd felt as relaxed as he was this evening. Working for Tony Summa had turned out to be more financially rewarding than he'd anticipated. He'd already put away $45,000 from the first assignment, and now Tony was talking about a second assignment. Maybe he'd accumulate enough money to purchase the country house in Quaddick that he'd been renting for the past two years. He inserted a Tony Bennett CD in the car stereo. Although he had a tin ear and couldn't carry a tune in a bucket, Phonz couldn't resist the temptation to sing along when the disc reached "I Left My Heart in San Francisco."

Cicci's watch read a little after 8:00 p.m. when he turned into the marina parking lot and locked the car. He walked across a suspended gangplank that led to the floating docks and boat slips, turned right, and strolled toward Summa's boat. It was a quiet walk. The only audible sounds came from his leather healed shoes hitting the wood planks of the dock, the sound of small waves bouncing off the hulls of boats in the slips, and clacking halyards against the masts of the sail boats. During the summer months, people would be milling about on the docks tending to chores or relaxing with a drink on their boats. Not tonight. Phonz didn't encounter a single person or see one boat light turned on as he walked to the end of the dock. Boating activities tended to slow down to a crawl in October.

In contrast to the darkness everywhere else in the marina, Summa's boat was lit up like a Christmas tree. Phonz stopped when he reached the foot of a gangplank and called out, "Tony it's Phonz. Should I come aboard?"

"Yeah, we're in the salon. Do you want a drink?"

"A scotch sounds good." Cicci was surprised to find that his host was not alone when he entered the salon. Two members of Tony's organization from Providence were with him. "You remember Angelo and Ernie."

"I met you guys at the Labor Day party." He shook hands and sat down opposite Tony.

"Ernie, fix Phonz a scotch. Did you get a look at that sky tonight, Phonz? It's magnificent, filled with stars. We think we saw the shuttle pass over about an hour ago."

"There must be millions of stars. When I stopped at the foot of the gangplank, I was able to locate the Big Dipper. It was as clear as a bell. I hadn't taken time to look for the Big Dipper since I was a kid."

After a few moments of small talk, Tony said, "Phonz, we have a problem with that job you did over in Riverside."

Cicci stiffened and sat up straight. His senses were immediately alerted to possible trouble. With his keen peripheral vision he located Angelo and Ernie, and rubbed the inside of his arm against a holstered revolver under a sweater. "What kind of a problem, Tony?"

Tony gestured with his hand. "Angelo, Ernie, go take a pee, or go out on the deck and enjoy the stars."

When they were alone, Tony described what had transpired prior assigning Cicci the task of eliminating Dr. Simpkins and the individuals involved. "Mario Nardello owns a trucking company here in Pawtucket. He's been in business for years and his company is a staunch supporter of the Teamsters. Paul DeCurcio is the union treasurer. I've known Paul since high school, and he's still one of my best friends. Mark Aquavia is one of the lawyers the union retains during labor negotiations." Tony smiled. "He's defended me on a few occasions when I had minor skirmishes with the local fuzz. Here's the problem, Phonz. When I agreed to help Nardello, I didn't know that his daughter worked for the city of Riverside or that she's Aquavia's niece." Tony stood up and began to gesture with his hands. "It turns out that this Nardello broad not only works for the city, she's one of the managers. I talked with Aquavia and DeCurcio yesterday. Apparently, the Nardello broad is beginning to suspect that her father and uncle were somehow involved with Simpkins' death. If she noses around much more, she's bound to find out that I was involved. I can't let that happen, Phonz. We need to convince her to keep quiet."

"It sounds like you have a plan, Tony."

"I'm building one. But it ain't complete. You wore a disguise when you met with Osborne, right?"

"Yeah, I used two different ones."

"If Osborne walked onto this boat tonight, would he recognize you?"

Cicci smiled. "Not a chance, Tony. My disguises are good. I was one of the F.B.I.'s best make up men."

"Good. Here's what I'm thinking."

46

Rose left the City Center parking garage at 5:30 p.m. and began the half hour drive to her apartment in Westwood. She was a careful driver: her father taught her to be cautious and defensive when operating a motor vehicle. He'd emphasized that to be accident free, she needed to be aware of her surroundings at all times. Even a minor distraction could be devastating. Rose was aware that his advise would be especially true this evening: her stress level was unusually high. The City Council had suggested that she and City Attorney Barry Sandler travel to New York to visit with Jason Roberts to approve the final drafts of the two lawsuits against the Diesel Engine Corporation before they were filed. The disagreement with her father over the Winston Osborne affair only exacerbated her level of stress.

Jason Roberts had faxed draft copies of the lawsuits to Riverside late that afternoon, but Rose had only enough time for a cursory review. Studying the documents at home was out of the question: she had a dinner date with Jerry Nichols. Reviewing the documents in the morning was also out of the question: she and Sandler were meeting at the Railroad Station in Stamford at 7:00 a.m. The only time Rose could concentrate on the content of the draft documents would be on the train or during the drive home.

Rose placed a tablet of yellow lined paper on the passenger seat to record notes, ideas, and questions as she drove. She was keenly aware that writing notes as she drove would violate everything her father had taught her, but she had no other alternative. She allowed her concentration to drift from defensive driving to thinking about the documents. The east/west route to her home was mostly straight, but it did include a few nasty curves and hills: passing slow moving vehicles could be an adventure. Trees along both sides of the road restricted the view of oncoming traffic, especially when navigating a curve or ascending a hill. As thoughts about the draft documents kept flowing through her mind, she kept shifting her attention from writing notes on the tablet, to her driving, and then back to the tablet again.

When Rose finally noticed that the broken yellow line at the center of the road had changed to a solid line, the road was beginning a gradual curve to the left. She looked in her rear view mirror and saw a car sitting on her tail. The automobile had caught up with her and was now just a few yards behind. Rose sat up straight. She refocused her attention on the road and the tailgating vehicle. Within seconds, the vehicle was along side her car. Her peripheral vision caught sight of the driver. It was a man and he was looking at her. When Rose turned her head to return the look, the driver smiled, and flipped her off. When Rose returned her attention to the road wondering why he'd done that, she saw a truck begin to round the curve and approach in the opposite lane. She realized immediately that a head on collision would result unless the truck driver, or the driver of the vehicle passing her, took evasive action. Rose gripped the steering wheel with such intensity that her knuckles turned white.

The truck slowed, and moved off the road onto the shoulder. Rose braked, but when she did, the rear end of her car fishtailed slightly to the right. The passing vehicle sped by and nudged the left end of the Rose's front bumper, causing her to lose control. Her car left the road and bounced along the grassy shoulder for over 30 yards before she could position her foot on the brake pedal and regain control, stopping only inches from a massive tree. Rose couldn't move. She just sat looking at the tree with her mouth open.

Cicci saw the truck begin to round the curve and realized that he had only one choice: exit the lane he was in as quickly as possible or face eternity. He swore as he took evasive action pressing the accelerator to the floor and turning the steering wheel to his right. He felt the impact of his rear end colliding with Rose's front end, but was able maintain control and reenter the appropriate lane.

The oncoming truck had thwarted his clever plan: he'd wanted to give the girl an unambiguous message. After giving her the finger, he was going to force her off the road. He slapped the steering wheel, swore again, and sped west. When he reached the next major intersection, he turned south, and pulled into the first gas station he encountered. He parked behind the building, shut off the engine, and contemplated his next move.

The truck driver ran across the road yelling, "Get out of the car! Get out of the car!" Rose opened the driver's side door, released her seat belt, and slowly climbed out. She stumbled and nearly fell. She leaned against the driver's door to regain her equilibrium.

"Are you alright, lady?" Rose looked around, and nodded. The truck driver helped her walk to the tree and gently lowered her into a sitting position with her back against the tree. "Should I call 911, lady?"

"No. I'll be all right. Just let me sit for a minute."

"Can you believe it? The son-of-a-bitch just kept going. It happened so fast I didn't see the guy's license plate number. I'd better go back to my truck and call the State Police. Will you be okay while I make the phone call?"

"Please don't call the police. I don't have time to talk with them. The car is undamaged and I live only a few miles down the road."

"Okay. You're the boss. But I think I'd better stick around and make sure the car will start."

"Thank you, sir." Rose stood up and added, "I'll be fine." The man helped her walk back to her car. She thanked him, climbed into her vehicle, and drove off.

Rose's hands were shaking badly when she pulled into her carport. She experienced some difficulty inserting the key into the front door lock. When the door finally opened, she stumbled in, pulled off her coat, and tossed it on the first chair she came to. Thoroughly exhausted, she flopped down on the bed on her back, and placed her arm over her eyes. She was unsure how long she lay there, reliving the accident. The thought that she could have been killed monopolized her mind. She began to shake again. When she was finally able to sit up, she remembered she had a date. *I don't feel like going out tonight. I'll call Jerry and cancel.*

Jerry Nichols understood immediately. He even volunteered to drive over and prepare dinner for the two of them.

"Thanks Jerry, but not tonight. I just want to soak in the tub and get to bed early."

"I'll take a rain check, Rose. Call me when you return from New York."

The bath water was relaxing. Rose lay her head back against a bath cushion and tried to prepare her mind for the meeting with Jason Roberts in the morning. The circumstances related to the accident, however, kept replaying in her mind. Was it an accident, or was it a deliberate attempt on her life? She was certain that the driver flipped her off when his car was along side hers. *It was a childish. Why would anyone want to do that?* As she dried off, she had another scary thought. *If the person or persons who killed Dr. Simpkins considered her a threat, would they kill again?* That possibility just added to the high level of stress she was experiencing.

47

Rose was unusually quiet during the train ride to New York City. She purchased a copy of the New York Times at the Stamford railroad station and worked the crossword puzzle until she and Barry Sanders arrived at Grand Central Station. The subject of the accident the previous evening wasn't mentioned until she and Barry were riding in a cab to the downtown offices of Roberts and Spencer. She described the hair-raising experience, and then added jokingly, "Fortunately, the damage to the front end of my car was minimal. But, with my luck, the repair cost will be less than my deductible."

Jason Roberts stood up when Rose and Barry were ushered into his office. "Welcome. We ordered rolls and coffee for you. They're in the conference room. I'm sure you had to leave home before sunrise and didn't have time for breakfast."

Rose said, "That's very thoughtful, Jason. A cup of coffee and something to eat is very appealing."

When John Dowling joined them, Sanders encouraged Rose to recount the story of her accident the previous evening. With three lawyers in the room her story elicited differing legal interpretations of what may have happened and what should be done in response. Jason Roberts checked his watch and decided it was time to move on and discuss more substantive matters. "If you're ready, let's get started." Rose sat alongside Sanders on one side of the conference table while Dowling and Roberts sat facing them. Jason said, "We have two documents for you to review." He slid one document across the table toward Rose. "The first is the Rado family's wrongful death claim. Since you're more familiar with the harmful health effects of diesel emissions and the specifics of young Robert's emphysema, I suggest you concentrate on that document, Rose. Pay particular attention to the references to the emissions data that you'll be collecting at the two monitoring stations.

The presentation of that data has to be clear and accurate. We're requesting compensation for pain and suffering, medical and funeral expenses, anticipated lifetime earnings, and punitive damages. You'll notice that we've named the city as a 'friend of the court.' Unless you uncover something that requires major revision, our goal is to file the complaint with the state court in Hartford next week.

"Barry, we'd like you to review the wording of the class action filing and the application for class certification. Pay special attention to the way we're presenting the data from the monitoring stations. The presentation must be clear and concise.

"We've designated the deceased Robert Rado as the class representative. We have him suing on behalf of the over 10,000 Riverside children under age ten. I'm a little concerned that the court will have a problem accepting Robert as class representative. We'll have to wait and see. If the court rejects him because he's deceased, we'll ask the court to allow us to name Riverside as the class representative. John and I will adjourn to my office while you're reviewing the documents. We want you both to review each document, so when you finish one, trade off."

The digital clock in the car read 7:45 p.m. when an exhausted Rose Nardello pulled into her carport. Darkness had already enveloped the village of Westwood. She unlocked the front door to her apartment, switched on the hall light, and placed her briefcase by the closet door before hanging up her coat. Unbuttoning her blouse, Rose turned and began the short walk to her bedroom.

"Welcome home, Miss Nardello."

Rose placed her hands on her cheeks and screamed.

Cicci, who'd been standing in the dark by the front door, grabbed her around the neck and placed his hand over her mouth. "Quiet! I'm not gonna hurt you, so calm down. We're just gonna have a little talk, you and me." He pulled her toward the sofa, forced her to sit and then stood over her.

Rose mumbled, "Who are you and what do you want?"

"It's not what I *want*. It's what I *don't* want. I don't want you talking with anyone about the Diesel Engine Corporation or about who your father talked with about the Diesel Engine Corporation." He bent over, moved to within a few inches of her face and looked into her eyes. "I don't think I have to elaborate." He placed his large hand on her head and squeezed. "You know exactly what I'm talking about, don't you, Miss Nardello?" When Rose didn't respond, Cicci squeezed harder. "Don't you, Miss. Nardello?" Rose nodded. "Good. Now that we understand one another, you'll keep your mouth shut, or I'll have to come back." Cicci turned and walked toward the door. He placed his hand on the knob, and then spun around and pointed a finger at Rose. "Remember what I just said, Miss Nardello. Don't talk with anyone. I don't want to hurt you or your father. Let this little encounter be a lesson: I can get to you or your father, whenever or wherever I choose." He exited as suddenly as he'd appeared.

Rose began to shake. She lowered her head into hands and sobbed. Slowly, she became aware that the chair cushion was wet: the intruder had knocked over a glass of water Rose had left on an end table the night before. Rose stood up and screamed, "Bastard!" She rushed into the kitchen, grabbed a handful of paper towels, and patted the wet spot until most of the water was absorbed. Rose shed her clothes, dropped them in a heap and stepped into the shower, where she remained until the hot water began to cool. After toweling off, she climbed into bed; pulled the covers up to her chin; and lay there with her eyes wide open, thinking about what had just transpired, and what if anything, she should do about it.

Robert Cicci entered the lobby of the Diesel Engine Corporation just before noon the following day, sporting the disguise he'd used when he met Osborne at the Newport bowling alley. He walked over to the receptionist and said authoritatively, "Tell Mr. Osborne to drop everything. His buddy from the Newport bowling alley is in the lobby to see him." The receptionist stared at him, and said, "I beg your pardon. What did you say?"

"You heard me. I'm in a hurry, lady, so get with it."

The startled secretary picked up the telephone and without taking her eyes off Cicci, called Osborne's secretary and repeated the message. She ended with, "I'll hold." While on hold she attempted to judge the importance of this rude, demanding man. A few minutes passed before she hung up the phone and said, "Mr. Osborne will be out to talk with you shortly. Please have a seat." Cicci didn't move. He remained standing in front of her desk, staring at her with a menacing smirk on his face.

Less than two minutes passed before Osborne was seen hurrying down the hallway toward the reception area. He studied the man standing before him and then said, "Let's go outside." Osborne led Cicci to a remote section of the parking lot. "You were paid the full $60,000. What the hell do you want now?"

"Is that any way to talk with an employee, Mr. Osborne? Not even a 'job well done.' Only, 'what do you want now?' That's not nice."

"I don't have time for your bullshit Mr…whatever your name is. You pulled me out of an important meeting. What do you want?"

"This won't take long. As long as you cooperate, my employer will not to talk with the police about the $60,000."

"Cooperate? What the hell does that mean?"

"I understand that you and your sister own this company, right? No other owners?" Osborne's jaw dropped, but he didn't respond. Cicci smiled. "I guess my information is correct."

"Where the hell are you going with this?"

"My employer has a daughter who just graduated from business school. She'd like to own stock in a public company and serve on its Board of Directors, but she can't seem to make up her mind about which company. My employer likes the truck business and believes Diesel Engine Corporation would make a good investment. He put those two things together and decided the Diesel Engine Corporation is the company that can satisfy both his and his daughter's desires. He believes it's time for you to take your company public. In other words, Osborne, for my employer to remain quiet, he wants a chunk of stock in your company."

Osborne's face turned red and the knuckles on his clenched fists turned white. He hissed, "Get out of here and don't come back." Osborne spun around and began to walk back to the reception area.

"I wouldn't be so hasty, Mr. Osborne. Taking your company public and pocketing huge sums of money from stock options would be a lot better than spending the rest of your life in jail." Osborne stopped dead in his tracks and whirled. He wanted to respond but couldn't think of anything to say. "You go back to your meeting, Osborne. But, after you finish your day, you'd better go talk with an investment banker. After that you'll see the virtue in what I'm suggesting." Cicci smiled again. "I want an answer next week."

Seemingly without a care in the world, Cicci strolled toward his car, leaving Osborne standing alone in the parking lot with fists clenched, ready to explode.

48

It was considered a long shot when Rose first proposed it, but in the end her initiative proved successful. Exploiting his considerable political influence, City Manager Frank Mancuso arranged a meeting with Connecticut's governor. Frank, Chief Rocco Tarencelli, and District Attorney Caroline Anderson traveled to Hartford on a Friday afternoon.

The Riverside D.A. didn't pull any punches: as soon as everyone was seated, she requested that governor commit the Connecticut State Police to help the Riverside police capture Dr. Simpkins murderer, dead or alive. She was very persuasive. Her argument was based on the evidence Sergeant Godfrey provided. After an hour long briefing, the governor committed the State Police without hesitation.

The meeting was about to close when Frank said, "Sir, I have a suggestion."

"Yes, Frank, what is it?"

"You might want to assign an observer to record what happens during Cicci's arrest."

"Why would I do that, Frank?"

"At the time of his death, Dr. Simpkins was a resident of California, was an internationally recognized vehicle emissions expert, and was working on a critical environmental project with national overtones. The media will be all over the story of the killer's capture. We should be very careful."

"Hum. Not a bad idea. Do you have someone in mind?"

Frank proposed that Rose Nardello be the observer. He said that Rose had a clear understanding of what was at stake. The governor agreed.

Frank met with Rose as soon as he returned to Riverside. "The governor responded favorably to our request, Rose. To do otherwise, would have negatively impacted his 'tough on crime' reputation. The commitment came with two provisos, however. He stipulated that Police Captain Gerald Shute must be in charge of the operation and that you be assigned to the operation as an observer."

Captain Shute spent the following day in Riverside meeting with Police Chief Tarencelli, Joe Godfrey and Pete Desmond. All three agreed that Captain Shute should assign his most experienced undercover man to shadow Cicci for a few days to determine the man's regular movements. Captain Shute chose Trooper Dick Trinker. Trinker watched Cicci's activities for five days before returning to Hartford to report on his findings.

"Cicci left Quaddick only once, Captain. The rest of the time he either worked in his garden or remained inside the house. The one time he did leave, I tailed him to a tobacco shop in Pawtucket. He stayed inside for about ten minutes." Trinker smiled. "He was madder than hell when he came out. He pounded his fist on the roof of his car and then sped off in his BMW to a condominium development in East Providence. He was going so fast I had one hell of a time keeping up. I thought I'd be picked up for speeding. He stayed inside the condo for over three hours before returning to Quaddick."

Joe Godfrey asked, "What was the name of the tobacco shop, Dick?"

Vincent checked his notes. "Mike's."

"I know the place, Captain. I stopped there two weeks ago and talked with the owner's wife. She's the one that gave me Cicci's address. I'll bet she told Cicci about my visit and he went ballistic. I think we all know what that means. Cicci knows we're on to him. We'd better be very careful from here on out."

Trinker added to Joe's warning. "My guess is that the guy is heavily armed. When he came out of the tobacco shop, his jacket was open and flapping in the breeze. I saw a shoulder holster. I suspect the guy also has a rifle stashed somewhere inside the car, probably in the trunk, or on the floor of the back seat. I suggest that we don't try to apprehend him while he's out in public. We should wait and go after him at his home where he could be more relaxed and, therefore, vulnerable."

Joe asked, "Who lives in the East Providence condominium, Dick?"

Trinker said he didn't know. He'd called the Rhode Island tax authorities when he returned to Hartford, but their records didn't list a name, only a corporation.

Captain Shute asked, "Rocco, can your people obtain information about Cicci's house? Does he own it, or is he renting it? We need to get our hands on a floor plan."

After numerous phone calls, Joe Godfrey determined that Cicci was renting the house in Quaddick and was able to locate the Putnam realtor who'd brokered the rental. When the lady heard why Joe was calling, she agreed enthusiastically to cooperate. She located a floor plan in her file and faxed it to Joe in Riverside.

Joe went over the plan with Pete Desmond. It appeared to both men that it was probably conventional for a ranch-style house. It showed the front door opening into a living room from a small, covered stoop, and the back door opening into the kitchen from a small uncovered deck. A living room and master bedroom suite were at the east end of the house. The kitchen, dinning area, a guest bedroom and a garage at the west end.

Joe called the realtor again to see if she had any additional information about the house that didn't show up on the floor plan. The realtor cautioned that she'd been in the house only once since Cicci rented it, but she did recall thinking that his usage of the space and his furnishings were "let's say, different." He was using the guest room as his bedroom. He'd converted the master bedroom into a gym: she remembered exercise and weight lifting equipment in the room. She recalled seeing only one chair in the living room, a recliner, a roll-top desk in one corner, and a large entertainment center with a large big screen TV and a sophisticated sound system with wall speakers in another. Given this critical information, Joe called Captain Shute and arranged to meet in Hartford to formulate an assault plan.

Armed with a first-degree murder indictment handed down by the Riverside Grand Jury, Joe Godfrey led a four-man law enforcement team from Riverside to a rendezvous with a group of experienced personnel from the Connecticut State Police. In addition to Godfrey, the Riverside contingent included detectives DeCarlo and Desmond, and the designated observer, Rose Nardello. The state team included Captain Shute, and officers Trinker, Mahoney, and Jefferson. The rendezvous site was a State Police Station on Interstate 395 north of Putnam, Connecticut, only eight miles south west of Cicci's home in Quaddick.

When everyone was assembled, Captain Shute presented the assault plan. "We want to catch the suspect while he's asleep, so we'll initiate the attack at 2:00 a.m. Godfrey and DeCarlo will enter the house through the back door and attempt to capture Cicci in his bedroom before he can cause trouble. Desmond and Jefferson will enter through the front door and provide backup support to Godfrey and DeCarlo. Trinker and I will be stationed about 20 yards from the back door with rifles, and Mahoney will take up a similar position at the front of the house. It will be our job to watch the windows. We want to disable the suspect, if at all possible, and take him alive. But if that's not in the cards, shoot to kill. Rose, you must stay out of the way. We'll find a spot at the side of the house. I want you to lie down flat with your tape recorder turned on. Don't move from there unless I tell you to."

Each person was given an opportunity to critique Captain Shute's plan. He wanted to avoid any chance that the mission would be jeopardized because of a misunderstanding or miscommunication. Shute closed the briefing and recommended that his troops try to get a few hours of sleep. The Putnam station was equipped with a half a dozen army cots and two roll away beds. Rose was given the couch in the station commander's office.

Instead of sleeping, however, Joe Godfrey, Dom DeCarlo, and Pete Desmond elected to talk awhile longer. They went over the attack plan again. Although each officer would be issued a bulletproof vest, Joe was concerned. "It's a clear night and there's a three quarter moon. That could be good or bad for us. Cicci probably has a weapon within easy reach of his bed. He'll start shooting as soon as we break down those doors. The moonlight will provide enough light for him to see us more clearly than we see him. If he has an automatic weapon, we could have a serious problem. What's your opinion of the size of the poles the captain gave us, Pete? Do you think they're strong enough to knock the doors off their hinges?"

"They sure look heavy enough, Joe. They're not as big as telephone poles, but they're big. They look like 4' x 8's."

Joe leaned back in his chair. "We're gonna have to drop to the ground as soon as those doors fall. Dom, you and I will have to crawl on our hands and knees through the kitchen toward Cicci's bedroom. Are you ready for that?"

"Yeah, but it's been awhile. I did that sort of thing in the Army."

Joe smiled. "You were probably in shape then, but how about now?"

"Listen, Joe, when my life's on the line, I think I can motivate my big ass to move." Pete and Joe laughed.

"Pete, you'll have to drop down to the prone position and crawl, too. Be alert. It'll be a lot more difficult to fire our weapons from the prone position."

"What do we know about the black dude, Trooper Jefferson?"

"Captain Shute took me aside and told me not to worry about Jefferson. He's a little guy, but Shute said he's reliable and courageous. I hope the hell he's right."

Unbeknownst to the assault teams, Robert Cicci was a stickler for security. Within a week of moving into the rental house, and without informing the realtor or the owner of the property, Cicci installed an elaborate security system. The system was designed to detect the slightest movement at the windows or on the front and back stoops. His cell phone would vibrate and make low buzzing sound when movement was detected. He carried the cell phone on his person at all times and even tucked it in his pajama pocket when he slept. Cicci had been trained to react immediately to any unusual sound, whether he was sleeping or he was awake.

49

Two SUVs rolled through the village of Quaddick at 1:30 a.m. They approached Cicci's country home from the south, pulled off the main road onto a remote dirt road about a quarter-mile from the house, and stopped. Captain Shute assembled his attack team and reviewed the plan once again. "We'll walk single file until we reach the entrance to Cicci's driveway. That's where we stop. Don't move until I give you the signal. Rose, at that point you take up a position at the side of the house. Make sure you can see both the front and back doors. Remember to turn on the tape recorder.

"When I give the signal, the rest of you are to take up your assigned positions. At exactly 2:00 a.m. Desmond and Godfrey will smash down the front and back doors. All hell will break loose, so be ready with your weapons." He repeated the specific assignments for each man, and then asked, "Any questions?" No one responded. Shute sighed. "Okay. Check your watches. I have 1:48 and 20 seconds. No conversation from now on until the exercise is complete. Good luck and let's go!"

At 1:58, Desmond and Trooper Jefferson quietly climbed three steps to the front stoop and took up positions on each side of the front door: Desmond on the left side holding, a 4' x 8' battering ram, and Jefferson on the right side, holding both weapons. Shute's plan called for Desmond to break down the door, drop the piece of wood, take his weapon from Jefferson, and immediately drop to the floor.

At 1:59 a.m., Godfrey and DeCarlo stepped onto the concrete patio at the back of the house and took positions similar to Desmond and Jefferson next to the back door, with Godfrey held the battering ram and DeCarlo the weapons.

At 1:58, Cicci's cell phone began to vibrate. It woke him with a start. He slid off the bed onto the floor and grabbed his Colt .45 off the table. He rolled across the room and settled against the wall next to the bedroom door. He peeked through the open bedroom door toward the kitchen but was unable to discern any movement. He turned his head in the direction of the front door but again saw or heard nothing. Just then, the back and the front doors came crashing down.

Cicci instinctively ducked back against the wall. He recovered and peeked through the doorway into the kitchen. The moonlight enabled him to make out the silhouettes of two men dropping to the floor, one after the other. He rolled over on his stomach, took aim and opened fire, spaying bullets low to the floor at what was now a gapping hole in the wall.

Using just their elbows and knees for power, Godfrey and DeCarlo crawled ahead as fast as they could, DeCarlo moving to his left and Godfrey straight ahead. When DeCarlo reached an appliance of some kind, he placed his back against it, freeing his right hand to shoot.

Godfrey was only able to move a few feet before he felt the impact of a bullet that shattered his right shoulder. Joe reacted with a grunt. His hand involuntarily opened and his weapon dropped to the floor. The bullet had rendered him useless as a combatant. Joe knew it instantly. He did the only thing that made sense at the time: he hugged the floor and willed himself not to cry out from the searing pain.

DeCarlo heard Joe's reaction to being hit and realized instantly that he was on his own. He squinted, saw something move in the doorway of the guest bedroom, and fired. Cicci returned the fire with another outburst from his .45. Bullets ricocheted off the appliance and penetrated the wooden cabinets alongside the appliance, but luckily, none hit DeCarlo. At this point, the firing stopped. DeCarlo hunkered down next to the appliance and tried to detect movement in the bedroom doorway.

After breaking down the front door, Desmond and Jefferson dropped to the floor and began to crawl toward the guest bedroom. When Pete saw that Cicci was firing from the bedroom doorway, he fired two shots in that direction. Cicci turned his head and shoulders, took aim at where he thought the new shots had come from and returned the fire. His aim was bad and the shots struck the wall next to what was left of the front entrance. Desmond reached over and tapped Jefferson on the shoulder and whispered, "Back out and see if you can get him from the bedroom window."

Jefferson slowly backed out over the top of the broken door, catching a splinter in his knee in the process. When he reached the stoop he got on his feet and limped over to the bedroom window. He poked his head above the sill and peeked in. It was dark but there was enough moonlight for Jefferson to barely make out the silhouette of Cicci in the doorway. It looked like Cicci was lying flat on his stomach with his arm and head pointed in the direction of the kitchen. Jefferson raised his revolver, took aim at Cicci's back, and fired three shots in rapid succession. He watched Cicci's head snap up and then forward before slowly dropping to the floor. Jefferson waited a moment to see if there was any movement. He opened fire again. Three more shots penetrated Cicci's body. He waited again to see if there was any movement. Seeing none, Jefferson yelled, "I think I got him, Pete. I put six shots into him. He looks like he's had it. Can you check to make sure? Be careful."

Rose lay in the grass exactly where Captain Shute had ordered her to stay. She wasn't concerned about getting dirty: she wore an old pair of Levi's, an old UConn sweatshirt, and sneakers. She thought about the overused phrase "It's so quiet, you can hear a pin drop," and smiled. *That's a really dumb saying,* she thought. Just then, gunfire erupted, and she instinctively hugged the ground. Just as quickly, the gunfire stopped. Hoping she might be able to see something, Rose raised her head, but quickly dropped to the ground again when gunfire started up again. She counted six or seven shots, a break, then a few more, followed by another break, and then two bursts of three shots each in rapid succession. She heard someone yell, "I think I got him, Pete. He looks like he's had it. Can you check to make sure? Be careful."

Everyone on the attack team remained motionless and quiet while Pete Desmond crawled over to the prostrate Cicci, and cautiously felt for a pulse. A few moments passed before Desmond called out, "He's dead, Captain."

Rose lowered her head and touched the ground with her forehead. She thought, *Thank God. Maybe I won't have to tell Joe about what Dad did for Winston Osborne.*

Then a different voice shouted, "Joe's been hit, Captain. It's pretty bad."

Rose jumped up and ran as fast as she could toward the back of the house. She pushed her way past Trooper Trinker and Dom DeCarlo and knelt down next to Joe. He was grimacing from the terrible pain in his shoulder, but when he realized who was kneeling next to him, a smile lit up his face. "Hi, Rose. I didn't do very well, did I?"

Rose grabbed his left hand and said, "I'm so sorry, Joe." She turned around to look for Captain Shute. "Captain, we'd better get him to the hospital. I'll take him."

"Rose, I appreciate your concern and your offer to take him to a hospital, but I think it would be wise for us to call 911. Mahoney, get on the phone. Tell the dispatcher that an officer of the law is down and needs immediate attention." Turning back to face Rose, the captain said, "You can follow the ambulance to the hospital in one of our vehicles."

Pete Desmond said, "Captain, one of us should go with Rose. If it's okay with you, I'll go."

"That'll be fine, Pete."

50

In less than 30 minutes, the ambulance carrying Joe Godfrey was on its way to Putnam General Hospital. Pete pulled DeCarlo aside and asked him to call Chief Tanencelli at his unlisted number. "Tell Rocco what happened. He might want to drive over to Putnam to visit with Joe and meet with Captain Shute and the medical examiner." Pete turned back and spoke to Captain Shute. "We should get a forensics team over here right away, Captain. Should I ask Chief Tarencelli to gather a team from Riverside, or do you want the State Police to conduct the search?"

"I'll call Hartford. I'll have to wake a few people up, but I should be able to get the state lab folks to assemble a team and be here within three to four hours. When you get back, you can help."

"I'll come back as soon as I get a report on Joe's condition."

After examining the wound, the physician on duty in the Emergency Room determined that Joe needed immediate surgery to repair his badly damaged shoulder. He telephoned Dr. William Vincent, the only orthopedic surgeon living in Putnam, and gave Vincent a quick briefing about the identity of the patient and what had happened. "I'll be there in 20 minutes. Get him ready."

Godfrey was still in surgery at 5:30 a.m. when Rose called Frank Mancuso at his home. "Good morning, Frank. Sorry to wake you." Frank could hear the excitement in her voice. "We got Cicci!" She described the sequence of events that led up to the shoot out. "Cicci was alerted somehow, Frank. He opened fire on Joe and Dom as soon as they broke down the back door." Rose sighed, "Joe was hit in the right shoulder. He's in surgery as we speak. The good news is that State Trooper Jefferson was able put six shots into Cicci through a window. Cicci died immediately."

"Good news, bad news Rose. How serious is Joe's injury?"

"The bullet shattered his shoulder. I don't know any more than that. I want to stay here for awhile, Frank, if that's okay. I'll take a few vacation days. Joe will need moral support when he recovers from the anesthesia."

"You're beginning to care for that man, aren't you, young lady?"

"Yes, I guess I am. Joe's a wonderful guy, Frank."

"Forget vacation days. You stay as long as you need to."

"Thanks, Frank."

"Where's Pete?"

"He's with me right now, but he's going back to Cicci's house in a few minutes to help the state forensics team search the house for clues. He said he'll probably head back to Riverside this afternoon."

Frank said, "You'll be pleased to hear that the Air Resources Board agreed to send Charles Olson to Riverside as Dr. Simpkins replacement. He'll install the two Laser Trail systems, train the operators, and then stay here until the emission tests are complete. We've lost a couple of months, but it looks like we're back on track. We may be able to file the two lawsuits before the end of the year."

The surgeon walked into the hospital waiting room at 8:15, and said, "Sergeant Godfrey will be fine, Miss Nardello. He'll be incapacitated for a few months. If he follows a rigorous program of physical therapy, he'll regain full flexibility in the shoulder. The first few weeks will be difficult, however. Does he have family that can stay and work with him?"

"His only family in this part of the country is a cousin who lives in Granby. I'll call her today and we'll work out the arrangements. If she can't take care of him, I'll bring him to my home for a few weeks. I'll make sure he gets to the physical therapist."

"Good. I'd better be going. I've got patients waiting for me in my office." The doctor smiled, "I'll be back later this afternoon to check on *our* patient, Miss Nardello."

Rose reached out to shake Doctor Vincent's hand. "Thank you, Doctor."

After saying goodbye to Pete Desmond, Rose began her vigil by reading magazines in the waiting room outside the recovery area. The realization that she hadn't eaten since lunch the previous day finally penetrated her consciousness. She decided to take the elevator to the basement cafeteria. Before she left the waiting room she asked the lead nurse to page her in the cafeteria if Sergeant Godfrey recovered from the anesthesia. "Take your time, Miss Nardello. Sergeant Godfrey will be out for at least another hour."

The medical examiner bagged Cicci's body and hauled it off in a van. Captain Shute instructed the remaining members of his assault team not to touch anything, except try to reattach the broken doors. "The forensics team is on its way and will conduct a thorough search of the premises." Pete Desmond returned to the house just as the forensics team was about to start its search.

Captain Shute suggested that Pete and Dom DeCarlo be allowed to join the search team and were assigned the living room. Dom checked out the entertainment center looking for videos, tapes, and CD's that might contain information helpful to Simpkins murder investigation. Pete inspected the open roll top desk. He lifted and scanned a stack of letters and bills that were loosely piled on top of a large calendar pad. He was about to replace the papers when a word at the top of the calendar pad caught his eye: August. He thought that was strange. It was already October, but the pages for the months of August and September had not been removed. He bent down to have a closer look.

Numerous notes were written on the calendar. Pete removed a small notebook from his breast pocket and tried to decipher them. One note in particular, written on August 12, seemed to jump off the page: "Contact Winston Osborne in Newport." He studied the name for a few moments trying to recall why he recognized the name. His eyes opened wide when he made the connection. *Joe's been talking about a Winston Osborne lately. He's the President of the Diesel Engine Corporation. Why would Robert Cicci be in contact with Winston Osborne?* He grabbed the phone attached to his belt and initiated a call to Rocco Tarencelli.

"Rocco, I found a note on Cicci's calendar. Apparently, he had a meeting with a Winston Osborne, the president of the Diesel Engine Corporation, on August 12, just a few weeks before Simpkins was killed. I think we'd better have a talk with Mr. Osborne."

"Good work, Pete. I'm on the road. I should be there in less than two hours. We'll set up a meeting with the Pawtucket Police Chief for later today."

"Thanks for accepting my call, Chief Dunn. I'm Chief Rocco Tarencelli of Riverside, Connecticut. I'd like to meet with you this afternoon and talk about a recent murder that we're investigating. It's beginning to look like the chief executive officer of your largest employer may be a suspect."